MW00415495

MURDER AT THE DINNER PARTY

CLEOPATRA FOX MYSTERY, BOOK 8

C.J. ARCHER

WWW.CJARCHER.COM

Copyright © 2024 by C.J. Archer

Visit C.J. at www.cjarcher.com

All rights reserved.

No part of this book may be reproduced in any form or by any electronic or
mechanical means, including information storage and retrieval systems,
without written permission from the author, except for the use of brief
quotations in a book review.

CHAPTER 1

LONDON, JULY 1900

*M*iss Hessing and Mr. Liddicoat were blissfully unaware of the disaster that threatened to derail their engagement dinner party. They sat side by side at the main table in the Mayfair Hotel's restaurant, stealing glances at one another when they thought no one was looking. To most, it appeared to be a romantic scene. A couple clearly in love, candlelight flickering in the soft breeze coming through the open windows, the array of silverware glinting like stars against the black tablecloths, and dozens of white chrysanthemums filling the vases. If anyone thought the traditional flower used for funerals was an odd choice, they were polite enough not to say so, or perhaps they thought the flower had a different meaning in the bride-to-be's home country of the United States.

One person who did notice every altered detail was her mother. Mrs. Hessing asked Mr. Chapman, the hotel steward, why the pink roses she'd requested weren't on display.

He apologized profusely. "I'm afraid my order wasn't given due attention, and it failed to reach the florist on time."

Whether that was true, or an excuse to cover his own tardiness in submitting the order, I didn't know, but I doubted Mr. Hobart, the hotel manager, would have failed to sign off on the order on time if he'd known what it was for. On the other hand, he had been somewhat absent of late. He wasn't even attending the engagement dinner this evening.

Mrs. Hessing accepted Mr. Chapman's excuse with a purse of her lips and further scrutiny of the flowers. "At least they can't really be seen with the poor lighting in here. Is that so we won't be able to see what we're eating?"

Mr. Chapman laughed off the suggestion. "You will be delighted by the menu, Mrs. Hessing. Our chef is a marvel."

His assurance did nothing to wipe away her scowl, but at least she left him alone. She marched off, the end of her walking stick stabbing the floorboards with military precision. Mr. Chapman glared at her back with a sneer on his usually smooth features.

"Cheer up," I quipped. "You're right. Mrs. Poole and her team will make tonight's dishes taste like they came directly from a restaurant in the heart of Paris, despite everything."

Everything being another word for disaster. The lack of light Mrs. Hessing referred to was caused by a kitchen fire that had burned through the electrical wiring. Candles had to be sourced from the hotel's storeroom moments before the diners arrived. Fortunately, candles gave the occasion the romanticism it deserved. Unfortunately, the lingering scent of smoke did not. As to the last-minute change of menu, as insisted upon by Mr. Chapman, it remained to be seen if the cooks would live up to the praise I heaped on them.

The black tablecloths and chrysanthemums were courtesy of a local funeral home, due to the fact that a deceased's family had failed to pay the deposit on time. Our usual florist couldn't fulfil Mr. Chapman's order for roses, but she had enough of the mourning blooms ready. The funeral director was also willing to loan us his tablecloths, since he no longer needed them this evening.

The steward didn't seem to appreciate my attempt at reassurance. His rigid spine stiffened even more as he looked down his thin nose at me. "You should take your seat, Miss Fox. You know how Sir Ronald dislikes you fraternizing with the staff."

I wasn't quite sure if it was a threat or not. He knew I chatted to some of the staff during their time off, and that it would indeed anger my uncle to have his niece mingling with employees. But was he threatening to tell my uncle, and, if so, why? Although he'd been rude to me when I first arrived at the hotel, I thought we had an understanding now, albeit an unspoken one.

Perhaps he was snippy because he knew that I knew these disasters were not only his fault, but they could have been avoided if he'd accepted Harmony's offer to help him organize the party. He'd undertaken the task alone, determined to prove to Sir Ronald that he was capable. I'd wondered if he'd been upset to be overlooked in favor of Harmony when Floyd required an assistant to organize the opening of the new restaurant; his jealous guarding of the engagement party arrangements these past two weeks proved he was.

Mr. Chapman slipped away while I was still trying to decide if his comment was meant to threaten me. But I did as he suggested and found my seat between my cousins. Flossy was chatting with a guest on her other side, while Floyd surreptitiously admired his own reflection in the silver candlestick.

"You look as dapper as always," I assured him.

"I know."

I rolled my eyes. "Don't they look happy?" I nodded at Miss Hessing and Mr. Liddicoat, chatting to his cousin the polo player.

"She's happy because she's a month away from being free of her mother, and he's happy because he's marrying into one of America's wealthiest families."

"Don't be so cynical. They're happy because they're in love."

He snorted. "Don't pretend you believe in love, Cleo. You and I think alike on that, at least."

"I've never said I don't believe in love, just that I don't want to marry. Those are entirely different things. A woman can be in love but not want to lose her independence."

"Now who's being cynical? Marriage doesn't have to end a woman's independence. She just needs to choose her husband wisely." He tapped his chest. "I, for example, would allow my wife to do as she pleases. She can own property, have opinions contrary to my own, and spend all my money on frivolous things if that makes her happy."

"Can she work?"

He made a face. "Don't be absurd. Nobody wants to work if they don't have to."

"Floyd, please do the entire female half of the planet a favor and don't marry until you've matured."

He picked up his empty glass. "If I had a drink, I'd raise my glass to that." He signaled to the waiter and accepted another flute of champagne.

Flossy turned to us and tugged at one long white glove, attempting to pull it higher. "It's getting cool in here. Someone ought to close the windows."

"The windows are open to release the lingering smell of smoke," I said.

She sniffed the air. "It's all but gone. Do you think any of the guests noticed?" She looked around at the small private gathering, most of whom were family members and friends of Mr. Liddicoat. The Hessings had no family in England and few friends. "This wouldn't have happened if Mr. Hobart oversaw the event," she said as she turned back to us. "Where is he, anyway? I haven't seen him all night."

Floyd shrugged. "He ought to be here. Cleo, you must know where he is."

"Why?" I asked.

"Because you seem to know more about his private life than either of us."

"I doubt that."

"No?" he asked, innocently. "Doesn't Armitage discuss his family with you?"

"Rarely."

Talking about Harry brought up the memory of how we'd last parted, after a kiss in his office. He'd instigated the kiss, but I'd liked it very much. Too much. Even so, I'd ended it before it developed into something I couldn't walk away from, something I'd later regret when the implications had sunk in.

I'd hurried out of his office, my mind whirling. I couldn't recall if I even said goodbye. I walked for hours before returning to the hotel, hot and bothered by both the summer heat and the kiss. I tried to push all thoughts of it from my mind afterward. At night, when I couldn't sleep, I picked up a book and read until exhaustion overtook me. I avoided all mention of him, and even avoided speaking to his uncle, the hotel manager. And I'd avoided going anywhere near Harry's Soho office.

In the weeks since, he had avoided me, too. There'd been no correspondence from him, not even a brief note. I was grateful for that. It made it easier to forget the kiss, and him.

Thankfully, I was saved from dwelling on it now by Mr. Chapman announcing the first course. A train of waiters emerged from the kitchen with bowls of turtle soup, one of Mrs. Poole's signature dishes. Next came poached trout and deep-fried whitebait, another of her regular offerings. It would seem she would not attempt anything unfamiliar, after all, despite what Mr. Chapman wanted. Or perhaps her suppliers hadn't been able to accommodate the last-minute changes. From the look on Mrs. Hessing's face, she was pleased. It wouldn't surprise me if Mrs. Poole cooked the dishes she knew one of the hotel's fussiest guests would enjoy, despite instruction from Mr. Chapman to the contrary. Her professionalism and willingness to accommodate her diners' tastes were part of the reason she was an excellent chef.

The rest of the evening was just as much a success. The food was heavenly, the speeches eloquent, and the bride-to-be's mother not too overbearing. Before she left the restaurant, Miss Hessing clasped my hands and squeezed. She thanked me profusely, although I wasn't really sure why. I'd merely suggested the hotel restaurant as a venue for the engagement dinner; the staff had done the rest.

Once she departed with her mother, only my family remained to see that the staff had it all in hand before we also retired. Before passing through the doorway that led directly to the hotel, I overheard my uncle tell Mr. Chapman that he wanted to see him in his office first thing in the morning.

Floyd had also overheard. He leaned closer to me. "I wouldn't want to be in Chapman's shoes tomorrow."

"Cleopatra!" Uncle Ronald barked. "Wait there."

"I wouldn't want to be in your shoes now," Floyd muttered before hurrying ahead.

I smiled as my uncle strode up to me. It was clear from his scowl that he would not be thanking me for suggesting the engagement party be held in the restaurant. To be fair, he often scowled for no particular reason. It didn't always mean he was annoyed.

This time, however, it did. "Where's Hobart?"

"Why would I know where he is?"

"Because you two get along."

"Perhaps he had a personal matter that required his attention at home."

"Home?"

"Yes. He has one outside of the hotel, and a wife." It was a little acerbic of me, but I couldn't help it. Sometimes my uncle took Mr. Hobart for granted and it needed to be pointed out to him.

He grunted. "Tonight was important. Mrs. Hessing is a great supporter of the hotel, but now that her daughter is to marry, there's a danger she won't return. We needed to be out in full force to show her why she ought to come back here, even if her son-in-law can comfortably accommodate her during her future visits to London."

While I couldn't defend Mr. Hobart, I could allay my uncle's fear. I looped my arm through his and strolled with him along the corridor to the hotel foyer. "I have it on good authority that the guest bedrooms in the Liddicoats' marital home will be in a state of renovation whenever Mrs. Hessing visits."

"I thought they hadn't chosen a new home yet. How can Miss Hessing know the guest bedrooms will require renovation?"

I winked at him.

He finally understood. Indeed, he even chuckled, proving he had a sense of humor, after all. He patted my arm. "Well done with Miss Hessing, Cleo. You have been a good friend to her."

"They would have found a way to be together if Mrs. Hessing didn't approve of Mr. Liddicoat, but I do credit myself with playing a part in convincing her he was worthy."

"I meant by suggesting the engagement party be held in our restaurant. There's not a finer venue in the city!" He patted my arm again. Then, spotting Mrs. Short waiting at one side of the corridor, gave her his full attention.

The hotel's housekeeper didn't want to speak to *him*, however. "May I have a word, Miss Fox?"

Uncle Ronald bowed out and headed across the foyer to where Aunt Lilian was waiting at the lift.

Once he was out of earshot, Mrs. Short clasped her hands in front of her and regarded me with lips pinched slightly less sternly than usual. "I'm sorry to bother you at this hour, but I find it's best to broach unpleasantness as soon as possible to get it over and done with."

"Speaking to me is unpleasant?" I asked mildly.

"That's not what I meant, Miss Fox, which I'm sure you are aware. What I should have said was the topic I need to discuss with you is unpleasant. I'd ask you not to infer meanings when you know them not to be true."

"I'm sorry, Mrs. Short."

Mrs. Short had a way of making me feel like a naughty child. She was excellent at her very demanding job, but rudely abrupt when she wanted to be, even to members of the Bainbridge family. Most of the hotel maids were afraid of her. I knew of at least six who'd been dismissed since her appointment as housekeeper in January, for offences ranging from smoking to being lazy. Even Harmony was careful not to do something that would attract negative attention.

A thought occurred to me, one that had me scrambling to think of an excuse that would explain why Harmony, a maid, and one of my closest friends, joined me for breakfast each morning.

What was said next couldn't have surprised me more if the stout woman before me had ridden naked through the hotel foyer on horseback. "I need your help, Miss Fox."

"Oh…uh…in what way?"

"My sister is upset." Mrs. Short unclasped and re-clasped her hands in front of her. "I don't like seeing her upset. She's a good woman."

"How can I help her?"

"I was about to get to that, if you'd only be a little patient."

"Sorry," I muttered.

"My sister is the housekeeper for a family here in Mayfair.

Their butler died recently, just as he was overseeing a dinner party for the family and their guests."

"How dreadful!"

Mrs. Short glared at me for interrupting. "It was. My sister likes order in her house, and I'm sure you can appreciate the chaos that ensued. Not only did he fall into a footman carrying a tureen of soup, spilling it on the carpet and creating a stain she can't get out, but the staff are still in a flutter, days later. They say they're too upset to work, that the house is cursed, and that he was murdered."

I gasped, but didn't interrupt again.

"My sister tends to agree with them. Not about the curse, about murder. She told me the police concluded he died of natural causes, but he was only aged in his mid-forties and fit as a fiddle. She also thinks he was afraid in the days leading up to his death. When she tried to speak to her employers about her concerns, she was told not to meddle and that if she took her concerns to the police, she would be dismissed." She paused and arched her thin brows. "Well, Miss Fox? Will you take the case?"

"Me?"

"Don't pretend innocence. I know you investigate from time to time as Mr. Armitage's assistant."

"We're associates. I work alongside him, not as his assistant."

"My sister thinks she can scrape together a little money from the other staff to pay a fee, but it won't be much. Hence why I'm asking you and not Mr. Armitage. They can't afford him."

I sighed. My hope when I began as a private investigator was that I would save up enough money to one day move out of the hotel and no longer rely on the allowance my uncle paid me. Alas, although I'd received a little income so far, it was nowhere near enough to enact my plan. Harry's business, on the other hand, was going from strength to strength. According to Mr. Hobart, Harry was very busy. He'd gained himself a reputation for solving complex crimes, some of which I'd investigated alongside him. Some of those had made it into the newspapers. The free publicity had proved a boon. So much so that he was too busy to even write a note to me after we'd kissed.

Not that I wanted to receive one, but it was the polite thing to do. *I think.*

"Miss Fox?" Mrs. Short prompted. "Do I need to ask someone else?"

"No. I'll investigate."

Her shoulders relaxed and I realized she'd been eager for me to take the case. "I'll send Miss Cotton to your room in the morning with my sister's details. Goodnight, Miss Fox."

I crossed the foyer to take the stairs up to my fourth-floor suite, nodding at the night porter as I passed him. He was the only front-of-house staff member available this late. The rest had gone home or to the residence hall if they lived there. I realized I didn't know if Mrs. Short had moved into the residence hall after her room in the hotel was demolished to make way for the restaurant, or whether she rented a place elsewhere.

I met Floyd as he trotted down the steps, whistling a tune.

He doffed his hat as he passed me. "Goodnight, Cousin. Don't wait up for me."

"I won't. Don't lose what you can't afford."

He paused on the step below me and gave me quite a serious look. "I no longer gamble, you know that."

I felt a twinge of guilt for suggesting that he'd not learned his lesson after a recent dreadful experience. "In that case, I'd like to change my advice to don't do anything foolish."

"I suspect your idea of what's foolish differs from mine." He tossed his hat in the air and caught it by the brim, then settled it on his head in one smooth move. "If I promise not to do anything illegal, will that suffice?"

"It'll have to do, I suppose, although try to steer clear of doing anything where Flossy or I have to provide an alibi when your father asks where you've been."

"All right, but if you do find yourself in that predicament, try to think of something more convincing than 'He went to the museum.' Just because it worked when you used to sneak out to investigate with Armitage doesn't mean it works for the likes of me. It's quite unbelievable." He kissed my cheek. "Don't look so annoyed with me, Cleo. Or are you annoyed that I mentioned Armitage? I noticed you two haven't seen each other the last two weeks, which is a good thing, in my opinion. Not that I dislike the fellow, just that I dislike him for you."

I crossed my arms. "Don't you have opera singers to annoy?"

"A dancer, actually, and she finds me irresistibly charming."

Something he'd said finally sank in. I frowned. "How do you know I haven't seen Harry for two weeks? Have you been following me?"

He waved and trotted down the steps. "Must dash."

"Floyd!"

He was halfway across the foyer when he turned around and tossed me a grin. "Goodnight, Cousin." He clapped the night porter on the shoulder as he opened the door for Floyd.

With a sigh, I continued up the steps. I suspected Floyd guessed I hadn't seen Harry for two weeks based on the simple fact that I hadn't investigated a crime in that time. He wasn't following me or spying on me. He didn't get up early enough to see me leave the hotel. It would seem he still didn't believe me when I said I had no interest in Harry, however. It was quite irritating, but then my cousin was an irritating person. Loveable, sometimes, but most definitely irritating.

* * *

HARMONY USUALLY GREETED me with a hearty "Good morning" when I let her into my suite with the breakfast tray each day, but not this morning. "Why did Mrs. Short ask me to give you this?" She nodded at the folded piece of paper on the tray.

I removed it and read the name and address while she carried the tray through to my sitting room. "She accosted me after dinner last night. Her sister wants to employ me to investigate a murder that she believes occurred at the house where she works." I passed her the note.

She studied the address before handing it back. "That's not far from here."

"Do you know the family?" I checked the piece of paper. "Sir Ian and Lady Campbell?"

"No. If they have a London house, it's unlikely they've stayed here."

I would ask my aunt later. She had a wealth of knowledge when it came to the upper-class families of London.

Harmony removed the domed lid on the platter to reveal scrambled eggs arranged into a heart shape. She quickly messed it up with a fork.

"Victor's working the breakfast shift?" I asked.

"He needs to be more careful. Someone could see that and think he's sending *you* a message." She sounded cross, but the tilt of her lips gave away her true feelings. She and Victor were getting on *very* well lately. "Tell me what you know about the butler's death."

I did, but it only took a few moments. There was so little to tell. "I'll call on Mrs. Short's sister after breakfast and see what more I can learn."

Harmony placed toast on her plate and scooped scrambled egg onto it. "Well?" she asked as she stabbed a rasher of bacon with her fork.

I picked up the coffee pot but didn't pour. I blinked at her. "Well, what?"

"How was last night's party?"

"Oh. That. It had the potential to be a disaster, actually, but I don't think any of the guests noticed."

She lowered the bacon to her plate. "I heard about the kitchen fire and the lights going out."

I told her about the black tablecloths and the chrysanthemums. "I thought Mrs. Hessing was going to make a scene. Mr. Chapman did, too, by the worried look on his face. If she had, he'd only have himself to blame. He shouldn't have changed everything at the last moment. It threw everyone out, and now Mrs. Poole is probably annoyed. My uncle is definitely annoyed. And Mr. Hobart...well, who knows where he is or what he thinks. Do you know why he wasn't there last night?"

"He's not in the habit of confiding in the maids." Harmony accepted the coffee cup from me and sipped thoughtfully. "So Mr. Chapman made a botch of it, did he?"

"I feel a little sorry for him. I know he was simply trying to make it all grander to impress my uncle, but it failed. If only he'd enlisted your help. Or better still, if only you'd taken charge of the entire event from the beginning."

Harmony smiled into her cup.

"The wedding is next month," I went on. "I'm concerned that if it's left in Mr. Chapman's hands again, he might not be up to the task."

"Perhaps that's why Sir Ronald is currently having words with him in his office."

"You know everything that goes on here."

"I overheard his raised voice before knocking on your door, although I couldn't hear his exact words."

"You have to press your ear to the door for that." I gathered toast, eggs, and bacon onto my plate and picked up my knife and fork. I pointed the fork at Harmony. "*You* should be in charge of the wedding. You did all the work with the restaurant opening and look how well that turned out."

"Mr. Bainbridge was in charge of the guest list."

"The guest list was the easiest part. We both know Floyd did little else. You did it all. My uncle knows it, too."

"He gave me bonus wages, Cleo. I didn't do it for nothing."

"My point is, *you* should organize the wedding. I'll mention it to him."

She bristled. "You'll do no such thing."

"Why not?"

"I don't want any favors."

"But—"

"No, Cleo. Thank you, but I'd rather you didn't."

I didn't push the point further. Instead, we spent the rest of breakfast discussing what the ladies wore to the engagement party.

* * *

ALTHOUGH MRS. TURNER pointed out that she was two years younger than her sister, Mrs. Short, they could have been twins. There were many similarities, from their stout frames to the gray hair arranged into a tight bun at the back of their heads. Mrs. Turner's thin eyebrows formed a shallow V as she scrutinized my appearance in an almost identical manner to her sister. I used to think Mrs. Short was scowling at me, but came to realize her brows were always in that position and she regarded everyone the same way, even my uncle.

"You're prettier than I expected." Mrs. Turner turned away and strode down the corridor in the basement service area, the bunch of keys at her hip jangling with every step.

Assuming she wanted me to follow, I hurried after her. We passed the open door to the kitchen. A cook looked up from the central bench where she was chopping vegetables. Her young assistant stirred a pot on the range, humming softly to herself. A footman and maid seated at the table in the staff dining room also looked up from their mending. Mrs. Turner gave me no opportunity to study them in return as she bustled onward, past the larder, pantry and servants' staircase.

"Mrs. Short tells me—"

"Hush." Mrs. Turner used one of the keys to unlock a door. Inside was a small office without so much as a pen out of place on the desk. "Walls have ears. You ought to know that given your profession and where you live."

"Right. Yes." I waited until she'd closed the door and sat behind the desk, then I sat, too. "Your sister tells me you don't believe the butler died of natural causes, that he was relatively young and in good health. He was also fearful in the days leading up to his death."

"Not fearful. Merely...different. He'd been an even-tempered fellow, not overly stern with the staff. But before his death, he ceased to have idle conversations and seemed more introverted, reflective. It was unlike him."

"Did he simply drop dead in the dining room? There were no outward signs of murder?"

"Poison doesn't necessarily leave obvious signs."

"No, but poisoning is not the usual conclusion to jump to, even if someone has been acting oddly in the days before their death. People do die suddenly in their forties from natural causes, Mrs. Turner. However, I can already tell that you and Mrs. Short are alike, and I know Mrs. Short would not jump to the conclusion of murder without good reason.

So tell me, what reason do you have for assuming the butler was murdered?"

She leaned forward a little, causing the chair to creak, and locked her gaze with mine. "Because Mr. Hardy, the butler, started acting oddly after old friends of the Campbells came to dinner one evening. The couple acted oddly, too, upon seeing him, according to the footman who was also present in the dining room. He said they looked startled. Then, on the day of Mr. Hardy's death, someone snuck into his room upstairs. He mentioned it to me, saying things had been moved. One thing in particular that he mentioned having been moved seems relevant now, in light of his death."

"What was it?"

She unlocked the top drawer and removed a dark brown glass bottle of seltzer salts. She set it down with a thud on the desk between us. "I removed this before the killer could come back and destroy the evidence. I believe if you test the contents, you'll find the poison that killed Mr. Hardy."

CHAPTER 2

I removed the cork stopper and sniffed the bottle's contents. It smelled like ordinary bicarbonate of soda. "Why do you think the poison is in here?"

"Where else could it be? Mr. Hardy ate and drank the same as the rest of us and we're all well. The seltzer was beside his bed. He suffered from headaches, and a dose of the powder was the only thing that gave him relief."

I studied the bottle, but the label didn't list the ingredients. "Where do you keep the household poisons?"

"We don't have any. I refuse to have them in the house."

"Not even for mice control?"

"We don't get mice," she said snippily. "I run a tight, *clean* ship, Miss Fox."

I removed my notebook and pencil from my bag and flipped to a blank page. "Tell me about Mr. Hardy. How long had he worked here?"

"A month."

"And before that?"

"I don't know. He avoided answering questions about his past."

"Lady Campbell didn't tell you?"

"Why would she? It's none of my business."

"You mentioned Mr. Hardy's character changed after friends of Sir Ian and Lady Campbell came to dinner one evening. Was it the same dinner as the one during which he died?"

"No, it was earlier. Lord and Lady Whitchurch live not far away, although they also have an estate in the country. I forget where. No children, just his elderly mother who lives at the estate."

"What was their behavior like on the night they were served by Mr. Hardy?"

"I can't say for certain as I wasn't in the dining room. I did see them arriving and leaving, and all I can say is they seemed on good terms with the Campbells. It was all very cordial."

"But you said the footman noticed them looking oddly at Mr. Hardy."

"He did. You should speak to him before the Campbells return home. He'll be busy when they arrive, having to do Mr. Hardy's duties as well as his own now."

"I'd like to speak to the other staff, too."

"Of course."

"How much time passed between the two dinner parties, the one at which Lord and Lady Whitchurch were present and the one where Mr. Hardy died?"

"Only a few days."

"Tell me about the guests who were present at the fateful dinner."

"I don't think they're suspects. Both couples had seen Mr. Hardy on earlier occasions, and there was no change in their behavior before or his after those meetings. They were all very shocked when he collapsed. One of the ladies wouldn't stop screaming."

She gave me their names, although her account convinced me they were unlikely to be involved in the butler's demise.

Mrs. Turner led the way back along the corridor to the kitchen and adjoining staff room. She introduced me to the footman, maid, the cook, known simply as Mrs. Cook, and her assistant, a quiet girl of about fifteen who Mrs. Cook bluntly stated was simple and unable to answer any questions.

"I'm also unable to answer your questions," she went on.

"Why?" I asked.

"Well, I don't know anything, do I?" She picked up a large knife and sliced through a potato with more aggression than the humble vegetable deserved. "I knew nothing about Mr. Hardy or the dinner guests." She pointed the knife at the ceiling. "They all ate the same thing upstairs, and we ate the same thing, too, well beforehand, so it wasn't my food that done him in."

"You believe he was poisoned, too?"

"I suppose he must have been. He was hale and hearty, but he wasn't himself lately. Not ill, just…different. Almost like he was thinking something through, ever since the night of that dinner party with the Whitchurches." She scooped up potato pieces and placed them into a large pot. "Fill this with water, Birdy, and place it on the range."

The footman snatched a slice of uncooked carrot from the pot before the assistant, Birdy, removed it. He winked at her and she giggled.

"Leave the girl alone, Davey," Mrs. Cook chided.

Davey popped the carrot into his mouth. "You'll want to question me, Miss Fox. I was in the dining room the night Mr. Hardy died. He fell right into me, and I was carrying the soup tureen. Made a real mess, it did. All over the carpet. Betty here can't get the stain out, can you, Bet?"

The maid named Betty shook her head without looking up from her feet.

"Did he clutch his chest or throat before he fell?" I asked. "Did he vomit?"

Betty gulped loudly, then covered her mouth and ran from the room.

Mrs. Turner clicked her tongue. "Sensitive girl. Go on, Davey, answer Miss Fox."

Davey scratched the side of his face where many young men his age grew sideburns. As with most household footmen and butlers, however, he was clean-shaven. He was tall and quite good-looking, which seemed to be other features common amongst footmen. "His face went a little red just before he collapsed," Davey went on. "He seemed confused, too, like he didn't know where he was. But it was over in a blink. Then he just crumpled to the floor and sort of shook all over before going still."

"Did the seizure last long?"

Davey shrugged. "I'm not sure. One of the ladies started screaming, the men were shouting at each other and me, the soup was all over the carpet...it was chaotic."

I jotted notes in my book. I wasn't very familiar with the symptoms of different poisons, but disorientation and seizures were certainly symptoms of some, but could also point to natural causes, too. "How well did you know Mr. Hardy, Davey?"

"Not at all. He gave the orders and I followed them. We never discussed anything other than work, but I liked him. He didn't often get cross, unlike the butler before him." He pulled a face.

Mrs. Cook pointed her knife at him. "That's not true. I heard you two arguing in his office. The day before he died, it would have been."

"We weren't arguing. He was scolding me." Davey rolled his eyes. "I lost a button. He found it and gave me a talking-to about how I had to maintain standards, that my missing button was a poor reflection on Sir Ian and Lady Campbell and that I needed to do better in future. It was the only time he scolded me. Most of the time we got along fine."

Being scolded for a missing button sounded a little excessive to me. I tried to imagine Mr. Hobart getting cross with one of the porters for poor presentation, but couldn't. He would take them aside and tell them quietly to fix their attire at the earliest opportunity. He wouldn't raise his voice. Mr. Chapman, on the other hand, would certainly have stern words with his waiters in front of the other staff, so perhaps Mr. Hardy's scolding wasn't all that unusual, after all.

"Tell me about the night Lord and Lady Whitchurch dined here," I said to Davey. "Did you notice Mr. Hardy acting oddly after meeting them?"

"Before."

"Pardon?"

"He started acting strangely *before* meeting them. I don't know how long before, but it was definitely before. When I asked him what was wrong, he told me to mind my own business. Then when they came, he seemed tense. He always acted stiff when speaking to Sir Ian and Lady Campbell, but that night he was stiffer, not making eye contact with anyone. But *they* couldn't stop staring at *him*. Both Lord and Lady Whitchurch seemed to recognize him, but I reckon they couldn't place him. They kept frowning as if they were searching their memories."

"Did they speak to him?"

"No."

Betty re-entered the kitchen. She looked pale, drawn, and Mrs. Turner ordered her to sit on the stool in the corner. She signaled to the young cook's assistant, Birdy, to make her a cup of tea.

"Buck up, Child," Mrs. Turner chided. "You've got floors to scrub."

Betty nodded quickly. "Yes, Mrs. Turner. I'll be all right. It was thinking about poor Mr. Hardy that made my stomach turn. I can't believe he's gone." She pressed a hand to her middle, but fortunately didn't need to rush off again. "Why would that lord and lady poison him?"

"We don't know if they did," I assured her.

"But Miss Fox will find out," Davey said brightly. "I have a feeling she's very thorough." He winked at me.

"According to Mr. Hardy, someone entered his room on the day of his death," I went on. "Did any of you go into his room and move his things?"

They all shook their heads. Mrs. Cook and Mrs. Turner protested vehemently. "It wasn't any of the staff," Mrs. Turner said. "None have permission to enter Mr. Hardy's room. He cleans it himself."

I refrained from telling them that not having permission wouldn't stop anyone. Not even locked doors could. "Did any of you see someone else that day who shouldn't be in the house?"

They all shook their heads.

I closed my notebook and slipped it back into my bag. "Thank you. Mrs. Turner, I'd like to see the dining room before Sir Ian and Lady Campbell return, then I'd like to look around Mr. Hardy's office and bedchamber, please."

She marched toward the door. "Follow me, Miss Fox."

The dining room was a sumptuous statement of the Campbells' wealth. Masterful artwork in gilded frames decorated the deep red walls, and tall silver candlesticks stood proudly on the black marble mantelpiece. The large table and sideboard were polished to a sheen, and the velvet-covered chairs looked comfortable for a long evening chatting with friends. The only thing missing from the scene was the rug, which Mrs. Turner informed me had been thrown away since it couldn't be cleaned. They were waiting for a new one, which Lady Campbell was yet to purchase.

There was nothing more to see, so we headed up the stairs to the servants' quarters, housed on the top floor. The butler's bedroom contained a single bed, dresser, wardrobe, and a chair positioned by the window.

"It's as he left it, except for the seltzer bottle," Mrs. Turner said. "He was a neat and tidy man, with never so much as a loose button." She pointed to the bedside table with the lamp and a copy of an old Sherlock Holmes mystery. "That's where the seltzer salts bottle was kept."

I ran my hands over the bedspread then checked under the mattress, inside the pillow slip and other places for hidden objects, all under the frowning gaze of Mrs. Turner. She remained by the door, however, and didn't say a word as I moved to the dresser. Finding nothing of note, I opened the cupboard door. To see the highest shelf, I stood on the chair. Tucked into the corner was a sturdy metal box, the sort used to keep money or valuables. The padlock was still in place, locked, but the lid had been pried open. Whatever tool had forced it had scratched and dented the metal. I lifted the lid. The box was empty.

I showed it to Mrs. Turner. "Do you know what he stored in here?"

She shook her head.

I returned the box and checked the rest of the cupboard. Mr. Hardy kept a selection of neatly pressed suits, two pairs of polished shoes and a woolen coat. Other items were conspicuous by their absence. "Where are his underthings?"

"When my sister told me you were a young unwed lady, I removed them. Your virtue must be protected."

My virtue wouldn't be lost by seeing a man's under-clothes, but I bit my tongue. I checked the jacket and coat pockets, then inside the shoes. My fingers touched cool metal near the toe.

I removed a fine silver watch. It was very shiny and there wasn't a scratch on it. I held it up by its chain to show Mrs. Turner. Like me, she knew immediately it was a quality time-piece of the sort a wealthy gentleman would wear, not a butler.

"Where did he get that?" she murmured.

I checked the case, inside and out, but there were no initials or other way of telling whether Mr. Hardy owned it or had stolen it. "You've never seen him wear it?"

"No."

"It doesn't belong to Sir Ian?"

"No! Mr. Hardy wasn't a thief, Miss Fox. I hadn't known him long, but he struck me as a fine fellow of good moral fiber."

I didn't point out that if he'd come by it using legitimate means, he wouldn't have kept it in his shoe. The question was, why in his shoe and not the metal box? Unable to think of a good reason, I placed it back into the shoe only to discover another object tucked into the toe.

I removed it and laid it flat on my palm. It was a gold gentleman's tiepin shaped like a sword with small diamonds inlaid into the pommel and a sapphire the size of my smallest fingernail in the center. I didn't bother to ask Mrs. Turner if she'd seen it before. I knew by the shocked look on her face that she hadn't, and that she was as confused as me as to why Mr. Hardy had it and why he kept it in his shoe. I returned it along with the watch to its hiding place.

"Did he have family?" I asked.

"I don't know. I didn't find any correspondence when I came in here after he died. Lady Campbell will have his details in her writing bureau listing his next of kin."

"The day of his death, when he told you his things had been moved, did he mention which things?"

"The bottle, his pillow, some items in the top drawer of the bedside table. His bedcovers were wrinkled, too. He couldn't abide wrinkles."

I smoothed my hand over the bedcover when searching. If the intruder had left wrinkles, it would seem they'd been searching for something, too. The question was, what? And had they found it in the metal box?

"I'd like to see his office next, please, Mrs. Turner."

She locked the butler's bedchamber door and led the way downstairs to the basement. She was in the process of unlocking the butler's office when Davey the footman hurried past, adjusting his collar as he went.

"They just arrived home," he said over his shoulder before disappearing up the stairs. "Nice meeting you, Miss Fox. Pity we can't chat longer."

I waited until he was out of earshot before I asked Mrs. Turner my next question. "Will he be made butler now?"

She opened the door and indicated I should go ahead of her. "It's unlikely. He doesn't have the experience or the... how shall I put it? There's a foreign sounding word that starts with g..."

"Gravitas?"

"That's it. Mr. Hardy had gravitas. He was the perfect butler. Very knowledgeable, discreet and calm in a crisis. We all liked him." A shadow passed across her face before she cleared her throat and shook it off. "I once asked him if he'd worked in a grander place than this one in his last employment, but he didn't answer me. I could hazard a guess, though."

"Please do."

"I'd say he worked in the country, in one of those manors where they have large dinner parties and house parties that last for weeks. I could picture him butlering in one of those places with dozens of staff under him." The shadow returned. At the very least, she'd admired him. I wondered if there'd been more than admiration between them, hence her decision to investigate his death.

I scanned the contents of the desk. "The Campbells don't have a country property?"

"No. Sir Ian's father lost it some years ago."

She made it sound like he'd merely misplaced the estate. "How unfortunate."

"Quite."

"Are there any more staff here?"

"Just the five of us, now that Mr. Hardy's gone."

It didn't seem like many to me, but I wasn't an expert on the service requirements of Mayfair households.

Mrs. Turner unlocked the silver cabinet and watched me like a hawk as I looked through it, making sure I didn't tuck a napkin ring up my sleeve before leaving. She also unlocked the sideboard cupboard where the liquor was kept. There weren't many bottles inside, but I wasn't sure how much wine and spirits a butler usually kept close to hand and how much was stored in the cellar.

The desk drawers contained nothing out of the ordinary, just the most current ledger listing household expenses, a box of receipts, and spare stationery.

When I completed my search, Mrs. Turner followed me out of the office and locked the door. "Well? What are your thoughts?"

"It's difficult to say. There's very little evidence that he was murdered."

Her top lip twitched. "My sister tells me you're very good at solving murders. She doesn't offer praise lightly, so I'm inclined to believe her. If you think no crime has been committed, well, that will suffice, too."

"Suffice?"

"The staff are unsettled, particularly Betty. She's anxious and upset. Davey, too, despite outward appearances. He says he's going to leave, that he doesn't feel safe here anymore. I don't want either of them to go. It's hard to find good staff. So either find the killer, Miss Fox, or find out for certain that Mr. Hardy died of natural causes. Either result will assuage their fears."

"I'll do my best." I looked to the stairs. "I'd like to talk to Sir Ian and Lady Campbell. Can you announce me, please?"

For a woman who'd shown a limited range of emotions so far, she became positively animated with disapproval. "No, Miss Fox, I cannot just announce you."

"Why not?"

"You've not been invited."

"But I'm investigating the death of their butler in their own house."

"They don't believe a crime has been committed. They won't talk to you."

I huffed out a frustrated breath and once again glanced at the service staircase that led to the upper floors. It felt as though I'd asked to be let into Heaven without going through due process at the gates. "Very well. Try to convince them. If you do, contact me at the hotel at any time, either by telephone or in writing. A message will reach me."

"I will try my best, but I cannot be sure that Sir Ian or Lady Campbell will agree to a meeting." She glanced up the stairs and leaned closer to me. "It would be quite awful for them if the investigation into Mr. Hardy's death was reopened."

"I understand. But do try."

She escorted me to the front door of the service area. As we passed the kitchen, I spotted Mrs. Cook standing with hands on her hips as she studied a recipe book, while Birdy licked a wooden spoon behind her back. Betty the maid sat hunched over her sewing at the table again, a cup of tea within arm's reach. She looked up as we passed. The tea had done little to return the color to her cheeks.

I thanked Mrs. Turner at the door, then climbed the steps to the pavement. I was just adjusting my hat and gloves when a familiar voice greeted me.

"If it isn't the greatest female sleuth in the city. Nay, the country. Perhaps even the world!"

My heart leapt into my throat, but I knew if I hesitated, it would open a crack through which all the emotions I'd bottled up over the last two weeks could escape. And I did *not* want him to see that the kiss had rattled me. "You mean greatest sleuth, female or otherwise. Hello, Harry. How have you been?"

"Fine, although I could be dead for all you care."

"I would have heard if you were. Don't worry, I'd have come to your funeral and cried."

"Sobbing or merely a few silent tears slipping down your cheeks?"

"The latter. I'm an ugly sobber. Besides, silent tears are both beautiful *and* intriguing."

He grinned. "It's good to see you."

"And you." I hadn't realized how much I'd missed his company until seeing him standing there on the steps of the neighbor's townhouse, looking like he belonged here, in one of the city's most exclusive streets. It was that innate confidence he had, the effortless charisma, that made him fit in everywhere. The handsome face and broad shoulders helped, of course.

He joined me on the pavement. "What are you doing here?"

I nodded at the Campbells' front door. "The butler died. It was deemed natural causes, but the housekeeper has her doubts. She thinks he was poisoned. She mentioned her doubts to her sister, who happens to be the hotel's housekeeper, and she suggested I look into it."

"Are they paying you?"

"Yes." I didn't mention it wasn't much. I wasn't sure why.

We both started walking without either of us suggesting we continue on. It seemed we needed to go in the same direction, so it made sense to walk together. To avoid a small puddle, I stepped to the side, bumping him. I quickly put distance between us again. To distract from my reddening face, I tugged on the hem of my waistcoat, smoothed the fabric over my middle, then touched my hat to ensure it was still in place.

Harry laughed softly. He seemed quite unaffected by our meeting after more than two weeks without a word passing between us. Whereas I couldn't look at him without thinking of the kiss we'd shared last time, he was his usual unruffled self. It was annoying, not to mention a little deflating. While I'd purposely avoided him, it hadn't been easy. I'd told myself it was the right thing to do, the best thing, despite going against my instincts. He, on the other hand, seemed to take it in his stride. I supposed he was more experienced at kissing than me, but it would have been nice if he felt as tortured as I did about what to do next.

"Tell me about your investigation," he said. "If you want to, that is. I won't help you unless you ask."

"Why wouldn't I want your help? Your insights are valuable."

"Then it'll be my pleasure to be a sounding board for the world's greatest detective, female or otherwise."

I would have jabbed him in the ribs with my elbow if I

wasn't afraid of getting too close to him again. I entered into comfortably familiar territory by telling him what I'd learned so far about Mr. Hardy's demise, and why Mrs. Turner thought he'd been murdered.

He listened without interruption and didn't respond immediately. We'd come to an intersection and needed to cross the street. The sweeper spotted us and, sensing a tip, hurriedly cleared away the horse manure to create a wide enough path for us. The lad doffed his cap as we passed and Harry dropped a coin into it.

"Have a good day, sir, miss."

On the other side of the street, we continued walking in the direction of the hotel. It was a warm day and I was a little thirsty, which probably meant Harry was, too. Should I invite him in? Would he accept, given my uncle had vowed that Harry could never step foot in the hotel again? Where would we go if he did accept?

"The evidence for murder is flimsy," Harry finally said.

"I'm inclined to believe it was natural causes, after all, and the housekeeper says she'll be satisfied with that verdict. She wants to assuage the fears of the rest of the staff, either by catching a murderer or assuring them no murder took place."

"They'll be suspects if it was murder."

I proceeded to give him my opinion of each member of staff, even though he hadn't asked. It seemed natural to confide in him.

By the time I finished, we were on Piccadilly, almost at the hotel. I realized there was something I hadn't asked him yet. "Why were you calling on the Campbells' neighbor?"

"I had a telephone call from the occupant this morning. She's a regular client who asks me to investigate one thing or another from time to time. That was my fifth visit to her house."

"Fifth! Either she lives in a house riddled with crime, in which case you're not doing your job properly, or she simply wants to spend time in your company. A merry widow, is she?"

He grinned. "She is a widow, as it happens, and is also good company. I like her very much."

"Do you?" I murmured. I wished I hadn't brought it up.

"And what reason did she give for hiring you for the fifth time?"

Out of the corner of my eye, I saw his lips tilt with his smile. "Her housekeeper thought she heard a noise in the kitchen."

"How strange that a large house filled with servants should have noises coming from the kitchen," I said wryly.

"There are no other servants. Just the housekeeper. She and my client were in the sitting room at the time."

"Did your client hear the noise, too?"

"She's hard of hearing, so no, but she gets anxious if her housekeeper is concerned. She's eighty, you see, and her housekeeper is not much younger."

"Eighty!" I blurted out. "Ohhhhh. So she just wants to have *tea* with you."

"Probably." His lips twitched again. "Why? What did you think she wanted?"

"To, er, ask you to reach things on high shelves."

He laughed. "That and drinking tea have become my main tasks when I call on them. I no longer charge Mrs. Danvers a fee after the last time when I discovered her cat lapping up milk spilled from a bottle it had knocked off the table. The time before that, she tasked me with finding her missing jewelry. I found the necklace under the bed and the earrings in the bathroom. The housekeeper thinks Mrs. Danvers is losing her memory."

"The poor dear. It must have been upsetting when she thought she'd lost valuable jewels."

"They were paste. I gather she has sold off everything of value over the years. I think she and the housekeeper were more fearful of an intruder being inside. I checked all the doors and windows and assured them they would keep thieves out as long as they remembered to lock them at night."

It was good of him to take extra precautions, as well as not charge a lady in reduced circumstances for a false alarm.

He stopped before reaching the hotel. "I'll cross the road here." He paused. "Cleo..." He released a breath and shook his head. "Good luck with your investigation." He gave me a flat smile, touched the brim of his hat, and looked down Piccadilly for a gap in the oncoming traffic.

"Wait!"

He turned suddenly. "Yes?"

I removed the seltzer salts bottle from my bag. "You've got a knack for sciences, perhaps you'll know the answer to this. Do poisons all have a distinctive smell? Or do some have no smell at all?" I removed the cork stopper and held it out.

"Some have no smell or taste, so my reading of detective fiction tells me. I don't know which ones." He sniffed the bottle's contents. "It smells like bicarbonate of soda."

I replaced the stopper. "I'll take it to a pharmacist and see what he has to say."

"I may have a better idea. When my father left Scotland Yard, I met a fellow at his farewell party who works at St. Mary's Hospital. My father and his team sometimes took their medical questions to him. He should have the right chemicals on hand to test the seltzer salts for poisons."

"Is he a doctor?"

"More of a scientist. His specialty is dead people, not living ones." He put out his hand. "I'll take it to him now."

"We both will."

"Are you sure you won't be missed?" He glanced at the hotel where Frank was opening the door of one of the hotel's carriages as Goliath retrieved luggage from the back.

"I'm sure. I have nothing scheduled until afternoon tea."

"And if your family looks for you before then?"

"I'll tell them the truth. My uncle doesn't mind my sleuthing now, as long as it doesn't interrupt my social engagements and nobody finds out."

"I was worried Sir Ronald had changed his mind. He tends to do that."

I couldn't deny that my uncle could be fickle. For now, he had given his approval, and I wasn't about to let him forget it.

Cobbit, the coachman, spotted us and touched the brim of his hat in greeting. The acknowledgement wasn't for my benefit, I was sure of it. Harry had helped Cobbit and the other mews staff keep their jobs when they threatened to go on strike over the stabling of a guest's automobile. Harry had suggested a compromise that suited them and Uncle Ronald.

Although, if my uncle had known at the time that Harry had a hand in negotiations, he might have dug his heels in. He wasn't prepared to forgive Harry for lying about his past, even though Harry had been one of his best employees and losing him had interrupted the smooth running of the hotel.

Uncle Ronald was a stubborn man, and I feared he'd never forgive Harry. He might be allowing me to investigate alongside him, but I suspected that was only because he thought Harry was still courting Miss Morris. If he knew their relationship was over, he'd forbid our acquaintance for fear we'd develop feelings for one another.

That's why I was determined he should never know.

CHAPTER 3

$\mathcal{W}$e set off again, retracing our steps down Piccadilly to Apsley House where we caught an omnibus to take us part of the way to St. Mary's Hospital in Paddington.

"Uncle Alfred tells me all has been calm at the hotel lately," Harry said as we settled on the seat.

"Calm but busy, particularly with Miss Hessing's engagement dinner last night. It almost ended in disaster, but thankfully all crises were averted before guests noticed. Speaking of your uncle, where was Mr. Hobart last night?"

"He wasn't at the dinner?"

"No. In fact, he's been absent quite a lot lately. It's very unlike him. Is there a reason?"

"Not that I know of." He frowned. "You're right, though. It is unusual. I'll ask next time I see him."

"Oh, no, please don't. It makes me feel like I'm spying for my uncle."

The rest of our journey threatened to be ruined by awkward silence, so I filled it with chatter about the engagement party instead, as well as Miss Hessing's ideas for her wedding day. If Harry found the topic dull, he was polite enough not to mention it and let me prattle on uninterrupted. By the time we alighted, I was even more parched than before.

We entered the handsome red-brick hospital building and

asked for directions to Dr. Garside's rooms. A few minutes later, we found a man wearing a white coat peering into a microscope in a laboratory smaller than my sitting room. Harry cleared his throat. "Dr. Garside?"

"One moment," the doctor said, without looking up from his microscope. "Make yourself at home while I finish this."

Amongst the rows of bottles, racks of test tubes, and piles of papers, I spied some cups filled with water. "Do you mind if I take a sip? I'm dying of thirst." I reached for one.

"Don't drink that!" Dr. Garside plucked the cup from my grip.

"What is it?"

"Something that will make you very ill if you drink it." Dr. Garside set the cup back in line with the others. "I'm afraid I don't have any refreshments in here. I don't usually have visitors."

"You should have a warning label on those," Harry said tightly.

"As I said, I don't usually have visitors." Dr. Garside spoke just as tightly as he regarded Harry with a mixture of annoyance and faint recognition. "Have we met?" Based on his thinning hair and the creases around his eyes, I gauged him to be aged in his mid-forties. He was neatly attired, a green silk waistcoat and black bowtie showing underneath his laboratory coat, although the bowtie was a little crooked.

Harry reintroduced himself. Once the connection to the former Detective Inspector Hobart was established, Dr. Garside's face cleared. He smiled and extended his hand. "I remember now. We met at your father's farewell. You're a private detective."

"I am, and this is my associate, Miss Fox. Her current investigation is the reason for our visit."

Dr. Garside studied me anew, this time with all the attention he gave the object under his microscope. "A lady detective? Do you specialize in wayward husbands, Miss Fox?"

It was an obvious assumption, considering most female detectives tended to get lumped with cases that involved spying on, or catching out, philandering men. I tried not to let it annoy me. "I tend to find myself embroiled in murders."

"How fortunate!"

"Not for the victims."

Dr. Garside blinked. "Yes. Quite. I mean how fortunate for you to have interesting cases to investigate. I assume Mr. Armitage told you I can help identify the cause of death where it's not obvious, and that's why you're here? I ought to warn you, I need access to the cadaver for my work, and I doubt you brought one with you." He chuckled to himself. "Forgive me. It was a macabre little joke."

I removed the bottle from my bag. "We're hoping you can identify if there is poison in these seltzer salts and, if so, which one."

Dr. Garside's eyes brightened. He waggled his fingers as if he couldn't wait to wrap them around the bottle. "How intriguing! I do love a good poisoning."

I somehow kept a straight face as I watched him sniff the contents before distributing pea-sized amounts of the salts into test tubes. He then collected several bottles of liquid from the shelf and proceeded to drip three drops of one of the liquids onto the first batch of salts. Nothing happened.

"Do you know when the victim last ate or drank anything?" he asked as he dropped three drops of the second liquid into the second test tube. "Was it immediately before his death or much earlier?"

"Earlier. All the witnesses say he didn't have anything immediately before. When he did eat or drink, the others had the same thing. That's why I wanted the salts tested, as they're potentially the only thing that he had that the others didn't." I proceeded to tell him how the butler had seemed disoriented then collapsed and had a seizure before dying.

"Did he vomit? Froth at the mouth?"

"Not as far as I know."

"Was there discoloration around or inside his mouth? Or fingernails?"

"I'm afraid I don't know. I didn't see the body and the witnesses who did might not have noticed those things if they were present."

"The police believe it was natural causes, if that helps," Harry said.

Dr. Garside added droplets to the last test tube. Nothing happened. I thought that was the end of his experiments, but he then proceeded to use a pair of tongs to hold each test tube over a Bunsen burner. He muttered to himself then finally stood back, hands on hips.

"Based on your witness reports, I can inform you he didn't die of arsenic, antimony, mercury, or cyanide poisoning. Without doing an autopsy, I can only guess, but it's very likely your victim may have consumed hyoscine in the hours leading up to his death. It also goes by the name of scopolamine and is found in the seeds and leaves of henbane. If taken in small doses, it can actually be beneficial. The medical profession uses it to treat motion sickness, stomach complaints and even alcoholism. Larger doses, however, can kill. The victim will convulse, then lose consciousness, and finally suffer respiratory failure. If the fully grown male victim had any underlying conditions, like a weak heart, then as little as a quarter of a grain could be fatal. It's imperative that a patient taking a tonic or powder containing hyoscine hydrobromide ingests only the dose prescribed by their doctor."

I indicated the series of test tubes. Some of the seltzer had changed color or fizzed, while others looked the same. "Which one of these shows you that it's hyoscine?"

"None." He handed me the bottle of seltzer salts. "This doesn't contain anything other than bicarbonate of soda. Not only would a dose of the seltzer not have killed him, it wouldn't have cured him of anything either."

I tucked the bottle into my bag. "Thank you, Doctor. I'm sorry about almost drinking your experiment earlier."

"That's not an experiment. It's fluid from the brain and spinal cord of a recently deceased male."

I must have looked like I was about to be sick because Harry hastily thanked the doctor then steered me out of the laboratory, through the hospital and outside. The fresh air helped to settle my stomach, although it was warm and I was still thirsty. When Harry suggested we find a teashop, I gratefully agreed.

The brief walk did me good and my stomach made the most unladylike rumble of hunger as we sat at a table covered with a pretty blue-and-yellow checkered tablecloth. We ordered tea and sandwiches and fell into a discussion about poisons, keeping our voices low so as not to alarm our nearest neighbors.

"Without doing an autopsy, it's impossible to know whether Mr. Hardy was poisoned or died of natural causes," I said.

"Dr. Garside seemed quite sure that if the victim was poisoned, it was with hyoscine," Harry said. "The question is, how was it administered?"

"If at all."

His lips curved at the edges with his small smile. "But you don't believe he did. I can tell from the dint between your brows."

I pressed my finger to the space between my brows in an attempt to smooth out the dint. I wished I wasn't so easy to read, particularly by him. "I would be inclined to think he did die of natural causes if it wasn't for the forced lock on the lockbox and the fact his room had clearly been searched. Not to mention the other staff noticed Mr. Hardy seemed altered when meeting the Campbells' friends. Not the ones on the night of the murder, but the couple who dined there a few nights earlier, the Whitchurches. They all said he became more thoughtful and somewhat distracted."

"Tell me what you know about them. It might help to toss out ideas as to why the sight of them unnerved him."

"It wasn't the sight of Lord and Lady Whitchurch that brought about a change in him. It was the mention of their name when Lady Campbell informed him the Whitchurches were coming to dinner. He clearly knew them or knew of them. According to the footman, they recognized Mr. Hardy at dinner, although he thinks they couldn't place him."

Harry frowned. "Whitchurch? That name rings a bell."

"Were they guests at the hotel?"

He slowly shook his head. "I don't think so..." He continued to frown as we ate our sandwiches and sipped our tea. Every suggestion I made as to how the name could be familiar to him was met with another shake of his head.

Until I suggested that he might not have met them at all, but heard someone else mention them. He clicked his fingers. "You're right." He picked up his teacup. "Finish your sandwiches. I need to telephone my father."

* * *

HARRY PROMISED to telephone me after he'd talked to his father. He'd not been able to give me any other information about the Whitchurches except to say the name reminded him of an old case of Inspector Hobart's. It must have made an impact on Harry at the time for him to recall the name years later.

I returned to the hotel well before it was time to dress for afternoon tea. I informed Goliath and Frank about my new case, then repeated the information for Peter's sake, who told me that Mrs. Short had asked him to send me to her office when I returned. Once there, I again gave a report on the investigation so far. I had a question for her, too.

"What do you know of the Campbells, Mrs. Short? Your sister is inclined to protect her employers, but I believe you will give me an honest answer. Do they treat their staff well?"

She hesitated, then expelled a resigned sigh. "My sister won't like me telling you this. She'll assume it has no bearing on the case, but I think you ought to know everything. The Campbells have paid the staff their wages late on occasion. They've also let one of the maids go, as well as the coachman and groom, after they sold their horse and equipage."

So they were poor by the standards of their class. The sumptuousness of the dining room had belied their reduced circumstances. "Mrs. Turner mentioned Sir Ian's father lost the country estate some years ago."

"It seems the money from its sale may have run out."

It did indeed seem to be the case. "Thank you, Mrs. Short. If you think of anything else your sister may have told you that may be relevant, please inform me."

"One more thing, Miss Fox." She wouldn't immediately meet my gaze, but when she finally did, she held it as directly as always. "If my sister can't raise the funds to pay you, I would like to contribute something to your fee."

The way she worded it should have been a warning. "What would you like to contribute?"

"I'll allow Miss Cotton to continue to breakfast with you in your suite of a morning."

35

I stared at her, my mouth ajar. Should I deny it? Say nothing? Call her a blackmailer?

She spoke again before I'd made my decision. "I know she breakfasts with you, and I've been considering whether to put an end to it. If the other maids find out, it might cause jealousy. They'll think she gets special treatment from me because of her friendship with you. But I'll allow her to continue until someone discovers you, at which point I must insist that you end the practice."

I was still a little stunned, so only managed to say, "I see."

"Miss Fox..." She sighed. "I hesitate to say this, because I don't think you'll understand, but, if I were you, I'd consider ending the breakfasts anyway. You may think you're doing something nice for Miss Cotton, but all you're really doing is giving her false hope. She believes she's special because she has your ear, that you can help her rise above her station, but we both know she can't be anything other than a maid at this point in time. Perhaps one day she will be housekeeper here, when I am gone, but that's all a girl like her can hope for."

It wasn't often that my temper surfaced, but at that moment, it boiled up and spilled over. I couldn't contain it any more than I could hold back a sneeze. "Harmony is my friend, it's true, but it isn't our friendship that will see her take on more responsibility here. It's her intelligence, diligence and dedication. She acquitted herself superbly when she organized the opening of the restaurant. She doesn't need my friendship to help her, because it's clear to all who know her that she is extremely competent and capable. Indeed, she has asked me *not* to help her." I strode for the door, only to stop before opening it. "And why shouldn't she, or any of your maids, wish to take on a different role? What is wrong with aspiring to be something else?"

"Because very, very few women can ever fulfil their dreams, Miss Fox. You are privileged enough to be able to afford to dream. Girls like Miss Cotton and the rest of the maids cannot."

"You don't know my situation at all, Mrs. Short. Do not presume." I stormed out of her office before I said something I'd later regret. Despite my anger, she was right about one thing: I might not be wealthy, like she seemed to think, but I had a privileged life compared to the maids. I had an education and all the advantages that came with being the niece of Sir Ronald Bainbridge. I never had to worry about paying rent or going hungry. If I wanted to climb the ladder of society, I only had to marry the right man, as unpalatable as that option was to me.

Maids and other service staff could rarely move up to the next rung of the ladder, however. There was only the same rung, or lower. I couldn't name a single maid who'd risen beyond the position of housekeeper. While the senior position came with more responsibility and pay than a maid's, it wasn't what Harmony aspired to.

My temper had cooled a little by the time I came across Flossy emerging from the lift. She looked like she'd been crying. John, the lift operator, looked relieved that he no longer had to be enclosed in a small space alone with her. He must have been worried that she'd spill all of her woes out to him. Perhaps she already had.

"Flossy, what is it?" I caught her by the arms and tried to peer into her eyes, but she wouldn't lift her chin. "What's wrong?"

"It's Mother." She fished a handkerchief from the inside of her sleeve. "She's being beastly."

"What did she say?"

"She called me silly for not liking that fellow she made me sit next to at dinner last night. Apparently, she thought he'd be a good match for me, but he was frightfully dull, not to mention he had a lazy eye that wandered about independent of the other one. When I told her my reasons for talking to you most of the night instead of him, she got very cross and said I'd never find a husband if I set such impossibly high standards. But Cleo, if I lower them, who knows what sort of man she'll marry me off to."

Three guests approached to take the lift, so I steered Flossy away. "Don't take it to heart. Her illness is making her say things she doesn't mean."

Aunt Lilian had been taking a tonic containing cocaine for her nerves for some time. While it initially gave her renewed energy, when it wore off, she became lethargic and suffered debilitating headaches. She'd become addicted to it, needing more of it more often to give her the same benefits. We'd tried convincing her to stop taking it, but she refused, saying she needed it to get through the whirl of social engagements. Lately, her moods had changed again. Usually so kind and thoughtful, she now snapped at her loved ones and had become short with those around her.

"What's even worse is that Father is also in a dreadful mood because Mother is," Flossy went on. "I wouldn't go near his office if I were you, Cleo."

"I won't, but I am going upstairs. Are you coming?"

She shook her head. "I need some fresh air."

I took the stairs to the fourth floor rather than wait for the lift. I glanced at my uncle's office door, then walked in the other direction, to my suite. I passed Floyd emerging from his rooms.

"There you are," he said. "Come with me." He signaled for me to follow him, then strode off.

I stayed put. "To where?"

"My father's office."

"Why does he want to see me?"

He stopped. "He doesn't, but I think you should speak to him."

"Flossy told me to avoid him."

"You can't avoid him, so it's best to get it over with."

"Get what over with?"

"Hobart." With that cryptic response he knocked on Uncle Ronald's office door, then opened it. "After you, Cousin."

Sometimes, the best way to counter someone's ill temper is to attack it with positivity and brightness. I smiled. "Good afternoon, Uncle. I've just been outside for a walk. It's a glorious summer day out there."

He grunted. "Glad some of us have the time for walks. I've got work to do." He picked up a ledger then dropped it on the desk with a loud bang. A pencil rolled across the surface and tumbled to the floor.

I picked it up and returned it to the desk. "Don't you have an assistant to take some of the load from you?"

"He's busy. Besides, this is a reporting issue. Hobart should be taking care of it, but he's busy, too. Usually he does his reports at home if he doesn't get them done here, but lately he's been shirking."

"Is it shirking *not* to work out of hours? If he has so much to do that he needs to take work home, then perhaps he needs more help."

"He has an assistant," Uncle Ronald growled. "Anyway, this has never been a problem before. He never complained about taking work home. He simply did it. This lackadaisical attitude of his is becoming a problem."

"It's hardly lackadaisical to refuse to take work home," I said tightly.

"He should have been at the hotel last night for the engagement party. And he leaves right on time lately, not a moment later, and he takes an entire hour off for lunch. He used to work through the day without stopping."

I glanced at Floyd, standing a little behind me, but he remained silent. I suspected he didn't want his father's attention to turn to him. He appeared to be waiting for his father to say something, however.

"Floyd, why did you insist I come in here to speak to Uncle Ronald?"

Uncle Ronald frowned. "Why indeed? Afraid to talk to me alone, son?"

Floyd cleared his throat. "I thought Cleo might have an answer for you about Hobart's change of attitude. If not, she could find out, given they're on friendly terms."

I narrowed my gaze at him. "I don't have any answers for you. Perhaps Mr. Hobart simply needs a rest. When was the last time he had a holiday?"

Father and son both shrugged.

"There you are. Perhaps he's tired."

"Then why not just say so and ask for some time off?" Uncle Ronald snapped. He had a point. "I know what's going on with him," he went on. "I don't need you to find out for me, Cleopatra. I can make an educated guess. I have it on good authority that the Carlton Hotel is in need of a new manager. Hobart must be considering the position."

"Steady on," Floyd declared. "Hobart would never leave the Mayfair. He's been here longer than I've been alive. He's part of the furniture."

39

"Perhaps that attitude explains why he's considering leaving, *if* indeed he is," I pointed out. "You take him for granted."

Uncle Ronald narrowed his gaze at me. "So, you do think he's leaving?"

"I'm simply saying you should treat him with the respect he deserves. Don't give him so much work that he needs to take it home of an evening, and don't expect him to work through lunch or stay late."

Uncle Ronald stroked his moustache with his thumb and forefinger and grumbled a protest under his breath. Finally, he got to the point. "It's not just Hobart. I feel as though I can't trust any of the staff lately. Ever since Armitage left—"

"You dismissed him."

"The business with Armitage, then the former housekeeper, and lately Cobbit's unrest…it feels as though the staff are mutinying." He stabbed his stubby finger on the ledger's cover. "The problem is, there's no loyalty anymore."

"They will be loyal if they're treated with respect," I pointed out.

He went on as if I hadn't spoken. "As to Hobart, I thought I knew him. I thought we had a mutual understanding. But now…I'm no longer certain of his loyalty."

Floyd finally stepped forward. "I have a suggestion. Why don't you investigate him, Cleo?"

I spluttered a laugh. When I realized he was serious, the laugh turned to a protest. "I am not spying on Mr. Hobart for you, Floyd. Or for you, Uncle."

"Father will pay you."

"Is this why you hauled me in here?"

He dug his hands into his trouser pockets and rocked back on his heels, but the innocent look wouldn't work on me.

"Honestly, Floyd. If you want to know what's on Mr. Hobart's mind, why not ask him?"

When his response was to glance at his father, I turned back to my uncle.

"Hobart may not give a direct answer," Uncle Ronald said. "Cleopatra, I won't ask you to investigate him if you don't want to."

"Good, because I won't."

"Give it more thought. You're part of this family, and your loyalty should be with us and the hotel, not the staff."

He may not be asking me to investigate, but he was doing something even more unpalatable. He was using emotional blackmail in an attempt to coerce me.

I wasn't going to be persuaded, but I wasn't going to burn my bridges either. Fortunately, sometimes my temper could be reined in before it did any damage. "The needs of the family, the hotel and the staff are closely entwined. What benefits one, benefits the other two. Look how well the situation turned out with Cobbit and the grooms. I'm sure this situation will resolve just as well for everyone." There. It wasn't an agreement to investigate, but it wasn't an outright refusal either.

Uncle Ronald grunted, then opened the ledger and picked up a pencil. He concentrated on his work, dismissing Floyd and me with a flick of his finger.

I hurried out ahead of Floyd, not wanting to speak to him lest he asked me again to investigate Mr. Hobart. As I passed the door to my aunt and uncle's suite, I slowed. I wanted to ask Aunt Lilian about the Campbells, but the timing didn't feel right. If she was still in a sour mood, it was best to leave her alone. Besides, my own mood was positively black.

I returned to my suite and tried to read a book while I waited for Harmony to come as prearranged to do my hair. The moment she entered, I couldn't help blurting out what Uncle Ronald and Floyd had asked me to do. It wasn't until afterward that I regretted it. While she and I were friends, my uncle wouldn't want me discussing hotel business with anyone outside the family.

Harmony's response was to order me to sit at my dressing table, face the mirror, and tell her how I wanted my hair done for afternoon tea. She understood that I'd simply needed to vent my problems. I wasn't looking for answers.

I did feel better and was able to change the topic. I told her what Harry and I had learned today. At the mention of his name, her hands stilled.

"You're blushing," she said.

"I am not! It's hot in here." I picked up a fan from my dressing table and flapped it in front of my face.

She smiled and continued to arrange my hair.

Once that task was finished, she helped me dress in a pink-and-green tea gown with lace sleeves and more lace across my décolletage, then sent me on my way with a spray of Guerlain. I met my aunt and Flossy in the corridor, waiting for the lift.

Flossy gave me a knowing look and a subtle glance at her mother.

Aunt Lilian put out her hands to me and pecked my cheek. She looked flushed, her eyes brilliant and huge in her gaunt face. I didn't need to employ any detective skills to know she'd had a dose of her tonic to get her through afternoon tea. "My dearest niece, how pretty you look! Doesn't she look lovely, Florence?"

"She does," Flossy said.

"My two lovely girls, what beauties you are." She squeezed my hands before turning to the lift door. She tapped her foot on the carpet. "What's taking John so long?"

Flossy and I exchanged disappointed glances.

Downstairs, I caught sight of Mr. Hobart in the foyer. He must have been watching the lift doors and waiting, because he approached. For a moment, I thought he'd caught wind of my earlier meeting with Uncle Ronald and Floyd, but his announcement eased my conscience.

"Miss Fox, you have a telephone call. You may take it in my office." As he walked beside me, he whispered, "It's Harry." He peeled away to speak to a new guest looking lost near the entrance.

In his office, I picked up the telephone receiver and leaned forward to speak into the mouthpiece. "Hello, Harry."

His voice crackled over the line. "I spoke to my father and he confirmed my suspicion. I had heard him speak about the Whitchurches years ago. They were caught up in an investigation that he couldn't solve. It bothers him still, and he was very keen to hear more when I mentioned their link to your current investigation."

"What crime was he investigating back then?"

"Murder."

CHAPTER 4

*H*arry gave me the bare bones of the case, as told to him by his father. "Twenty-five years ago, one of the Whitchurches' maids was found dead in the kitchen, stabbed through the heart."

"Were the Whitchurches suspects?" I asked.

"He refused to tell me more over the telephone." Caution edged Harry's tone. He, too, was concerned about a telephone operator listening in to our conversation. "He suggested we call on him tomorrow morning. I'll meet you at my office and we'll catch the train."

"Together?"

Even though I thought I spoke mildly and without undue concern, Harry's laughter drifted down the line. "Afraid of being alone with me now, Cleo?"

I was surprised that he confronted the cause of my awkwardness head-on. Perhaps the physical distance between us made it easier for him. It didn't make it easier for me. I attempted a laugh, too, but it sounded flat. "Not at all."

"What if I promise not to kiss you again?"

"Harry!"

"I'll take that as you not agreeing to the promise, which is good because I had no plan to keep it."

I hastily said goodbye and hung the receiver on its hook as I flapped my hand in front of my warm face. I regretted not bringing a fan with me.

I entered the large sitting room where the hotel's famous afternoon teas were served on the finest china by impeccably dressed waiters. Mr. Chapman looked up from his reservations book with a ready smile, but it vanished upon seeing me.

"Good afternoon, Miss Fox." It was politely said, if lacking the enthusiasm he reserved for guests and Bainbridges.

"Good afternoon, Mr. Chapman. Oh look, we match." I indicated the pink rose tucked into his buttonhole with two green leaves still attached. They were the same shade as my dress.

"How delightful," he said blandly.

I joined Aunt Lilian and Flossy, seated alone at our regular table as our guests had not yet arrived. They chatted quietly to one another, although my aunt fidgeted with her napkin and her gaze darted around the room. Richard, the head waiter, swooped in and asked if I required anything while I waited. Neither my aunt nor cousin had any refreshments in front of them, so I declined, too.

Mr. Chapman signaled for Richard to join him. They spoke, then Mr. Chapman disappeared. He reappeared a few minutes later with a white carnation in place of the pink rose. I laughed to myself, not at all surprised.

"Why are you smiling like that, Cleo?" Aunt Lilian asked.

"Mr. Chapman changed his flower after I pointed out that his rose was the same color as my dress."

She looked to Mr. Chapman, once again manning the reservations desk, and spotted her friend, Mrs. Druitt-Poore, arriving with her two daughters. "Here they are!"

Just as they joined us, Mrs. Digby arrived with her daughter. The older women fell into the easy chatter of long-term friends catching up on the latest gossip, while the younger women passed along gossip about their peers. I knew some of the people they talked about, but not all. Even so, I listened intently. Gossip was an important currency in my work. One day the information they imparted today might be useful.

Neither they nor their mothers mentioned the names of anyone I was interested in for my current investigation, however. I waited until after the first round of tea and scones had been consumed before steering the conversation in a direction I wanted.

"What do you know about Sir Ian and Lady Campbell?"

The young ladies all looked at me blankly.

"Lord and Lady Whitchurch?"

More blank looks.

"Why?" asked Cora Druitt-Poore.

Before I could think of an innocent reason, Flossy turned to her mother's friends. "Cleo wants to know about the Campbells and Whitchurches. Is anyone familiar with them?"

Fortunately, they weren't as curious as to my reason for asking, but were quite keen to impart their knowledge.

"The Whitchurches keep to themselves," Mrs. Digby said. "There was a scandal many years ago, but I don't recall anything about it now." She looked at her friends. While Aunt Lilian shrugged, Mrs. Druitt-Poore picked up the explanation.

"It had something to do with the current Lord Whitchurch's older brother. He went missing. This was when their father was still alive, so the eldest was the heir at the time."

I leaned forward, eager to hear more. "Missing?"

"The eldest of the two brothers was quite unsuitable to be a viscount anyway, so I heard. He was a notorious trouble-maker, and a drinker and gambler. The younger brother was the opposite—serious, quiet, and generally thought to be a good egg. He inherited the title when his father died, since the elder brother had been declared dead by the authorities by then, despite his body never being discovered."

It must be the younger son and his wife who were friends with the Campbells.

Aunt Lilian made a sudden and surprising announcement. "Lady Campbell is here now."

Everyone glanced around until she hissed at us not to.

"She's seated with three others by the potted palm near the library. She's the one dressed in black with the large amethyst brooch edged with diamonds and pearls. She used to come to afternoon tea here regularly, although I haven't seen her in some time."

I subtly glanced in Lady Campbell's direction. She was about the same age as my aunt, with gray hair that she tried to cover with a large, feathered hat. She was dressed elegantly, albeit entirely in black. Her clothes were a little out of date, too, although not unacceptably so. Women her age didn't always follow the latest fashion like Flossy and her friends.

"What do you know about her, Aunt?" I asked.

"We've never been properly introduced, so we've never spoken." She picked up her teacup. Noticing it tremble in her shaking hand, she used her other hand to steady it. "She keeps to herself and her small group of friends. They rarely attend social gatherings."

"The Whitchurches are the same," Mrs. Digby said. "I never see them out."

My aunt abruptly changed the conversation to a different topic, not giving her friends the opportunity to ask me why I was making inquiries about the Campbells and Whitchurches. She probably suspected I was investigating them and so made sure I didn't have to face questions I couldn't answer. She wanted to keep my detecting a secret just as much as my uncle did, even from her closest friends.

The rest of the afternoon continued slowly, until our guests departed along with most of the other ladies in the sitting room. Flossy and I waited as Aunt Lilian thanked Richard for his service to our table. Near the door, Mr. Chapman was attempting to get Lady Campbell's attention, but she hurried off without acknowledging him.

Mr. Chapman asked to have a word with my aunt as we left the sitting room. We couldn't overhear him, so Flossy asked what he wanted when Aunt Lilian rejoined us.

"Nothing that concerns you," she said.

"But wasn't it do with Lady Campbell, who Cleo was just asking about?"

"That doesn't give her, or you, the right to poke your nose into other people's affairs. Nobody likes a busybody, Florence."

Flossy stopped and stared at her mother's back as she strode off toward the lift. I clasped her hand and squeezed.

"Her tonic wore off some time ago," I said. "She must have a dreadful headache."

To prove my point, Aunt Lilian pressed her fingertips to her temple as she waited for the lift.

"I know," Flossy said heavily. "But it doesn't make it any easier to bear." She glanced over her shoulder to Mr. Chapman, farewelling a pair of guests. "If you think it might be important, you should ask him why he wanted to speak to Lady Campbell."

"I doubt he'll tell me. He might be a busybody himself, but he doesn't like me and will be disinclined to help. Besides, it's unlikely to have any bearing on my investigation." I squeezed her hand again. "Come on, let's go for a walk. I could do with some fresh air."

* * *

SEVERAL CONVERSATIONS from the previous day still weighed on my mind when I met Harry the following morning in the café below his office. The one that weighed heaviest, however, was the one I'd had with Mrs. Short about Harmony. As we sat drinking coffee at the table by the window, I couldn't help bringing it up. Of all my friends, Harry would give the wisest and most honest answer.

"Should I stop having breakfast with Harmony each morning?"

He watched me over the rim of his cup, then set it down on the table without taking a sip. "Who suggested you should stop?"

I told him what Mrs. Short had said, including her comment that she'd refrain from forbidding Harmony, as a reward of sorts for investigating Mr. Hardy's death. "Is she right? Am I being cruel by giving Harmony false hope? The thing is," I went on before he could answer, "Harmony doesn't want my help, so she gains no advantage from our friendship. Mrs. Short is wrong about that." I felt pleased with my argument and looked expectantly at Harry.

He deflated my hopes with a shake of his head. "Mrs. Short's biggest concern isn't you giving Harmony false hope. It's what the other maids believe. If they think Harmony has an advantage by being friends with you, then they'll take their grievances to Mrs. Short. Mrs. Short will then have to do something about it. At best, she'll tell you to stop. At worst, she'll dismiss Harmony or take her concerns to Sir Ronald. Perhaps both."

He was right, but I wished he wasn't. "How did she find out, anyway?"

"You'll be surprised how quickly gossip is spread amongst the staff, particularly if it involves their employers."

"I'm not their employer."

"Your uncle is. Besides, you're pretty, young, unwed, and new to the hotel. What better fodder for gossip is there? If you want them to stop, don't do anything interesting and they'll turn their attention elsewhere."

I briefly toyed with the idea of encouraging Floyd to resume his hedonistic ways to provide a distraction, but dismissed it. I didn't want him thrown out of carriages in the middle of the night, drunk and miserable after losing at the gambling tables again. He still stayed out most evenings until very late anyway, attending private parties. He didn't give anyone a reason to stop gossiping about him.

"So, you do think I should end my breakfasts with Harmony?"

"No."

"But you just confirmed that Mrs. Short might be forced to act."

"And if she does act, I'm sure you'll manage to defuse the situation and smooth ruffled feathers, be they hers or Sir Ronald's. You're good at that, particularly where he's concerned."

I finished my coffee and said goodbye to Luigi, the proprietor, leaning against the counter as he flipped through an instruction manual for a new coffee maker. Harry said a few words in Italian to the two creased old men perched on their favorite stools. They both looked at me, gave a single nod, and muttered something back to Harry.

Outside, I commended him on the rapid improvement in his Italian. "You were very fluent and your vocabulary has already exceeded mine."

"Thank you. I've been practicing with them every day."

I waited for more, but he didn't elaborate. "What did you say to them?"

"It was just a little gossip to impart."

"About me?"

"Not everything is about you, Cleo."

"But they looked at me and nodded."

"That was their way of saying goodbye to you." Harry spied a cab pulling to the curb to let some passengers out. "Forget the train. This is more convenient."

He signaled to the driver to wait. When he reached the carriage, he put out his hand to me to assist me up to the cabin.

There's a way a gentleman holds a lady's hand to assist her. It's a light, impersonal touch, involving the fingers only. Harry held my hand as though we were courting.

He didn't let go until I was seated, then he climbed in and sat beside me. If he was aware that he'd held my hand intimately, he didn't show it. Although he did seem rather pleased with himself. He smiled at me as we set off.

"What is it?" I asked cautiously. "Why are you looking at me like that?"

"I'm simply remembering the look on your face after our kiss."

Of all the things he could have said, I'd not expected that. I was so surprised that I gulped in a gasp of air, causing me to choke. Harry offered his handkerchief as my coughing fit subsided. I pushed it away.

"This is how you looked at first," he said. "Startled. Then you blushed the brightest red I've ever seen, then you ran off, but not before I saw how much you liked the kiss."

"I did not!"

"It's understandable. It was a very good kiss, if I do say so myself."

His cockiness almost had me laughing out loud. I covered it with a derisive snort. "We need to change the subject."

"Why?"

"Because we can't let it happen again."

"Can't we?" he asked idly. "Why not, if we both enjoyed it?"

"I didn't say I enjoyed it. *You* said I did." I smoothed my hands down my skirt, over my thighs. My palms felt sweaty within my gloves, and my collar too tight. "Before we visit your father, I ought to tell you about yesterday's afternoon tea."

"*You* might want to pretend the kiss never happened, but I'm not going to."

"Stop changing the subject."

"You changed it first, Cleo. Very well. We don't have to talk about the kiss or how you've been avoiding me ever since."

"I have not! I've been too busy to call on you. Besides, there hasn't been a reason to see you until now."

With a smile playing at his lips, he pressed a hand to his chest. "Ouch."

"If you don't stop, Harry, I'll continue this investigation alone."

He stopped.

I spent the next few minutes telling him what I'd heard and seen at afternoon tea the day before. When I'd finished, we traveled in silence to his parents' home in Ealing.

His mother greeted us at the door with a hug and a big smile for Harry. The smile she gave me was less enthusiastic and I received no hug, just a cool welcome that wasn't quite as frosty as her usual greetings. I hadn't called on the Hobarts often, but when I did, Mrs. Hobart always made it clear that she hadn't forgiven me for getting Harry dismissed from his position at the hotel. She was fiercely protective of him, as most mothers would be. Even though she only became his mother when he was thirteen, she was no less protective of him than a natural mother would be. She and D.I. Hobart were wonderful parents to their adopted son.

A moment of melancholy welled within me as I thought of my own parents, both killed in an accident when I was ten. I didn't think of them as much as a daughter ought to, and that only made the melancholy worse. I loved my parents, and they'd loved me, but their marriage had been volatile. My paternal grandparents, who'd taken me in, blamed my other grandparents for not accepting their son, placing a strain on the marriage from the outset. I used to believe that, too, but as I grew older and saw more marriages, both good and bad, I began to realize the truth was more complicated. My mother's family's rejection of my father certainly hadn't helped, though.

Harry touched my elbow. "Are you all right?"

"Fine, thank you."

"If it's about the conversation in the cab on the way here, I'm sorry. I was just trying to clear the air. It was clumsy."

"It was."

"And a little childish."

"True, but it's all right."

He gave me a flat smile and indicated I should walk ahead of him into the parlor where his father rose from an armchair to greet us. D.I. Hobart—I still couldn't think of him as anything other than Detective Inspector, even though he was retired—shook my hand and indicated I should sit with a flap of the papers he held in his other hand.

"Good to see you again, Miss Fox. Harry tells me you have another murder to investigate."

Mrs. Hobart clicked her tongue. "Stephen," she chided. "You've forgotten your manners."

D.I. Hobart looked sheepish. "My apologies, Miss Fox. How have you been?"

Satisfied that the formality of exchanging pleasantries was being observed, Mrs. Hobart left.

The moment he gauged she was out of earshot, D.I. Hobart asked me to tell him everything about the investigation so far. He knew most of it, so I simply updated him on what I'd learned at afternoon tea.

As I finished, Mrs. Hobart bustled in carrying a tray. She poured tea and offered me a cup. While she didn't smile, she didn't scowl at me either. It was an improvement.

D.I. Hobart sipped his tea thoughtfully. "I'll get to the disappearance of the older Whitchurch brother in a moment, but first, I think you should find out why Chapman spoke to Lady Campbell. It may have no bearing on the case, but you never know what will lead to the unearthing of a clue." He pointed the teacup at me, then Harry. "Not that I need to tell either of you that."

"Did any of your cases for Scotland Yard involve hyoscine poisoning?" I asked.

"One, although there could have been others that I or my

fellow detectives attributed to natural causes, just as yours has been. While a body can be tested for hyoscine, if no one suspects murder, the coroner won't order a test. The symptoms don't obviously point to poisoning."

"It's a pity we can't dig up the body."

Both Harry and D.I. Hobart nodded.

Too late, I realized how unladylike I must sound to Mrs. Hobart. "I'm sorry," I said to her. "That was unfeeling of me."

"Don't mind me, Miss Fox. I've heard far worse in this very room."

Her husband chuckled. "Very true." He took a large gulp of his tea, then set the cup down. "Now, let me tell you what I know. Harry informed me yesterday that your investigation has a link to the Whitchurches, so I called on a former colleague. He and I were part of the team that investigated the murder of the Whitchurches' maid years ago. He still works at the Yard and was able to bring me the old case file."

He picked up the papers he'd been holding when we entered and placed them on the central table between us. Sensing we'd need more space, Mrs. Hobart cleared away the cups and saucers.

D.I. Hobart spread the papers out. "Twenty years ago, we were called out to Lord and Lady Whitchurch's home in Mayfair. That's the former Lord Whitchurch, now deceased, and his wife, the current dowager. A housemaid named Charlotte was found dead on the kitchen floor, a knife in her chest." He passed me the report detailing the observations of the lead investigator.

Seated beside me, Harry moved closer and read over my shoulder.

"Suspicion immediately fell on Rupert, the oldest son of the Whitchurches, the brother of the current Lord Whitchurch," D.I. Hobart went on. "Rupert was the heir. According to one of the other maids, Charlotte was having a liaison with him."

"Consensual?" Harry asked. "Or was he taking advantage of her?"

"The question was never asked, as far as I know. According to these files, the D.I. questioned the other maid."

He handed me another piece of paper with the maid's statement. "What she does imply is that Charlotte was…spirited."

According to the statement, the maid's exact words were that Charlotte "wasn't a good girl" and that Rupert had "fallen for her pretty face and low morals."

"Rupert fled before he could be arrested," D.I. Hobart went on. "He vanished without a trace. Despite an extensive search, he was never found. His absence cemented his guilt in everyone's eyes. Innocent men don't run away."

"I assume the Whitchurch family denied Rupert's involvement," Harry said.

"Strenuously."

"They didn't try to influence the police investigation or end it prematurely?"

"I don't know. If they did, it didn't work. The case has remained open, and Rupert is still the main suspect." He passed me the lead detective's final report and pointed to the last line, which stated he was leaving the case open until such time as Rupert was found dead or alive.

"You all assumed Rupert was guilty?" I asked. "Nobody thought he could also be a victim?"

"The idea was briefly bandied about after the family suggested it, but dismissed. There wasn't enough blood for there to be a second victim. And why remove Rupert's body, but not Charlotte's? If it was kidnapping, why no ransom demand? It was generally assumed he fled after he realized he couldn't get away with it."

"He was supposed to inherit the title," I added. "It went to Rupert's younger brother after Rupert was officially declared deceased."

"Arthur, yes." D.I. Hobart showed me Arthur's brief statement, in which he claimed he was asleep all night in his room and didn't hear anything. He was twenty-two at the time.

"My sources tell me he is a better viscount than his brother would have been," I said. "Rupert was wild and irresponsible. Arthur is more serious."

Harry found a list of witnesses and scanned it twice. "Hardy's name isn't on here. There's a butler and two footmen, which seems appropriate for a Mayfair household, but none are named Hardy. The remaining witnesses are women, except for the former Lord Whitchurch and the current one, Arthur. So where does Hardy fit in?"

"A good question," D.I. Hobart said. "Perhaps he doesn't fit into the household at all." He turned to me. "Are your witnesses sure Hardy recognized the Whitchurches?"

I nodded. "The other staff mentioned he changed after hearing they were coming to dine. It was the first time they'd come in the month he'd been working at the Campbell residence. According to the footman, the Whitchurches recognized Hardy that night, too."

"It doesn't mean he has a link to the murder of Charlotte. There could be another reason they recognized each other."

I still thought the connection was worth pursuing. While it wasn't out of the realm of possibility that Mr. Hardy's death had nothing to do with the Whitchurches, I'd rather know for sure before I attributed it to coincidence. "If there's a chance that looking into Charlotte's murder might help us solve Hardy's, I want to delve into it further."

"It won't be easy, given the case is so old. Some of the witnesses will be difficult to locate. Some may have passed away. The D.I. in charge certainly has."

"I'd still like to try. I'll begin by finding out where Hardy worked before becoming the Campbells' butler. I'll call on Lady Campbell and ask to look at his references. Inspector, may I borrow this list of witnesses?"

We finished our tea and headed off, but not before Mrs. Hobart made Harry promise to come for dinner the following night. It was the most she'd spoken the entire duration of our visit.

"Your mother was quiet today," I said as we walked to the station. "Last time I came here she blamed me for ending your relationship with Miss Morris."

"I set her straight."

"Still, that can't be the reason why she didn't glare at me today, not even once. I doubt she's forgiven me for getting you dismissed from the hotel."

"I told her to be nice to you."

"Oh."

He frowned at me. "You sound disappointed."

"I hoped I could win her over by being me."

"You will eventually. You have time."

I frowned back at him. "Time before what happens?"

He looked ahead to the railway station. "We should hurry. I think I hear the train coming."

It was a dreadfully clumsy avoidance tactic, but I didn't press him for an answer. I had an inkling it would make me uncomfortable again.

When we arrived back in Mayfair, I wasn't sure what to do about Harry. We'd teamed up for most of our investigations in the past, so it seemed natural to do so again. He was a good sounding board. Indeed, he was a good partner. We worked well together.

But asking him to help this time felt different. We'd been at a crossroads for some time, where we were both friends and colleagues, but lately a third factor had been thrown into the mix and it was unbalancing everything. I didn't like being unbalanced.

There was only one thing to do. I stopped near the line of cabs waiting to collect passengers outside the station. "Goodbye, Harry. Thank you for your assistance."

The look of disappointment on his face almost had me changing my mind. He quickly regained his usual air of self-confidence, however. "I'm glad I could help. I'll see you…at some point."

"I'm sure you will." Before I could stop myself, I put out my hand.

He stared at it, and for a moment, I thought he'd take my hand, pull me against his body and kiss me again. It was an alarming thought, but not a terrible one. Indeed, it was very far from terrible. That made it even more alarming.

Instead, he shook my hand before striding off without another word.

CHAPTER 5

$\mathcal{S}$ir Ian and Lady Campbell were both at home. I'd spent a mere two minutes in their company before wishing I'd not sent Harry on his way. He was very good at charming people and I badly needed someone to charm them. It was clear from the moment I introduced myself and mentioned the reason for my visit that I was going to fail miserably. Lady Campbell stiffened and her lips pinched into a thin line, while Sir Ian asked me to leave.

"We have no need of your services," he said with a haughty jut of his chin. "The footman will see you out."

Davey had remained by the door, awaiting further instruction. He now indicated I should walk ahead of him out of the drawing room. There was nothing of the cheeky fellow I'd met below stairs the day before. He was quite subdued and upright.

"You don't understand," I said to the Campbells. "I'm not touting for business. I've already been hired by others to look into Mr. Hardy's death."

"Who hired you?" Sir Ian demanded.

"I'm not at liberty to say."

He took a step toward me, his face and neck turning pinker by the second. They matched his bulbous nose. "I demand you tell me!"

"You can't make such a demand."

"I most certainly can. Hardy was our butler." When I

didn't respond, a vein in his neck began to throb. "This is outrageous! Hardy's death was not suspicious and that's the end of it."

"All I want is a list of Mr. Hardy's references. I'd like to know where he worked before he came here."

"You can't have it."

"Why not?"

Lady Campbell made a subtle motion to stop her husband's tirade. He dutifully shut his mouth and took a step back. Lady Campbell regarded me with an icy gaze. Where her husband was all bluster and bluntness, her anger was cold and sharp and far more intimidating. She sat on the sofa in a dress of black and cream that showed off her lush bosom and tiny waist. The hourglass figure was unusual on women her age and somehow made her more intimidating. I stayed silent as I waited for her to speak.

"What did you same your name is?"

"Cleopatra Fox."

She didn't seem to recognize me from yesterday, thankfully. I had no doubt she'd immediately complain to my aunt after this meeting if she had.

"Miss Fox, as my husband has explained, the police concluded that Hardy's death was the result of natural causes. Your inquiries are not only unnecessary, they are also upsetting. We are in mourning. Kindly inform your client that there is no need for an investigation."

I didn't believe they would be mourning a butler who'd only worked for them for a month, but I kept my mouth shut. "That may be the case, but I'd like to know for certain—"

"We are *telling* you, there is no need for an investigation. Now, if you don't leave, Davey will throw you out."

The footman swallowed heavily.

"If you come back, we'll press charges for trespass. Is that clear?"

"Very." I walked toward Davey, but turned back to her. "Are you blocking my investigation because you're protecting the Whitchurches?"

The mention of their friends startled both Sir Ian and Lady Campbell. She suddenly stood, revealing a threadbare patch on the sofa cushion that she'd been hiding with her skirts.

Now that I'd seen it, I noticed other signs of wear and tear on the furniture. They were all old, solid pieces with beautiful carvings and intricate inlays of different woods. But they were scratched and stained, the lamp shades had faded, and the chairs didn't match. It was as if they'd once belonged to different sets in different rooms but the other pieces had been thrown away or lost over the years and these were all that were left. It was the sort of furniture found in an ancestral country manor. Too good to throw out, but too costly to restore to its former glory. It seemed the Campbells used the dining room to impress their guests, but left the other rooms to gradually lose their luster.

"What have the Whitchurches got to do with anything?" Sir Ian demanded.

"Mr. Hardy behaved oddly after he learned they were coming here, and on the evening they dined with you, they recognized him."

I was a little concerned that they'd realize Davey had given me that information, but it didn't seem to occur to them that he was my source. They were blinded by their anger, or perhaps they'd forgotten that servants were capable of making observations.

"How did the Whitchurches know Mr. Hardy?" I persisted.

"You should go, Miss Fox," Lady Campbell snapped.

Sir Ian clicked his fingers at Davey.

I saved Davey the trouble of manhandling me and left of my own accord. At the front door, I whispered that I'd like to speak to Mrs. Turner. I left, but instead of walking down the street, I trotted down the stairs to the basement service area and knocked.

The maid, Betty, opened the door. "Miss Fox! Weren't you just upstairs?"

Davey came up behind her, a little short of breath. He must have run from upstairs after closing the front door. "That was a trial by fire. You all right, Miss Fox?"

"I'm made of sturdy stuff, Davey, but thank you. May I come in? I'd like to speak to Mrs. Turner."

Betty led the way along the corridor while Davey brought up the rear.

"I reckon you'll need a nice cup of tea after that. Or something stronger."

"I'm all right, thank you."

"What happened?" Betty asked.

"Sir Ian and Lady C blew their hats off when Miss Fox here asked to see Hardy's references. I've never seen them like that. I'm surprised you didn't hear him from down here."

"They don't usually lose their tempers?" I asked.

They both shook their heads.

Mrs. Turner emerged from her office upon hearing our voices. Davey told her what had just occurred in the drawing room.

"All because Miss Fox here wanted to see Hardy's records." He shook his head. "Real angry they were. Real angry. I hope I don't have to see them before they cool down."

Betty pressed a hand to her stomach and glanced anxiously up the staircase.

One of the service bells rang and Davey grumbled under his breath.

"Buck up," Mrs. Turner said crisply. "Remember, they're not angry with you." She watched him go then invited me into her office. "Please sit, Miss Fox."

I declined the offer. "I only need to ask you one thing. I really do need to see Mr. Hardy's references. There's a possibility he used to work for the Whitchurches during a difficult time in their household, twenty-two years ago."

"Is that when the current Lord Whitchurch's brother died?"

"Their maid died. The brother went missing."

Her eyes widened. "I see."

"You told me Lady Campbell keeps employee records in her writing desk. You refused last time to get Mr. Hardy's for me, but will you reconsider now?"

She'd remained standing, too, and now clutched the back of the chair. "You want me to steal it?"

"Borrow. You can put it back after I've looked at it."

She regarded me levelly. "No, Miss Fox. I draw the line there. I won't break her ladyship's trust in such a way. If I'm caught..." She shook her head vigorously. "And don't ask

Davey or any of the other staff, either. I won't place them in such a position. You'll have to find another way."

Another way was already forming in my head, so I didn't persist. I removed Mr. Hardy's bottle of seltzer salts from my bag. "There are no traces of poison in this."

She frowned as she accepted the bottle. "Then how was it administered?"

"If it was, it was some other way."

She tucked the bottle into her skirt pocket. "I still can't believe he died of natural causes. I just can't."

I gave her a sympathetic look but didn't tell her she may have to come to terms with it. "Does anyone else in the household take a medicinal tonic or powder, something that's ingested, not rubbed onto the skin?"

"No. Fit as a fiddle, all of us."

As I walked back to the hotel, I couldn't help wondering why the Campbells had become so cross over my request. Were they trying to protect themselves or the Whitchurches?

I dearly wanted to discuss it with Harry.

Instead, I headed home.

* * *

THE HOTEL'S staff parlor became a makeshift meeting room when I needed to discuss my investigations with the staff members who occasionally helped me. My presence was accepted by most, although there was always a flurry of movement when I entered of an afternoon. The cooks who'd put their feet up on tables or spare chairs would lower them to the floor, the maids pretended they hadn't been gossiping, and the footmen and waiters sometimes sprang up and stood to attention until I told them not to mind me.

My own group of friends no longer bothered to make a fuss. My arrival in the parlor didn't even warrant a greeting from Frank. He was too busy grumbling about a guest who'd moaned about the sun being too hot as she left the hotel.

"What did she expect me to do about it?" he whined.

"She probably wasn't expecting you to do anything," Harmony told him. "She may have simply wanted to complain, and you happened to be there."

Goliath stretched out his long legs and crossed them at the ankles. "Of all people, you should understand the need to complain, Frank."

Frank nudged Goliath's foot. "Move those big clown feet before someone trips over them."

Peter had just poured a cup of tea for himself, but handed it to me instead. "Welcome to Bedlam, Miss Fox."

I gratefully accepted the cup. "There's never a dull moment when you're all together. I'm glad everyone is here, actually. I want to discuss my latest case." Although I encompassed them all, it was to Victor that my gaze drifted.

His chef's uniform was unstained, meaning he hadn't started his shift yet. When he worked the dinner shift, he usually finished about eleven. That was perfect timing. Sensing my interest, he lazily arched his brows in question. Seated close beside him, Harmony sat up a little straighter. An observant onlooker would know by now they were in a relationship, even though they hadn't declared it. I wasn't sure when they would. My attempt to find out more from Harmony was always met with a wall of silence.

Peter poured himself another cup from the teapot warming on the portable stove and joined our little circle. "Harmony told us about the butler. It's good of you to investigate, Miss Fox. Not everyone would bother for a servant."

"Those who work in them fancy houses are hard done by," Frank said with a shake of his head. "They're not treated with the same amount of respect by their employers as the Bainbridges treat us."

Goliath scoffed. "Two weeks ago you were about to go on strike in sympathy with Cobbit over the future of the mews staff. You did nothing but complain about Sir Ronald, then."

Frank sniffed. "That was a one-off. And anyway, Sir Ronald capitulated to our demands. Few employers would."

"I wouldn't tell my uncle to his face that he capitulated," I said. "He remembers it differently."

Frank opened his mouth to continue, but Peter got in first. "Tell us about the case, Miss Fox. Harmony says the victim may not have been murdered, after all."

"I'm not sure yet. One particular poison, hyoscine, causes death in a manner consistent with witness reports of Mr.

Hardy's death. But just how he may have ingested it, I don't know. The housekeeper thought it was in his seltzer salts, but I had them tested and they were harmless. However, there has been an interesting development that could link Mr. Hardy's death to another, much older, murder investigation." I told them about the Whitchurches' maid, and the subsequent disappearance of the prime suspect, the eldest son and heir.

"So the younger son inherited instead?" Goliath asked. "Lucky devil."

"Hardly," Peter said. "He lost his brother."

"But gained a title and all the benefits that go with it."

Arthur certainly had gained from Rupert's disappearance. I wondered if he was the only one. "I have an inkling that looking into the maid's murder will help solve what happened to Mr. Hardy. It's just an inkling, mind."

No one seemed to think it unusual that I wanted to continue based on so little evidence of a crime having been committed. They knew me well enough to know I needed to do something productive with my time.

"Will you call on the Whitchurches?" Victor asked. "It's unlikely they'll offer assistance."

I removed the list from my bag. "D.I. Hobart was able to get his hands on this list of witnesses. I'll try to interview each of them again."

"Our Mr. Hobart's brother?" Frank asked. "You speak to him?"

"Harry put me in touch with his father."

"Armitage? I've seen you with him outside." He shook his head. "Sir Ronald won't like it if he finds out you two still spend time together."

Harmony narrowed her gaze at him. "Which he won't."

Frank put his hands in the air. "Not from me. I don't mind the fellow." That was an improvement. Being a Bainbridge man, Frank had taken against Harry after my uncle dismissed him, even though he didn't know the reason for it. It seemed Harry's involvement in brokering peace between my uncle and the mews staff hadn't gone unnoticed or unappreciated by Frank.

"Uncle Ronald doesn't mind if Harry and I see one another," I said. "He says we can investigate together."

"Then you'd better not see Armitage between investigations," Frank said. "You don't want to give anyone the wrong idea."

"By anyone, do you mean only my uncle?"

"No, I mean everyone, including Armitage himself."

"Frank," I said on a sigh. "Harry and I are just friends."

He merely grunted. Goliath and Peter exchanged glances, while Harmony studied her fingernails.

Victor got to his feet and collected the empty cups. "I have to start my shift soon."

I finished my tea and passed him the cup. "Before you go, I need to ask you to do something." I lowered my voice further so that the staff who were not part of our group couldn't hear. "I need to find the link between Mr. Hardy and the Whitchurches. If he did know them at the time of Charlotte's murder, then I'll have a clear path forward."

"You think Hardy is the key to finding Charlotte's murderer after all these years, and the Whitchurches killed him to keep him quiet?"

"Blimey," Goliath muttered. "Is that what you think, Miss Fox?"

"It's one theory," I said. "But I'm not sure it holds water. Why would they worry that Hardy would go to the police now, when he's had years to do it?" I shook my head, trying to shake loose more theories, but they wouldn't come. "Whether that is the link or not, I have to know for sure. I need to see Hardy's references and find out where he worked before becoming butler for the Campbells. On reflection, I think it's extremely unlikely he listed the Whitchurches as his former employers when he applied for the position. Lady Campbell would have asked her friend, Lady Whitchurch, about him if he had, however we've learned that Lady Whitchurch was surprised to see him serving them dinner."

"You want Victor to break into the house and look for the references?" Harmony asked.

I chewed on my lip and glanced between her and Victor. I wasn't sure which one I needed approval from. She might worry about his safety and forbid it. From the look on her face, I could see she was imagining all the things that could go wrong.

She hesitated too long, however. "I'll do it," Victor said.

Harmony stayed quiet, which I took as her assent.

"Thank you, Victor. Perhaps take Goliath with you as a lookout."

Frank snorted. "He'll stand out like an elephant at a tea party. Take me. I'm good at blending in."

"That's because you're unremarkable," Goliath said, getting to his feet. "Come on, we've got to get back."

The men filed out while I stayed to gauge Harmony's thoughts. She made no comment about my request, however, and seemed more concerned with what I was wearing that evening to a ball I needed to attend with my family.

"I know you wore the blue dress with the white trim three weeks ago, but it does look very fetching on you, so I think you should wear it again." She tilted her head to the side and studied me. "May I try something different with your hair?"

"I'm in your expert hands, Harmony. As for the gown, I think everyone has ceased to notice who wears the same ones. Nobody could possibly wear a different one to every single ball. Their frequency has become ridiculous at this point and I, for one, am quite sick of them."

"They are good for information gathering," she said with a wicked smile.

She had a good point. While she helped me dress and did my hair, we tossed around ideas for ways I could subtly find out more about the Campbells and Whitchurches.

* * *

MY FIRST TARGET for the evening wasn't the friends of Lady Campbell or Lady Whitchurch, but my aunt. She was excitable after having taken her tonic, and I wanted to question her before her good mood faded and she became sulky and riddled with pain. Upon entering the ballroom, she spied a cluster of her friends and looked as though she'd forge a path to them. I wrapped both my hands around her arm to keep her at my side. Her muscles twitched beneath my grip.

"May I ask you something, Aunt?"

She looked at me, although her enlarged pupils seemed to peer right through me. "Of course, Cleo, dear. Is it about the maharaja's son?"

"Who?"

She nodded to where Flossy had cornered a young man I recognized from the hotel. He'd been a guest with his father in April, before heading off to Oxford University for the term. Flossy seemed quite taken with him this evening. His expression was more reserved and I couldn't tell if he liked her company or would prefer to chat with his chums.

"It's not about him," I said.

"He's very handsome." Aunt Lilian shifted from foot to foot. "Shall I go and help her, do you think? She's likely to say something silly and put him off. I hear he's very intelligent and she can be a little foolish. Oh, wouldn't it be wonderful if they married!"

"I think he's moving back to India when his education is complete. Flossy wouldn't like the heat."

Aunt Lilian waved off my concern. "Ronald can find him a position here in London. He's very well-connected. There he is now, looking quite dashing and not at all troubled. Have you noticed that about him lately, Cleo? How troubled he is? He's not himself. When I ask him what the matter is, he won't tell me. I don't know why. He used to tell me everything." She sighed. "That's the way with marriages, I suppose. After a while, they become stale. A couple who once talked all the time stop talking. I never thought it would happen to us, but here we are."

"I don't think your marriage is stale."

"He married me for my money, you know. There. I've shocked you, haven't I?"

"I—"

"Don't pity me, Cleo. I married him because his family is nobility, albeit a minor branch." She giggled behind her fan. "At some point, we grew to love and respect one another. I'm not quite sure when it happened. He was so full of energy and ideas that one couldn't help admiring him." She lowered the fan. "He adored your mother more than me, however, but she had no interest in him. She'd met your father by then and nobody could compare in her eyes."

Good lord, I needed to stop her before she told me something she'd later regret. "Aunt, what did Mr. Chapman want with Lady Campbell yesterday?"

Her gaze darted around the room, although I wondered how much she was taking in. "Hmmm?"

"At afternoon tea, Mr. Chapman tried to speak to Lady Campbell, then he approached you. What did he want?"

She fluttered her hand in the air, wriggling her fingers. "I don't recall now, Cleo. Hotel business, I should imagine."

"Yes, but—"

"Enjoy your night, my dear. Dance with all the handsome men you can. Oh, to be young again." She strode off, the feathers in her headpiece bouncing with each step.

I sighed and went to join Flossy, only to be waylaid by a gentleman wanting to add his name to my dance card. I politely agreed and secretly wondered if he knew the Campbells or Whitchurches. I'd find out when we danced the waltz.

I was waylaid a second time by a more welcome interruption, Miss Hessing. I'd hardly spoken to her since the engagement dinner, and she was eager to relive every minor detail with me.

"My mother says the food wasn't what she ordered, nor the flowers, but I didn't notice. Did you, Miss Fox?"

I didn't want to ruin her memory of the dinner, so I simply smiled. "I thought the evening was wonderful. I had a lovely time. Did you?"

"Oh yes, it was heavenly. Although Mother disagrees. She's a little annoyed, as it happens." She stopped herself and bit her lower lip. "I shouldn't be discussing this with you."

"You can confide in me, Miss Hessing. We're friends."

"I suppose so. It's just that Mother can be cruel. Perhaps forewarned is forearmed, as they say."

"That sounds ominous."

She looked around and, seeing her mother deep in conversation with her friends, leaned closer to me. "She's thinking of having the wedding reception at the Savoy."

"The Savoy!"

At my exclamation, heads turned toward us, including Uncle Ronald's.

I took Miss Hessing's hand and led her to a quiet corner of

the room. "What do you mean she wants to hold the reception at the Savoy? The Mayfair is her favorite hotel. She always stays with us when she comes to London."

"Oh yes, she adores it. Rest assured, she doesn't think it inferior to the Savoy or any other London hotel. The staff are wonderful, the rooms are modern and a good size, and the new restaurant serves excellent food. But the Savoy are very good at hosting special occasions, and she feels my engagement party was underwhelming. She wanted something grander. I didn't care, you understand. This isn't coming from me. But you know Mother."

I did indeed. Tonight, Miss Hessing wore a demure gown of cream and pale pink, whereas her mother looked like a peacock in bright green and blue. Even her headpiece had long peacock feathers shooting into the air. She was a tall woman with a booming voice that drew everyone's notice. If it failed to be heard, she stamped the end of her walking stick into the floor like a child stomping her foot to get attention. A woman like that wanted to make a bold statement to the world to announce the engagement of her only child. Not only had the engagement party hosted in our restaurant been a modest affair, but Mr. Chapman had also failed to deliver the few requests Mrs. Hessing had made. No wonder she was considering the Savoy. They'd built a reputation hosting extravagant parties for society's most influential members.

It wasn't entirely Mr. Chapman's fault, though. We'd all made the mistake of thinking Miss Hessing was the one we needed to please, since it was her engagement party. But her mother was paying for it, and she was more particular than her daughter.

I clasped Miss Hessing's hands in mine. "Don't let your mother talk to the Savoy. Insist your wedding reception be held in our ballroom. I'll see that Mr. Chapman understands what's required."

She breathed a sigh of relief. "Thank you, Miss Fox. I knew telling you was the right thing to do. I'd certainly rather have my reception at the Mayfair, not the Savoy. Your family wouldn't come if it was there, for one thing, and I would like all of you to attend."

I squeezed her hands. "I'll come, no matter where it is."

"You're a dear friend and I am so glad I'll be living in London instead of on the other side of the world. We won't be in Mayfair, but it will only be a short train journey from our house to the hotel."

She talked about the house they were moving to after they married, until it was time for the first dance.

My dance partners proved no help when it came to imparting gossip about the Campbells and the Whitchurches, so when refreshments were served I made sure to attach myself to a group of middle-aged ladies I'd met on a few occasions. It wasn't easy steering conversations in the directions I wanted them to go in, but by the end of supper, I'd heard how the two couples were long-time friends. I had also confirmed that speculation had swirled for years after the eldest son of Lord and Lady Whitchurch disappeared, but he'd finally been declared dead seven years after going missing, leaving Arthur to inherit upon his father's death.

Not all believed Rupert was dead, however. Those who remembered the maid had been murdered thought he was living overseas under an assumed name to avoid capture. It seemed most of the details of the murder had not made it to the newspapers, but one or two ladies had heard the more sordid aspects from friends who knew the Whitchurches. They speculated that Rupert had been involved with the maid, but differed on whether *he* had seduced *her* or the other way around.

"He was a known philanderer," one woman said.

"He was no different from other young gentleman," another pointed out. "She was trying to trap him."

"He was lazy and a drunk. He didn't care about the tenants on his father's land, or the responsibilities he would one day inherit. He should have been helping his father and learning how to run the estate, but instead he was running around after anything in a petticoat." When she realized we were all staring at her, she cleared her throat. "So I heard."

"Wasn't he betrothed?" a third woman chimed in.

"To the current Lady Whitchurch, yes." That information was met with several gasps from those listening, including me. "She went on to marry the younger brother, Arthur. *He* has acquitted himself well as viscount. Nobody can fault him. Not even his mother can complain."

Several of the women made a face.

"The Dowager Lady Whitchurch is still alive?" I asked.

"Oh, yes. She's a recluse now. Her health is failing and she doesn't leave the estate."

"Yes, she does," said another. "I heard she's currently in London to see her physician."

I already knew the address of the Whitchurches' London house from D.I. Hobart's file. It was just around the corner from the Campbells.

Although my dance card was quite full for the rest of the evening, I didn't have the opportunity to dance again. Uncle Ronald rounded up Flossy and me and told us it was time to leave, as Aunt Lilian wasn't well.

"But I want to stay." Flossy cast a longing glance toward the maharaja's son.

"If Floyd were here, I'd leave you both in his care, but he isn't." Uncle Ronald walked off before either of us could protest again.

Flossy pouted all the way home, while Aunt Lilian sat like a wilting flower in the corner of the carriage, her eyes closed. Uncle Ronald stared out of the window at the passing lights.

I wasn't ready to retire, so I looked in on the diners in the restaurant instead of going upstairs with my family. Mr. Chapman stood near the entrance, his hands clasped behind him, overseeing proceedings like a headmaster. He would remain there until the last guest left. From the raucous behavior of the furthest group, they wouldn't be leaving for some time.

I retraced my steps and paused near the corridor that led to the offices of Mr. Chapman and Mrs. Short. A handful of guests in the foyer ahead paid me no mind. I was alone.

I ducked into the corridor and tried the handle on Mr. Chapman's office door. To my surprise, it wasn't locked. I switched on the light and went straight to the filing cabinet. I knew he kept a file for the regular diners in it. If Lady Campbell had afternoon tea often at the hotel, she would have a file. I found it quickly, but a scan of the neatly handwritten notes told me nothing of importance. She preferred cucumber sandwiches and was polite to the staff. She and Sir Ian had once dined in the old restaurant two years ago, but not since.

I put back the Campbells' card and searched for the Whitchurches' file. Again, the notes were brief. They'd dined a few times in the old restaurant, but not since the same night as the Campbells had dined there. The two couples must have dined together. Apparently, Lord Whitchurch liked French food and wine. There was no other note on the card.

I returned it to the cabinet and pushed the drawer closed. As the drawer clicked into place, the office door opened. I spun around to see Mr. Chapman standing there, looking smug.

"Sneaking around again, Miss Fox? What will Sir Ronald say this time?"

CHAPTER 6

r. Chapman and I didn't get along and never had. He was a busybody who listened at doors. Perhaps he'd learned that I was also a busybody who listened at doors, but at least I'd given him a chance at the beginning of our acquaintance. He'd looked down his nose at me ever since my arrival at the hotel.

I'd thought his attitude toward me would soften after I didn't tell anyone that he had intimate relations with men, but it appeared it hadn't. Perhaps it was time to remind him that I knew something about him that would damage his reputation and get him thrown into prison.

"I thought you and I had an understanding, Mr. Chapman."

His eyes widened with alarm. "Are you threatening to tell Sir Ronald about me if I tell him about this?"

"That's not what I'm saying at all. Your secret is safe with me and always will be, no matter what you say about me to him. But I thought you'd be more inclined to forgive this since I've not told a soul."

He passed a hand over his mouth and jaw. When it came away, he was visibly more relaxed. "What else am I supposed to do, Miss Fox? You clearly have no regard for my privacy. Would asking you not to break in have made a difference?"

"I didn't break in. The door was unlocked."

He gave me an icy glare.

"I do have regard for your privacy, Mr. Chapman. I simply came in here to find out why you wanted to speak to Lady Campbell at afternoon tea."

"You could have asked."

I waited. When he did not go on, I said, "I'm asking now."

"I can't tell you. It's hotel business."

I sucked in a breath in an attempt to ease my frustration. It didn't work. "I am a member of the Bainbridge family and therefore as much a part of the hotel as my aunt. You can tell me since you told her."

"You have no authority here."

He would never give in, out of sheer spite and stubbornness. Unless I offered him something in return, something that would help him make a good impression on one of our best guests and therefore my uncle. "I spoke to Miss Hessing at the ball tonight. She gave me a friendly warning about her mother's plans for the wedding. Unfortunately, she doesn't think we're capable of putting on a reception grand enough, so she's considering the Savoy."

"Not grand enough!" He planted his hands on his hips and paced the floor, shaking his head. He suddenly stopped in front of me. "Is this because of the engagement party? It wasn't my fault the flowers she wanted couldn't be delivered on time, and the electrical wiring caught fire. The event was tasteful and elegant, which is more than I can say for Mrs. Hessing."

I was regretting bringing it up now. "I think that's the entire point. Mrs. Hessing wants the wedding to be…grand."

"You mean she wants it to be vulgar, like her. Well, I won't do it. *She's* not getting married anyway, her daughter is, and Miss Hessing has better taste than her mother."

"*Mrs.* Hessing is the one paying for it."

He didn't seem to hear me as he started pacing again. "I have an excellent reputation. I've organized over a dozen balls and countless exclusive dinners for the Mayfair, and they've all been a success." He stopped and wagged a finger at me. "This is about the restaurant opening, isn't it? Mrs. Hessing wants an ostentatious display akin to that ridiculous spectacle."

"The opening dinner was the talk of London and will be remembered for years. So, yes, I think that's what she wants."

He crossed his arms over his chest. "She can't have it. That was Mr. Bainbridge's style, not mine. Not that he did any of the arrangements, mind. It was all that upstart maid, getting above herself. Another one who wouldn't know a fish fork from a dessert fork."

I suspected he was referring to me as the other. In the household I was raised in, we only had one style of fork and it wasn't made of silver. "Miss Cotton did an excellent job. Not a single thing went wrong."

He bristled. "I told you, the problems with the engagement dinner were not my fault."

They were, but I wasn't going to tell him that. He was riled up enough as it was, and I had no interest in letting the argument continue. I left his office and headed upstairs to my suite. It took me some time before I'd calmed down enough to fall asleep.

* * *

MY USUAL BREAKFAST had to serve three the following morning. It helped that Victor had stopped in at the kitchen on his way and added more toast and eggs to the tray. He sat beside Harmony at the table in my sitting room and gave his report while spreading butter on his toast. It was very brief.

"We didn't find any records for the butler. We found the references for the other staff in Lady Campbell's writing bureau, but nothing for Hardy."

"If the others were there, it means his have been destroyed." I frowned as something he said sank in. "'We?' Did you go with him, Harmony?"

They glanced at each, giving me my answer.

"You invited Harry along, didn't you?"

"It was my idea," Harmony said. "Victor wouldn't let me go with him, and I didn't want him going alone. Frank's right: Goliath is too tall for clandestine activities, and Frank himself isn't suited, nor is Peter. It requires someone competent, with iron nerves. It could really only be Harry."

Victor gave me a shrug, as if to ask why it mattered.

I supposed it didn't. Harry wouldn't have minded.

But given I'd been resolved not to ask him for further assistance with the case so as not to complicate our relationship even more, I wasn't sure it was wise to involve him again. Even so, he'd helped me and I ought to thank him. It was the least I could do.

Or so I told myself.

Before heading to the Whitchurches' house, I walked to Soho. I paused outside the Roma Café, but decided against taking coffees up to Harry's office. I didn't plan on staying long.

Out of habit, I entered without knocking. He sat behind the desk, one of Luigi's small coffee cups cradled in one hand, his sleeves rolled to his elbows. He sat side-on to the desk with his legs stretched out, staring at the wall. I felt sorry for disturbing him. Going by the blank way he blinked at me, he'd been consumed by his own thoughts and it seemed a shame to drag him from them.

"Working hard, I see," I quipped.

"I'm thinking."

"What about?"

"Your case, as it happens."

His admission caught me by surprise. "Oh. Well, that's what I came to talk to you about."

He indicated I should sit, but I shook my head.

"I'm not staying long. I'm going to call on the Whitchurches, and simply wanted to drop in on my way to thank you for accompanying Victor last night. It put Harmony's mind at ease. Mine, too."

His lips curved with his slow, easy smile.

"Why are you smiling like that?"

"Because my office isn't on your way to the Whitchurches. So why are you really here, Cleo?"

"To thank you, Harry, that's all. Don't read something into it that isn't there."

He set the cup on the desk and began to roll down his sleeves. "Harmony told me how the Campbells treated you yesterday. It sounds like it was an unpleasant encounter."

"Thoroughly. I don't think I handled them very well. I'm

sure you would have done it differently and achieved a different result."

"I was available."

"I know."

"I'm also available now."

I knew precisely how the rest of the meeting was going to unfold, so I simply skipped the part in the middle where he tried to talk me into letting him come and I resisted at first, but eventually gave in. "You may as well join me. I'm sure the Whitchurches will be just as prickly as the Campbells, if not more so. If the encounter goes as badly as it did yesterday, at least I'll have someone to commiserate with."

"I'm happy to commiserate with you, Cleo." He rolled down his second sleeve as he stood. It occurred to me that he'd expected me to ask him ever since I entered. Surely, he wasn't that intuitive. Perhaps I was simply that obvious.

I peeked at the open file on his desk. The client wanted him to spy on her neighbor whom she suspected was operating a brothel out of the house. "You don't have work of your own that requires your attention here?"

He closed the file and placed it in the top drawer. "Nothing that can't wait."

"Very true. Brothels are busier in the evenings."

He shot me a withering glare.

* * *

FORTUNATELY, it was a short walk to the Whitchurches' townhouse, so we had no opportunity to discuss anything other than the case. We decided to tackle the master and mistress first, but if they weren't home, or weren't very forthcoming, we'd speak to the servants.

We gave our names to the young footman who answered our knock, but not the reason for our visit. He led us through to the drawing room, where the butler waited with us while the footman fetched his employers. Under the guise of making idle chatter to pass the time, Harry asked the butler how long he and the other staff had been employed there. The longest serving member was the housekeeper, at seven years, well short of the twenty-two since the maid died.

While Harry questioned the butler, I took a turn around the room. The paneled walls were painted soft green, which was rather calming against the high white ceiling and pink-and-green rug. There were no signs of wear and tear like I'd witnessed at the Campbells' residence. The sumptuous furniture and furnishings were in good condition, even though most pieces were over a hundred years old, going by the Grecian aesthetic, the ormolu mounts and acanthus leaf motifs. I glanced at the framed photographs scattered across various tables. Most were taken in the countryside, at shooting parties, hunting parties, and picnics. One photograph struck me as odd. It wasn't the subject matter—a middle-aged man standing beside a horse—that had me taking a closer look. It was the position of the photograph within its silver frame. The horse was up against the edge of the photograph, butting up to the frame. Neither horse nor man were centered. Stables could be seen in the distance, but they didn't add anything of interest to the photograph. The size was also odd. It didn't fill the frame and a gap was left at its edge.

Something or someone on the horse's other side had been cut off.

The man and woman who entered the drawing room introduced themselves as Lord and Lady Whitchurch. They were both aged in their forties, with lines fanning from the corners of their eyes and plump waistlines thanks to decades of comfortable living. Lady Whitchurch didn't attempt to hide the gray in her hair, as some ladies did with hats. She wore it plaited and arranged high on her head with a center part at the front, a style that went out of fashion years ago. Her dress was more modern, but quite plain, with no color to lighten the dark gray and black trim. Her husband sported a full gray beard and a moustache that was still ginger. I recognized him from several of the photographs. He wasn't the man in the photo with the horse, although they looked similar.

They studied Harry and me with curiosity, but not wariness. That all changed when we mentioned we were private investigators. Their open countenances closed and their backs stiffened. While they didn't order us to leave, I sensed answers wouldn't come easily.

"I've been tasked with looking into the death of Mr. Hardy, the butler at the Campbell residence," I began.

"By whom?" Lord Whitchurch asked.

"I'm not at liberty to say."

"I don't understand. He died of natural causes. What is there to look into?"

"There is doubt in some minds as to whether the verdict was accurate."

Lord Whitchurch looked surprised. Lady Whitchurch looked confused. "If it wasn't natural causes, how did he die?"

Her husband, standing beside his seated wife, placed his hand on her shoulder. "I'm sure there's been a misunderstanding. Reassure your client that the coroner doesn't come to these verdicts lightly. He and the police are competent and thorough."

"Sometimes they make mistakes, particularly if the poison used can mimic death by natural causes."

Lady Whitchurch clutched her throat. "Poison?"

"I'm not sure what this fellow's death has to do with us," Lord Whitchurch said. "You're better off speaking to the Campbells."

"I have," I said. "The household staff were most helpful, and it's their responses that bring me here." If they noticed I spoke of the household and not the Campbells specifically, neither commented. "Apparently, Mr. Hardy recognized you when you dined there a few nights before his death."

Lord Whitchurch swallowed heavily. "Did he say something to another member of staff about us?"

"No. His reaction was noticed. As was yours. You recognized him, too."

"I didn't. Did you, my dear?" The hand that still clasped her shoulder squeezed.

She shook her head. "I'd never seen him before. He was new to the Campbells, I believe. That dinner was the first time we'd seen him."

"He has never worked for you?"

"No," they both said.

Pursuing that line of questioning wouldn't get me any further. It was time to use a different one. This time, as discussed with Harry on the walk over, I left the questions to him. We were heading into dangerous territory, and he was better at navigating than me.

"My father used to work for Scotland Yard." His manner was amiable, chatty, as if he were simply engaging in idle conversation. "When Miss Fox was telling me about her case, my father overheard her refer to Lord and Lady Whitchurch. The name was familiar to him. He told us about a dreadful incident that occurred here years ago. Your maid was stabbed, and your older brother was accused of her murder."

Lady Whitchurch gasped. She covered her mouth with her hand and visibly paled.

Her husband's fingers flexed on her shoulder again. I expected him to order us to leave, but he did not. "Your father has a good memory. I'm afraid I don't recall any policemen named Armitage, but it was such a chaotic time and there were so many police involved."

Harry didn't correct him on the name. "It must have been upsetting for the family."

"It was. But we've put it behind us." Lord Whitchurch's answer held a note of caution in his tone. He was wondering where Harry was heading with his questions.

Harry addressed Lady Whitchurch. "It must have been just as upsetting for you, ma'am, even though you weren't married yet. You were engaged to Rupert, weren't you?"

Lady Whitchurch blinked rapidly. "I, uh…" She glanced at her husband. "It was a long time ago."

"Indeed it was," Lord Whitchurch said tightly. "We would appreciate it if you let sleeping dogs lie. As you can see, dredging up old business is very upsetting for my wife. Are there any more questions?"

A thin yet authoritative voice came from the doorway. "There will be no more questions." An elderly woman approached with the aid of a walking stick, all her wrinkles— of which there were many—drawn into a fierce frown. Her pale face was tinged yellow and as she drew closer, I could see that the whites of her eyes were yellowed, too. Her black silk dress hung from her frame and her back was so rounded that she was probably shorter than her fully erect height by several inches.

Lord Whitchurch rushed to her side to assist her to a chair, but she clicked her tongue at him and he hesitated, uncertain.

She eased herself onto a chair unaided and pointed the walking stick at Harry. "You are impertinent, young man. Who are you and what do you want?"

Harry gave a shallow bow. "Do I have the honor of speaking to the Dowager Lady Whitchurch?"

"You do, and I am too old to fall for your charm, so don't bother. Just answer the question."

Harry gave a light laugh as if he respected being caught out by her sharp observation. Her scowl deepened, but it held a hint of acknowledgement. With that simple exchange, he'd earned a modicum of respect. Whether it would help or not remained to be seen.

He introduced us. "Miss Fox has been tasked with looking into the death of a fellow named Hardy. It's come to her attention that he may have known your son and daughter-in-law."

"If Miss Fox has been hired, then what is your purpose here, Mr. Armitage?"

"Moral support."

"Poppycock. You've been asking the difficult questions while Miss Fox asked the easy ones."

Harry's gaze wandered to the doorway. She must have been standing there eavesdropping for some time. There was certainly nothing wrong with her hearing.

"Yes, I listen at doors," she said. "What of it? It's my house."

Lord and Lady Whitchurch exchanged glances, but neither corrected her. In fact, it wasn't the dowager's house. Not since her son had inherited it, along with the country estate and title, upon his father's death.

"I didn't hear the beginning of this interrogation," the dowager went on. "Tell me, what do your questions about my daughter-in-law's prior engagement to Rupert have to do with the death of the man named Hardy?"

She addressed her question to Harry, but I answered. "Mr. Hardy was the butler at Sir Ian and Lady Campbell's residence and I was informed that he recognized Lord and Lady Whitchurch when they dined there recently."

The dowager's hand rubbed the end of her walking stick as she glanced at her son. It was the first time she'd looked at him, and her brows raised ever-so slightly. He gave a slight shake of his head.

"And then you had the audacity to ask about...prior events that occurred here years ago," the dowager went on. "All of that is none of your business and has nothing to do with your case. Now get out. Arthur, see that Miss Fox and Mr. Armitage find the door."

Lord Whitchurch signaled to the footman, and he stepped forward.

The dowager stamped the end of her walking stick into the floor, causing her daughter-in-law to jump and the footman to return to his position. "I ordered *you* to do it, Arthur."

"Yes, Mother." He politely indicated that Harry and I should walk ahead of him.

Before I exited, I glanced over my shoulder. Lady Whitchurch sat with her head bowed and her hands clasped in her lap.

The dowager poked her daughter-in-law's foot with the end of her walking stick. "You lack spine, girl. That's always been your problem. If only you'd been stronger..."

Lady Whitchurch hurried from the room in tears.

Outside, Harry and I trotted down the steps to the pavement. He indicated the descent to the basement service door. "Do you want to question the staff?"

"None of them worked here when Charlotte died, so I don't think there's any point. If Hardy was employed by the Whitchurches at that time, it's very unlikely he stayed long afterward." We both mulled on that for a while as we walked back the way we'd come. "Did you notice the dowager didn't recognize Hardy's name? It wasn't until I explained he was the Campbells' butler that her demeanor changed. I think her son and daughter-in-law told her they saw him at the Campbells that night, but never mentioned his name to her. There's only one reason they wouldn't."

"It meant nothing to them. They knew him by a different name."

"Precisely. The question is, why did he change it?"

Harry suddenly stopped. "Do you have the list of witnesses my father gave you?"

I dug it out of my bag and handed it to him, but he didn't want to see it.

"We need to re-interview them," he said.

"I agree, but how do we find them? The Whitchurches won't help."

"You could ask the current staff while I telephone my father. If any of the former staff have committed a crime, their names will be on record at Scotland Yard." He didn't sound hopeful, however, and I agreed it was unlikely. "If we both fail, we'll make inquiries at employment agencies that specialize in domestic staff."

We parted company, he going in search of a public telephone while I headed to the basement service area.

The Whitchurches' housekeeper must have heard that we'd been ousted from the drawing room, because she refused to talk to me. With more primness in her tone than her mistress's, she told me she couldn't answer my questions.

The butler who'd been present during our exchange with the Whitchurches appeared behind her. "We should help if we can. It's about that maid who died here years ago."

It would appear solidarity amongst the serving class counted for something, because the housekeeper nodded. Or perhaps they were curious to get to the bottom of the maid's murder, too. As Harry had said, servants liked to gossip about their employers.

"How can we help?" the housekeeper asked.

"Do you know where to find the staff who worked here at the time the murder occurred?" I asked.

"Most have either passed away or found employment in other households. I'm not sure where. There's only one that I have a current address for, but I don't know if she worked here at that time. Lady Whitchurch organizes a care package to a former maid once a month. It's delivered to Mrs. Hatch at The Female Servants Benevolent Society in Southampton Row, Bloomsbury."

I'd looked at the list of witness names so often I knew them all by heart. There was no Mrs. Hatch. I almost gave up, but the butler had a suggestion.

"Perhaps Mrs. Hatch went by her maiden name or first name when she worked here. Do you know it?"

The housekeeper nodded. "It's Virginia."

There was one servant named Virginia on the list, and she was perhaps the most important witness to be interviewed that night. She'd gone by a different surname then. It was from her witness statement that we knew Rupert had been having a liaison with Charlotte before her death.

I thanked them and headed back up the steps to the pavement. I met Harry coming out of the pharmacy where he'd found a silence cabinet the public could use to make telephone calls. "Any luck?" I asked.

He shook his head. "He says requesting a search of the records will only draw attention to himself and our investigation, plus it would take too long. He thinks we're better off making inquiries at employment agencies."

"We may not need to do that. Do you know where Southampton Row is?"

"I do."

"Can you give me directions?"

"I can do much better. I'll show you."

I no longer felt inclined to investigate without him. We achieved results when we worked together, so I smiled and asked him to lead the way.

CHAPTER 7

$\mathcal{T}$he boarding house on Southampton Row had seen better days. It may have once been a mansion belonging to a wealthy family, but it had either been acquired by The Female Servants Benevolent Society or donated to them, and it was showing signs of neglect. Paint flaked off the window frames, the carpet was worn bare in places, and the air had a sour smell that seemed to emanate from the walls themselves. I was glad to see it was clean, however, without a speck of dust or grimy windowpane in sight. It would have been a cruel indignity for women who'd spent most of their lives cleaning for others to be subjected to a dirty home in their later years.

According to Harry, the home was run by a charitable organization for former maids and housekeepers who could no longer work due to infirmity or age. The women had nowhere else to go, no family to take them in, and their former employers couldn't, or wouldn't, accommodate them. Earning so little in their lifetime that they could never save enough to retire comfortably, they now had to rely on charities.

We were following the matron's directions to Virginia Hatch's room on the third floor when it suddenly occurred to me that the hotel's maids were just as poorly off as domestic servants for large households. "What happens to the

Mayfair's staff when they can no longer perform their duties?" I asked Harry.

"Lady Bainbridge set up a fund some time ago. Sir Ronald pays a sum into it each year and guests are encouraged to donate to it upon their departure. There's a suggested amount on their bill. Some don't pay a penny, but most do. Some pay a great deal more than asked. When a staff member can no longer work, they receive a sum according to the number of years' service they gave to the hotel. It encourages them to be loyal to the Mayfair."

"Is it enough to live off in retirement?"

"That depends how long they live for."

Indeed. "Will Cobbit receive a payment from the fund after he leaves, even though he negotiated a settlement with my uncle after the strike?"

"Cobbit is considered senior staff, even though he has only two grooms under him. He, my uncle, Peter, the house-keeper, cook, steward, and your uncle's assistant are paid higher wages, so won't have access to money from the fund when they retire. It's only for maids, porters and the like."

That seemed fair, but it also seemed like a lost opportunity to ensure loyalty. Perhaps if the senior staff were promised a payment upon retirement for every year they served it might encourage them to stay, too. From what I could see, there was no incentive to keep good senior employees. All another hotel had to do was offer better wages. I wasn't sure if the Mayfair could compete with company-owned hotels like the Savoy.

Perhaps Uncle Ronald was right and Mr. Hobart was considering taking the vacant manager position at the Carlton Hotel. If he could negotiate better wages for himself in the final years of his working life, he and his wife would have a more comfortable retirement. With Harry gone, he had no need to stay at the Mayfair to oversee a smooth transition of the manager's role to his nephew.

Harry seemed to sense something was on my mind because he didn't knock on Mrs. Hatch's door straight away. "Sir Ronald has many faults, but fortunately your aunt doesn't. It's kind of you to worry about the staff, Cleo, but it's not necessary."

I decided to encourage Uncle Ronald to have a word with

Mr. Hobart as soon as possible. He needed to find out for certain whether the manager was leaving or not. If he was...

I pushed the thought from my mind. I didn't want to think about it.

Harry's knock was answered by a voice inviting us to enter. He opened the door and greeted the woman occupying the bed. Propped up by pillows, Mrs. Hatch removed her spectacles and put down the pamphlet she'd been reading to invite us into her room. She tried to sit up, but winced and clutched her back before returning to her original position.

"Please, don't get up," Harry said. "Can we get you anything?"

"A new back," she said wryly. "Are you with the Society board?"

"We're private investigators. I'm Harry Armitage and this is Miss Fox." He handed her his card. "I'm assisting Miss Fox with her investigation." He indicated I should continue.

I put out my hand for Mrs. Hatch and she shook it. Her palm was calloused. She looked frail, dressed in her night-gown and mob cap, both embroidered with pale blue flowers. According to the witness list, she'd been twenty at the time of Charlotte's murder, which would make her forty-two now. She seemed much older.

"I've been commissioned to look into the death of a servant," I said. "His death might be linked to the Whitchurches."

"Do you mean the current lord and lady, or the dowager and former Lord Whitchurch? The latter were my employers, not the current ones. Do you know the Whitchurches, Miss Fox?"

"We've just come from there. Mrs. Hatch, what can you tell us about the death of Charlotte, one of the Whitchurches' maids?"

Her eyes widened and she clutched the small crucifix on her necklace. A wooden crucifix was affixed above the bed and the only picture on the wall was a print of Jesus with his hands clasped in prayer. "What does your current investigation have to do with that?" she asked.

"There may be a link, but we're not entirely sure yet. We

need to re-interview some of the witnesses, and I understand you were a key one. Will you assist us, Mrs. Hatch?"

She smoothed her hand over the coverlet and nodded. "You'd both better sit. This could take some time." She tried adjusting her position again, only to suck in air between her teeth and wince. "What do you want to know?"

"Can I first confirm that you are Virginia Fryer?"

"That was my maiden name. At the time of Charlotte's murder, I was unmarried, although I was being courted by my Stanley. We married twenty-one years ago, but I remained in service to the Whitchurches until I had our daughter. I stayed home to raise her and my husband supported us until he died. My daughter was old enough to go into service by then and I returned to work, too. Not for the Whitchurches, mind, although Lady Whitchurch—the younger, not the dowager—was very kind and gave me a good reference even though I hadn't been employed there for years. I wasn't in my new position for long when I had a fall. All I did was climb a stepladder to get a jar of polish from a high shelf, something I've done thousands of times before. I lost my balance and landed awkwardly." She sighed heavily. "Now I need help to get out of bed."

"You've lived here ever since?" Harry asked.

She nodded. "I need full-time care and my daughter has to work. But when she's married, she'll look after me." Mrs. Hatch smiled. "She's hopeful there'll be a proposal soon."

"The Whitchurches send you a care package every month," I said. "That's generous."

"Lady Whitchurch is kindness itself, always thinking of others. Unlike the dowager. She was a dragon when I worked for her years ago, and the one time I met her afterward, when I went to ask for a reference, it was clear she was still a dragon. She wasn't going to give me one, because she said my character may have changed in the intervening years. Her daughter-in-law overheard and sent the reference to me the next day. She's a good woman." She frowned at me. "Is any of this relevant to your investigation, Miss Fox?"

"It may be. You were Charlotte's friend, is that right?"

Her lips pinched in distaste. "Not friends. We shared a bed, as young maids often did. I know it's not nice to speak ill of the dead, but Charlotte had loose morals. One of the footmen called her Charlotte the Harlot, which sums up everyone's opinion of her."

"You said in your statement to the police that Charlotte was having a liaison with Rupert, the eldest of Lord Whitchurch's sons."

"She was. She told me. I didn't believe her at first, but I followed her one night when she slipped out of our room. She entered his room and didn't come back until dawn." Her lips pinched in disapproval and she shook her head.

"So, she wasn't forced by Rupert?"

"She went willingly. I don't know how it all began, but I suspect she seduced him. She was very pretty and she knew how to attract a man with her flirtations. She used to put color on her cheeks and lips." She shook her head again. "Silly girl. If only she'd kept to herself and not attracted attention... Now, I'm not saying she got what she deserved, Miss Fox. No one deserves to die like that. But good girls don't get themselves murdered, do they?"

I managed to keep my retort to myself, but only just.

Harry must have been concerned that I'd say something to jeopardize the interview, because he took over the questioning. "Was there any trouble between Charlotte and Rupert? Did she ever seem upset after spending time with him?"

"Quite the opposite. She was happy, and refused to hear anything against him, even though I and the housekeeper tried to warn her."

"Warn her about what?"

"That she wasn't his only girl. Everyone knew he had others. He'd be out until all hours and always return drunk or smelling of perfume. Despite his faults, I liked him. He was kind to the staff."

It never ceased to amaze me that women often judged other women harsher than men, particularly when it came to intimacy before marriage. Charlotte was criticized for having one partner, whereas Rupert's multiple partners didn't matter. He was remembered for his kindness while she was remembered for being promiscuous. I wondered if that attitude would ever change in my lifetime.

"You say he was kind, but the police concluded that he

killed Charlotte," I pointed out. "Are you disagreeing with their finding?"

She clutched the crucifix necklace again. "I can only speak to my own experiences. It's true that Master Rupert had a temper, but he never turned it on the servants. He and his father, the late Lord Whitchurch, had terrible rows though."

"About anything in particular?"

"Lord Whitchurch wanted him to settle down. Rupert was too wild, he said. He wanted Master Rupert to be more sensible and studious like his younger brother. As the future viscount, he had a duty to be responsible and steady. I can't fault his lordship for thinking that, but some young gentlemen just need to get the wildness out of their system. Master Rupert would have matured in time. Marrying would have settled him, I'm sure. Do you know he was engaged to the current Lady Whitchurch? After Master Rupert was declared dead, she went on to wed his brother, Arthur."

"Do you think that is strange?"

"That's toffs for you, Miss Fox. Once a suitable girl is found, they don't want to waste her. It can take a long time to find a good one from the right family, and Lady Whitchurch is as good as they come. I suppose the dowager and the late Lord Whitchurch thought it best to keep her for Arthur. They waited until Master Rupert was declared dead after seven years missing, then they married the following week. It was all very sudden."

Seven years didn't seem sudden to me, but I kept my opinion to myself. "Tell us how events unfolded the night Charlotte was murdered."

She settled into the pillows and released her crucifix. "I woke up to screaming, just before dawn. I found out later it was the scullery maid who'd just discovered the body in the kitchen, but at the time, I thought it was Charlotte. She'd told me when we went to bed the night before that she was going to meet Master Rupert, so I assumed something had happened to her, that she'd had a fall or some such. That's why I went to the floor where the family's bedchambers are located when I heard the scream, not all the way down to the kitchen. Once I was there, I heard the scream again and realized it was coming from the kitchen, so I didn't bother to check Master Rupert's room. Luckily I didn't, or I might have been caught coming out by Master Arthur."

"He'd heard the scream, too?"

She nodded. "He came out of his room and ran along the corridor. If he wasn't putting his jacket on, he might have seen me where I was hiding behind a potted palm, but his view was obstructed by his arm. Lord and Lady Whitchurch were too distracted to see me, too, thankfully. They ran past in their dressing gowns, but they were glaring at one another and didn't notice me."

Her statement was fuller than the one she'd given the police. There'd been no mention of the clothing they'd worn, just that they'd passed her while she hid. Something struck me immediately. "Lord and Lady Whitchurch were wearing dressing gowns, which is understandable given the early hour. But Arthur was putting on a jacket. Was he putting it on over his pajamas?"

She frowned. "No, I don't think so. He was wearing trousers, a waistcoat, shirt and tie."

As if he'd just come home. Yet, in his statement he said he'd been in bed all night and was asleep when the body was discovered. He certainly wouldn't have had time to change into a suit if the scream awoke him. Like his parents, he should have been wearing a dressing gown over nightclothes.

So where had he been? And why did he lie? I asked her a few more questions, but her answers gave no new information.

I removed the list of witnesses from my bag and handed it to Mrs. Hatch. "Do you know where we can find the other staff who are on this list? We'd like to interview them again."

She picked up her spectacles from her lap and scrutinized the list. "The butler has passed away, the housekeeper, too. I don't know where the cook or scullery maid are now, but one of the footmen worked for the same family as me before I had my accident. He's the butler there now and he remained friends with Ralph, the Whitchurches' second footman, so he should be able to help you find him. Have you got a pencil and paper, Miss Fox? I'll give you the address."

I wrote it down, then returned my notepad and pencil to my bag. "You've been most helpful, Mrs. Hatch." She smiled, pleased. "One more thing. Do you think Rupert killed Charlotte?"

She sighed. "I suppose he must have done. Innocent men don't run away, do they?"

"Where do you think he went?"

"Overseas, somewhere where a person can change their name and not bump into anyone they know. Africa or Australia, for example."

"Why do you think he killed her?"

Her lips flattened. "It wouldn't surprise me if Charlotte got above herself and made demands on him. Either she wanted to be ensconced as his permanent mistress in her own flat, or she wanted money. They argued and he lashed out." She shook her head sadly. "Silly, silly girl."

"She was a victim, Mrs. Hatch. Whatever she did, she didn't deserve to be murdered by her lover."

"True enough, Miss Fox, but the fact is, if Charlotte had been more careful, more modest, she would still be here today."

It was a point we may never know for sure, but I had the heavy feeling she was right. I wished it could be otherwise.

After we left the charity boarding house, we headed to the address Mrs. Hatch had given me, where the butler gave another statement. It matched the one he'd given the police on the night of Charlotte's murder and provided no new clues. He gave us an address for his friend.

We found Ralph Gannon at his place of employment, a tailor's shop on Savile Row. The display in the front window sported a lightweight jacket and boater for summer, but the bolts of fabric neatly slotted into the shelves appeared to be heavier winter tweeds, worsted and cheviot.

After we introduced ourselves, the very upright and impeccably dressed Mr. Gannon proudly informed us that he left domestic service some years prior and changed careers to become assistant to the tailor. He did all the front-of-house duties, such as taking measurements and writing up orders, while a tailor and his apprentices made the clothes in the workshop out the back. Mr. Gannon claimed he had the skill to make the suits himself, but preferred to talk to the customers.

"I used to act as valet to the young Whitchurch masters, while also performing my footmen duties," he said. "The butler took care of old Lord Whitchurch when he was in London, but the sons were both in my care. I learned a lot about a gentleman's clothing needs from them, which has served me well in my new career."

"Did a man by the name of Hardy work for the Whitchurches?" I asked.

"Not that I recall."

"I'm investigating his death."

He pressed a hand to his chest. "Goodness me."

"He was butler to the Campbells and died while serving at a dinner party. Do you know the Campbells? They're friends of the Whitchurches."

"No, sorry, but it's been some years since I worked for the Whitchurches."

"Witnesses say Mr. Hardy knew them and they him. Does his name ring a bell at all?"

"No."

"Do you remember when Charlotte died?"

"Lord, yes. It was a dreadful day." He gasped. "Does your dead butler have something to do with Charlotte's murder?"

"That's what we're trying to discover."

"I see." He picked up the box of ties he'd been rearranging when we entered and returned them to the display shelf on the counter. Once it was in place, he did not look up, but seemed to be thinking something through.

Harry and I exchanged glances. "Mr. Gannon, is there something you'd like to tell us?" I asked.

He adjusted his tie, even though it was perfectly straight, and cleared his throat. "I'm afraid I didn't tell the police everything. I didn't lie," he quickly added. "Unless omitting something is a lie." When he did not go on, Harry stepped in to reassure him.

"You won't get in trouble for it now. The investigation into Charlotte's death hasn't been reopened. We're simply curious to know if it is connected to Hardy's."

Mr. Gannon smiled gently at Harry. "You're very kind to reassure me, sir." To me, he added, "I told the police how drunk Master Rupert was when I saw him that night. He could barely stand up and I had the devil of a time undressing him and getting him into his pajamas. He also wasn't making much sense, just rambling, which he tended to do when he was drunk."

"That was at about two in the morning?" I asked, recalling his statement.

"That's right."

According to the coroner, the murder had occurred at around four. "Did Rupert have blood on his clothes?"

"No, but that's the thing I omitted to inform the police. Rupert didn't have blood on his clothes, but his father did."

"Why did you keep such a thing from the police? It could have been important."

He put his hands up in defense. "I was afraid of losing my position, and I needed work desperately at the time. His lordship told me he fell and grazed his arm. The blood was inside his jacket, not the outside." He took a jacket off one of the dressmaker forms used for display and unbuttoned it. He indicated where he'd seen the blood on the lining, mostly at the back.

Mrs. Hatch had told us that she saw Lord Whitchurch throwing on his dressing gown as he passed her just before dawn. "At what time did you see him in bloodied clothes?"

"You misunderstand. I didn't see him *wearing* the jacket. I saw it the next day. He asked me to clean it. This was after the police had left. That's when he told me about grazing himself."

If he'd never seen Lord Whitchurch wearing the jacket, then Mrs. Hatch's recollection of seeing him and his wife at the time of the scream still held water.

"Was it definitely Lord Whitchurch's jacket?" Harry asked. "Could it have belonged to Rupert?"

"No. They were a different size. I would have noticed something like that."

"What about Arthur?" I asked. "Could it have been his?"

"He was also a different size to his father. Old Lord Whitchurch was a large fellow." Mr. Gannon patted his stomach. "Besides, I believe Arthur was asleep in his room all night."

"We have evidence to the contrary."

His eyes widened. "Really? Where was he?"

I didn't answer. "What do you think happened that night, Mr. Gannon? Do you think old Lord Whitchurch killed Charlotte and that's how he got blood on his jacket?"

He parted his hands before re-clasping them on the counter. "I've thought about it a lot over the years, and no, I don't think he did it. He wasn't a violent man. Argumentative with his wife and eldest son, yes, but he wouldn't kill a maid. Why would he? If he wanted to get rid of her, he could simply dismiss her without a reference. Unable to work in service without one, she'd vanish from his life. I don't know where the blood came from, but I don't think he murdered her."

"What about Rupert?"

"Ah. That's a different matter. He couldn't have Charlotte dismissed without his parents asking questions, and he wouldn't want that."

"Why would he want her dismissed? Did they have a falling out?"

Mr. Gannon shrugged. "There could be a number of reasons. He may have got her with child, or she could have been blackmailing him, threatening to tell his parents if he didn't pay her. Lord and Lady Whitchurch were upright people, very concerned about appearances, and would have been furious with him for taking one of the maids as his mistress."

"You don't think they knew?"

"I'm not sure. If they didn't, they certainly found out after Charlotte's death. It all came out then. I think Lord Whitchurch tried to hush it up, but a scandal like that can't be contained. So he did the next best thing."

"Which was?"

"Encouraged the police to give up the search for Master Rupert."

"That's a bold accusation," Harry said.

I suspected he was referring to the police obeying Lord Whitchurch's demand to end the search, but Mr. Gannon assumed he meant the accusation that Lord Whitchurch tried to affect the outcome of a murder investigation.

"They may have clashed dreadfully," he said, "but Rupert

was his son. I think his lordship worried that a public trial would ruin the family more than Rupert's disappearance. Lady Whitchurch was very fond of Rupert and wouldn't want to see him hang."

"Do *you* think he helped Rupert escape?"

"It's possible."

"What was Arthur's relationship like with his brother?" I asked. "Could *he* have helped Rupert escape?"

"Unlikely. Arthur loathed Rupert. He was terribly jealous of his older brother. Jealous that his father invested more time and effort in him, since he was the heir, and jealous that his mother loved Rupert more. Rupert had charm and wit, courage and confidence that many adored, including their mother. Of course she knew he had faults, but she thought he'd grow out of them, in time."

It reminded me of something Mrs. Hatch had said. It sounded like she'd also been enamored of the dashing Rupert. "Arthur resented his brother?"

"Oh, yes. When they walked into a room, all eyes went to Rupert. The worst of it was, Arthur was hopelessly in love with the girl his parents had chosen for his brother, and Rupert wasn't in the least interested in her."

"Was *she* interested in him?"

"It was hard to tell. She was a very quiet thing, very reserved. She was most *unsuited* to Rupert, of course. He would have grown bored with her very quickly. Anyway, Arthur got her in the end. They married when Rupert was declared dead seven years after his disappearance."

"Do you think he's still alive?" I asked.

Mr. Gannon shrugged. "I don't know. Wherever he went, he would be doing something with horses. He adored them, whether it was riding them, caring for them, gambling on them…if you're looking for him, try looking at racetracks or stables."

"That narrows it down," Harry joked.

Mr. Gannon chuckled.

"Can you describe Rupert's appearance?" I asked. "If we were to look for him, we should know what to look for."

"He was tall, although not as tall as you, Mr. Armitage." He smiled at Harry. "Good-looking."

"Rupert was?" I asked, just in case he was referring to Harry.

"Oh, yes. Light brown hair, blue eyes, and a light sprinkle of freckles on his straight nose. A strong jaw and chin with a cleft, but it wasn't too deep. A dimple formed in his left cheek when he smiled, which made his smiles seem boyish and innocent, but I can assure you there was nothing innocent about him."

"You're very observant, Mr. Gannon," I said.

The wistful look on Mr. Gannon's face vanished. He fussed with the top hat perched on the marble bust at one end of the counter.

We thanked him and left. I didn't get far before I started firing all of my theories at Harry. "Perhaps Arthur encouraged his brother to leave after the murder. He benefits from Rupert's disappearance the most. Not only does he inherit, he also gets to marry his brother's fiancée. If they were in love, that's two rather large motives."

"And the blood on old Lord Whitchurch's jacket?"

"Perhaps *he* murdered Charlotte because…well, I don't know why yet, but say he did, but Arthur didn't know his father was responsible. Arthur tells his brother that he, Rupert, did it and Rupert is too drunk to remember so believes him. Then Arthur helps him escape to get rid of him."

"It's a bit far-fetched. Besides, the blood was on the *inside* of the jacket. If old Lord Whitchurch stabbed her, he would have got blood on the outside and at the front, not the inside back."

"Perhaps *Charlotte* was wearing it. They were together and she was cold, so Lord Whitchurch wrapped it around her shoulders to keep her warm. Then they argued and he killed her, getting her blood on his jacket, which he removed before returning to his bedchamber." I rather liked that theory. Just because Lord Whitchurch was supposedly upright, it didn't mean he wasn't having an affair with the maid, too.

"The only person alive who'd know is the dowager," Harry said. "She'll never admit it."

"There might be evidence to prove the theory. We just haven't found it yet." We walked on in silence, but my mind was still reeling. "There's one more theory we haven't considered yet. One that has been gnawing at me for some time, but now that I've spoken to Mr. Gannon, it's taken root."

Harry stopped and took me by the elbow, steering me out of the way of other pedestrian traffic on busy Savile Row. "You look like you're going to explode if you don't say something soon."

I fished my fan from my bag and fanned myself. I wished I'd brought a parasol. I glanced around out of habit, then leaned closer to Harry. "What if Rupert and Mr. Hardy are— were—one and the same man?"

CHAPTER 8

*H*arry seemed as excited by my theory as I was. He walked quickly along Savile Row and I had a devil of a time keeping up with his long strides while also avoiding bumping into other pedestrians. We hadn't discussed where we were heading, but I suspected we had the same destination in mind.

We needed to find out what Mr. Hardy looked like. Considering what we suspected, it made sense to try to get answers from Mrs. Turner at the Campbells' house rather than confronting the Whitchurches again.

Once we were clear of Savile Row and the throng of shoppers, I fell into step alongside Harry. I picked up the conversation where we'd left off, even though I doubted I was telling him anything he hadn't already realized. *"That's* why the Whitchurches recognized Hardy on the night they dined with the Campbells. He was the current Lord Whitchurch's brother, and Lady Whitchurch's former fiancé. He didn't escape overseas all those years ago. He'd been hiding in plain sight. Cut off from his family, he needed to work to support himself, so he took employment as a butler. Given he grew up with a butler always nearby, he knew how they behaved and what tasks they performed."

Harry agreed with one amendment. "It makes more sense if he was a footman first, given he was young at the time of

97

his disappearance and he had no references. He would have worked his way up to the position of butler."

"So you like my theory?"

He cast me a crooked smile without breaking his stride. "It's just as far-fetched as the one about the old lord giving Charlotte his jacket then murdering her, but I like it more."

Instead of bolstering my confidence in the theory, he'd deflated it. The theory *was* quite far-fetched. "I'm sure I'm wrong. Usually, the simplest explanation is the correct one. This one is mad."

"But sometimes the mad explanations are the right ones. There's only one way to know for sure." He picked up speed and I had to trot to keep up.

"Harry, slow down. Not everyone has stilts for legs."

He paused and took my hand. It was an impulse on his part, a way of keeping us in step with one another. It took him a moment to realize what he'd done.

I noticed immediately, however, and couldn't decide whether I wanted to be released or not. I liked the way my heart skipped in response to the simple gesture.

But once my thoughts cleared, I became aware of what holding his hand meant. It was giving him the wrong impression. It was encouragement, when I wanted to discourage tender feelings, both mine and his. It was creating closeness when distance was the better course for a couple with no future together.

I slipped my hand free and focused on the pavement ahead, not on the way Harry cast a disappointed look in my direction. We didn't speak the rest of the way to the Campbells' residence.

Betty the maid couldn't take her eyes off Harry when she opened the door to us. Her pale cheeks suddenly flushed with color, and she developed a stammer as she invited us inside. The effect Harry had on some women was getting tiresome, and I was a little short with her when I asked to see Mrs. Turner.

She led the way along the corridor toward the housekeeper's office. Mrs. Cook and her assistant, Birdy, looked up from the pies they were assembling. I greeted them with smiles but received only nods in return. Davey the footman was more agreeable. He hurried out of the kitchen, carrying a domed silver platter balanced on the tips of his fingers.

"Miss Fox, what a pleasure! Can't stop for a chat today. Work to do."

We stepped aside to allow him to pass. When he reached Betty, he caught her hand and spun her with all the grace of a dancing master.

She giggled and blushed again.

Mrs. Turner saw them through her open office door. "Be off with you, Davey, they're waiting upstairs." Once we'd joined her in the office and Betty had closed the door, the housekeeper sighed. "That boy has caused me enough of a headache. I don't need him flirting with Betty. He seems to think it's all right now that he's leaving."

"He definitely is?" I asked as I sat.

She sighed again. "He applied for the position of butler, but Sir Ian and Lady Campbell won't give it to him, so he's given his resignation. Now we need a new butler *and* footman. I can't blame them, of course. He's not ready to be a butler. In a few more years, certainly, but not yet." She shuffled some papers on her desk with the shake of her head. "That's the problem with the younger generation. They want everything now, without working their way up to it. They don't understand they have to earn it." She suddenly stopped, perhaps realizing she was speaking to two people from the same generation as Davey.

I introduced her to Harry, calling him my assistant, not my associate.

He huffed ever so slightly, then smiled at Mrs. Turner. "Miss Fox doesn't need my assistance, but she likes to have me around."

She blinked at him. "Is that because people take her more seriously with a man at her side?"

"No, it's because I'm excellent company." His smile warmed.

The look she gave me left me in no doubt that she now assumed precisely what Harry wanted her to assume—that I liked him in *that* way. The fiend.

I launched into our reason for returning before he could

cause any more trouble. "Is there by any chance a photograph of the staff that includes Mr. Hardy?"

"I'm afraid not. He wasn't here long enough for one to be taken. Why do you need a photograph?"

"We're trying to find out where he worked before coming here. If Hardy is an assumed name and he went by another, it will be easier to show his photograph to see if he's recognized."

"I see. There are no photographs that I've come across, and I've searched through his desk and his personal belongings. There's nothing of a personal nature at all, not even the name of a family member to send his things to. It's very sad."

It was also odd. "Can you describe his appearance?"

"He was tall, slim, but not too thin, and quite handsome. He wasn't going bald, like some his age. He had a full head of thick gray hair."

Her description was almost as thorough as Mr. Gannon's had been. There was one telling feature she'd omitted, however.

"Did he have a cleft in his chin?" I asked.

"I don't know. He had a beard. It was neatly trimmed, but it obscured his chin and jaw."

I was disappointed, but Harry's suspicion was piqued. "In my experience, butlers and footmen are always cleanly shaved."

"The Campbells didn't seem to mind the beard. They don't worry about appearances like some. Oh, I did forget one thing. Mr. Hardy had a limp. I never asked how he got it. I didn't like to pry, and I worried he might be sensitive about it. You know how some men are, Miss Fox."

"Indeed. But a limp is also an unusual trait for a butler. You say the Campbells weren't concerned about appearances, but a limp is different to a beard."

She glanced at the door, then leaned forward. "While I was cleaning out his belongings, I saw his letter of offer. He wasn't being paid much. In fact, he was paid the same as me. Usually, a butler receives more, even though they do less. I've been thinking for some time that the Campbells might be in some financial difficulty and seeing that letter confirmed it. I think they hired a butler with a limp because he was inexpensive. He couldn't get work in the better households with a deformity, so he took the position here where he had to accept less. Not that it was a deformity in my eyes, you understand. I thought it made him even more dashing. But you know how toffs are, Miss Fox."

The limp didn't matter to me as much as the beard did. If Hardy had a cleft in his chin, the beard would hide it. It was quite possibly the reason he grew it in the first place. If he was indeed Rupert, it was definitely the reason he'd grown it.

"Speaking of the Campbells," Harry said. "Do you know how long they've been friends of the Whitchurches?"

Mrs. Turner thought about it for a moment. "Ten or eleven years, I'd say."

Not long enough to have known Rupert then. They could very well have unwittingly hired their friend's brother.

Mrs. Turner followed us out of her office after we thanked her and called for Betty to see us to the door. Betty couldn't be found, however.

"Was she summoned upstairs?" Mrs. Turner asked the cook.

Mrs. Cook shrugged and returned to her workbench.

Mrs. Turner sighed. "I know she's upset about Mr. Hardy, but we all are, and we don't disappear at the drop of a hat, do we? She needs to learn to get on with it when there's work to be done."

While she went in search of Betty, Harry and I saw ourselves out.

He waited until we were walking away from the house before speaking. "Do you still think Hardy and Rupert are the same person?"

"Even more so," I said. "There are no photographs of him, nothing personal from family members, and he grew a beard. What better way to disguise his appearance? The rest of Mrs. Turner's description could match an older Rupert, except the limp, which could have been acquired in the last twenty-two years."

"My thoughts exactly. So where to now, Lead Detective?"

I eyed him carefully. "Are you upset that I introduced you as my assistant, not associate?"

"No. I am your assistant this time. It's your case."

We walked on, but I could feel the tension thickening between us. I really didn't like it, but I didn't know what to say to alleviate it.

Harry, however, had no such qualms. "Are you upset that I made a joke in there about you enjoying my company?"

"You said you were excellent company, not that I enjoyed having you around. And no, of course I'm not upset. Some people do find you excellent company."

"You being one."

I laughed. "Have you always been this arrogant, or am I just now being exposed to it?"

"It's not arrogance, it's confidence. I'm confident that you like having me around."

I quickened my steps to get ahead of him to hide my heating face. Unfortunately, his long legs meant he easily kept up.

"You should slow down, Cleo. You look hot and bothered." He said it with a heavy dose of humor that had my face heating more.

I must remember my parasol tomorrow. If Harry continued to tease me, I was going to need it to hide my blushes.

I was so disoriented that I forgot to answer his question. He asked it again. "Are you going to tell me where we're going, or shall I guess?"

"If you stop distracting me by changing the subject, I would."

"It's not the change of subject that has you distracted, Cleo." The humor was still in his voice, but the undertone of flirtation was unmistakable.

I studiously kept my gaze focused forward. "We're returning to the Whitchurches' house. We're going to sneak in and look for a photograph of Rupert."

My suggestion wasn't met with an ounce of surprise, which meant he already suspected that was my plan. "And how will we do that?"

"I don't know yet. I'm hoping for inspiration on the way."

He laughed softly. "Just when I think you're being predictable, you surprise me."

"Here's another thing that will surprise you. You're not joining me."

He stopped. "You said 'we' will sneak in."

"I've changed my mind. You can't afford to be caught, Harry. You know that. I didn't want Victor to include you when he broke into the Campbells' residence, and I don't want you included this time."

Harry wasn't often annoyed, but he narrowed his gaze and glared daggers at me. "You need me in there, Cleo. You can't go in alone."

"I can and I will."

"The Whitchurches know you, as do some of the staff. They won't let you in, and without their permission, you can't sneak in."

"You didn't meet the housekeeper, Harry, only I did. That will do."

"Do for what?"

"For you to perform your role. I want you to create a distraction. If you do it well, not only will I not be discovered, but no one will know you were involved at all." I set off again, leaving him staring after me, still annoyed but also confused.

When he caught up, the annoyance had vanished altogether. Harry's bad moods didn't last very long. "What sort of distraction do you want me to create?"

"I'll tell you on the way to the hotel. Your costume is there."

* * *

THE COSTUME HARRY needed was in the maintenance room, located in the basement next to the coal cellar. The maintenance engineer was tall, like Harry, but unlike Harry, he looked like he lived in the basement with his pallid skin and fleshy sacks under his eyes and at his jowls. If ever a man resembled a sad hound, it was him.

I was keen to avoid him. Indeed, I was keen not to be seen in the basement at all. My uncle didn't like me mixing with the staff. If he knew I sat with them in the staff parlor, he'd scold me. If he knew I'd been breaking into the maintenance engineer's cupboard to steal his spare overalls, he'd be livid.

I asked Harmony to do it instead. As a maid, it was acceptable for her to be down there. She agreed to do it and told me to meet her in the lane near the service entrance where Harry waited for me. I'd entered the hotel via the front door so that I'd be seen, before heading to the staff parlor where I suspected she'd be enjoying a cup of tea after cleaning rooms all day.

As she went down to the basement, I returned to the foyer to spend a few minutes in full view of the guests and any of my family who happened to pass. It was mid-afternoon, a rather busy time as new guests checked in. Peter and Mr. Hobart were doing their best to greet guests and make sure all was as it should be. Peter looked so much more comfortable in his role as assistant manager these days. He was very agreeable to everybody, and good at calming demanding guests, although the most demanding were usually left to Mr. Hobart.

Mr. Hobart looked at ease this afternoon. Even when Uncle Ronald entered the foyer, hat in hand as he headed for the door, Mr. Hobart didn't bat an eye, despite the glare my uncle gave him.

Upon seeing me, Uncle Ronald approached. "He took an hour for lunch again today."

"I assume we're discussing Mr. Hobart?"

He grunted.

"Uncle, there is nothing wrong with taking his full allocated lunch hour."

He grunted again. "I heard the Carlton is close to filling the position of manager."

"That is good news. Then we won't have to worry about Mr. Hobart taking it."

He looked at me like I was a fool.

"Oh," I said quietly. "Unless they're close to filling it because Mr. Hobart has almost accepted."

He fidgeted with the hat in his hands, lightly skimming his fingers along the brim. "I know you told Floyd that you wouldn't investigate Hobart's change of attitude, but you didn't refuse *me* outright." He gave a hopeful lift of his brows.

I stared at him, trying to think of a delicate way to escape the conversation.

"It will give you something to do, Cleopatra, and you do want to be a detective."

"I am a detective already. I'm in the middle of an investigation now, as it happens."

He looked genuinely interested. "Is that so? What are you investigating?"

He wouldn't like me being involved in another murder. He thought a lady detective should only investigate gentle crimes. Death, divorce and violent crimes were all unpalatable topics.

So I skirted the truth, just a little. "I'm looking for a man who went missing more than twenty years ago."

"That's very noble, Cleopatra. I'm sure the family will be grateful to you, whether you find him or not. Make sure they pay you well."

I smiled as he put his hat on his head. It was a relief when he finally left the hotel. I was about to make my way to the kitchen exit when Miss Hessing and her fiancé, Mr. Liddicoat, emerged from the lift. She spotted me, said something to Mr. Liddicoat, then approached.

He continued on, greeting me as he passed before leaving the hotel.

"I'm so glad I caught you, Miss Fox," she said. "We've just been discussing wedding plans with my mother."

"How pleasant." At her frown, I changed my opinion. "Or not. Is something the matter, Miss Hessing?"

"Mother has booked my wedding reception at the Savoy."

I clasped her hands. "Oh, no. This is a disaster! Did you tell her you wanted it here?"

"We tried, but she says Mr. Chapman isn't listening to her."

The situation was grave indeed. Mrs. Hessing would rather trip over her own feet in the street than have no one notice her. "Mr. Chapman believes the reception to celebrate your wedding should suit *your* tastes, not your mother's."

"He doesn't understand," she moaned. "The wedding ceremony is for me, the reception is for Mother." She clutched my hands. "Miss Fox, will you talk to him?"

"It has to come from you." I squeezed her hands. "I must dash, but you must be strong, Miss Hessing. Go to Mr. Chapman and tell him to listen to your mother. Then go to your mother and tell her to cancel the Savoy, that you want your wedding reception here."

She assured me she would, but I wasn't convinced. For one thing, she did not go to Mr. Chapman even though she saw him emerge from the senior staff corridor. Instead, she hurried to catch the lift.

Mr. Chapman's gaze shifted from her to me. Then, with a tug on each of his cuffs and a tilt of his chin, he strode past me to the sitting room to prepare for afternoon tea.

I left the hotel via the service entrance and found Harry in the lane, chatting with Harmony and Victor. He already wore the maintenance engineer's overalls over his clothes and carried a clipboard.

Harmony, holding his jacket and hat, stepped back to study him. "You'll do. Just remember not to look so…" She wiggled her fingers at him.

He arched his brows. "So…what?"

"Polished."

Harry ruffled his hair, messing it up. "Better?"

"Hunch your back a little."

Harry hunched. "Now?"

Harmony lifted one shoulder, giving up.

Victor told us to wait, then disappeared inside. He returned moments later with a cloth blackened with soot. He drew a smudge on Harry's cheek, then told him to wipe his hands on the dirty cloth.

"I'm a gas inspector, not a chimney sweep," Harry said even though he obliged.

Harmony sent us on our way, then returned inside with Victor, still carrying Harry's jacket and hat.

"Are they a couple yet?" Harry asked.

"Yes."

"Can we expect wedding bells soon?"

"Not everyone wants to marry, Harry. Perhaps they're quite content as they are."

He gave me a sharp look, but made no comment about the irritation underpinning my tone. He was wiser than most men when it came to understanding when a topic was best left alone.

We briefly discussed our plan, then separated well before reaching the Whitchurches' house. I headed into the mews to wait at the rear of the residence. The moments ticked by slowly, but eventually Harry appeared and signaled for me to enter.

"Sorry it took so long," he whispered. "The dowager is refusing to leave. According to the housekeeper, she says she couldn't smell gas so is staying put. She's in her room. I had the housekeeper assemble everyone else down the street, including Lord and Lady Whitchurch."

It would seem the dowager was prepared to risk her life. Gas leaks could prove deadly. I'd lost count of the number of reports I'd read of corroded pipes and fittings leaking gas that exploded. If a resident or passerby smelled gas, the gas company would send a gas fitter to fix the problem, but due to the volatility of the substance, the residents had to vacate the premises in the meantime. Given no one had smelled gas, the dowager was smarter than the rest.

"You'll need to be quiet or she'll become suspicious," Harry went on.

"I will."

"I'll help. It'll be twice as fast with two."

"No." I pointed at the service stairs that led to the basement kitchen and storerooms. The gas tanks would be down there. If anyone who might recognize him checked on his progress, he could keep his face averted as he pretended to work. I suspected the fear of an explosion would keep the household away, however.

He obeyed, albeit reluctantly.

I snuck upstairs and checked all the photographs on display in the first-floor drawing room, the only room I'd already been in. I recognized Arthur, the current lord, and quickly realized which other man was his father. With various family members I'd met appearing in all other photographs, and based on their age in each, I was able to determine that not a single one was of Rupert. I took a closer look at the oddly sized photograph with the late Lord Whitchurch standing beside a horse. I'd suspected a section had been cut

C.J. ARCHER

off, and a second look proved I was right. Part of another person's shadow appeared on the ground.

I checked the rest of the rooms on the first floor and was surprised to find the second reception room was a dining room. Usually in grand townhouses they were on the ground floor, so that it wasn't far for the food to travel from the kitchen. There were no photographs in the dining room, but there was a large painted portrait over the fireplace. Closer inspection proved it was the late Lord Whitchurch and the dowager aged in their late thirties or early forties. She wore a lustrous gown of white satin and a necklace of diamonds and aquamarines. But it wasn't her clothing and jewels that interested me. It was Lord Whitchurch's tiepin. It was shaped like a sword with a sapphire embedded in the pommel.

Why was his tiepin hidden in the toe of Mr. Hardy's shoe?

I hurried out of the dining room and stood on the landing, uncertain whether to go downstairs to the ground floor where there ought to be a library and whatever had replaced the dining room space, or upstairs to the bedchambers where I suspected I'd have more success but might stumble across the dowager.

I decided to go up, but only search rooms where the door was open and I could see that it was empty. Unfortunately, there were only two rooms that fit that criteria. One was a guest bedchamber that held nothing of interest. The other was Lord Whitchurch's study. Despite a thorough search of his desk and shelves, I found no photographs of his brother, nor any correspondence from him or relating to him. If any existed, they'd probably be in the wall safe, which I found behind a painting, but cracking the code was beyond my limited skills.

I crept past the closed doors on both the second and third floors, wondering which one the dowager's bedchamber was behind. I didn't bother with the fourth floor, as the servants' quarters wouldn't contain anything relevant.

With only the ground floor left, I tiptoed down the stairs. I had to be careful searching the library. Located at the front of the house, the window overlooked the pavement, so I limited my search to the desk. Finding nothing, I exited via the rear door that led to the staircase, instead of the one leading to the entrance hall. The only main room left to search was the one that should have been the dining room, beyond the staircase. Curious as to what it might house since the dining room had been relocated to the first floor, I headed toward it, only to stop dead when the door opened.

Too late, I realized why the dining room had taken over the reception room on the first floor. The elderly dowager's bedchamber had been moved into the ground-floor room usually used as a dining room, so that she didn't have to climb up and down stairs all day. She'd refused to vacate it during the gas inspection and had stayed behind, not on the second or third floors where I'd been so careful to remain quiet, but on the ground level.

And now she was coming out.

I opened the nearest door and ducked inside. Before the light was blocked out by the closing door, I took note of thick, long coats and fur stoles. The enclosed space smelled of cedarwood, used to keep the moths away. Hopefully, the smell hadn't wafted out when I entered the coat closet.

"Who's there?" came the dowager's brittle voice. "Arthur? Is that you?"

I stayed silent.

The *clomp clomp* of her walking stick passed the closet door, heading away from her bedchamber then fading altogether.

I opened the door a crack and checked the vicinity. The dowager was nowhere in sight, but her bedchamber door was wide open. If anyone kept a photograph of Rupert, surely it would be his mother.

I didn't allow myself any more time to think through my actions. I didn't want to give doubt time to creep in. I slipped out of the closet and raced into her room, closing the door behind me.

The room was divided by a screen, behind which was a chair and space for dressing. In the main part of the room, aside from a bed and chest of drawers, was a dressing table and writing desk. If I were to keep photographs of my banished son, I'd keep them on the dressing table. It felt more private.

A quick search produced nothing but hair combs and pins,

perfume and jewelry. I moved to the writing desk and checked each of the drawers. Finding nothing, I searched the small compartments at the back. Again, there was nothing related to Rupert. Perhaps his own mother hadn't liked him and had kept nothing of his after he disappeared. By all accounts, she'd been fond of him, but the witnesses could be wrong.

My hand skimmed over something protruding at the back of one of the desk's compartments. My father had owned a similar desk, and behind the small drawers was a secret compartment that I'd discovered one day when I was bored. Perhaps this one had something similar. Guided by my childhood memories, I easily found the latch. I flicked it up and the compartment revealed itself.

Letters spilled out onto the desk surface. There were dozens, all in the same hand, all signed with the name "Oblitus." Each was dated a few months apart, beginning mere weeks after the murder of Charlotte, and were sent from various countries. The most common was France or Italy, but there was quite a variety, including Malta, Greece, Russia and finally America. Oblitus was well traveled.

If Oblitus was a coded name for Rupert, then he'd been in correspondence with his mother throughout his exile, until a month before Mr. Hardy had begun working at the Campbell residence. After opening a few letters at random, I concentrated on the most recent ones. All were brief, some a mere paragraph. They said nothing of interest, most simply describing the weather, his health, and that he hoped she was well. The last few letters changed, however. He talked about being low in spirits, and missing home and the life he used to lead. These last ones asked for money, saying he couldn't continue with his former employment. In the final letter, the tone turned to begging. He asked her to send financial assistance "just this once" to get him back on his feet. The implication being she'd not sent money after his earlier requests.

I heard the *clomp* of the walking stick against the floorboards first, followed by the voices of the dowager and Lord Whitchurch. I hurriedly shoved the letters back into the compartment and closed it.

"There is no leak, Arthur!"

"The gas fitter said—"

"Can you smell gas?"

They were right outside the door! If I tried to escape, I'd be seen. Even if I hid my face and ran, they'd alert the staff to my presence, and I'd be stopped outside and my identity revealed. Hiding under the bed or behind the privacy screen would only be a temporary solution. And how long would I need to remain hidden before the dowager left again? It was too much of a risk.

"No," the dowager was saying in response to something her son said. "I can't either." The voices were close, but they seemed to have stopped at the door.

I had only moments to make my escape.

The good thing about being on the ground floor was escaping via a window meant I wouldn't need to put life and limb at risk. All I had to do was climb through.

Unfortunately, the bad thing about being on the ground floor was that the windows were usually locked to keep burglars out. The dowager's bedroom window wouldn't budge, and there was no time to search for a key.

The door handle turned as someone on the other side opened it.

I'd have to brazen it out. I drew in a fortifying breath, faced the door, and tried to think of an excuse.

CHAPTER 9

*T*he blood rushed like a torrent in my ears, drowning out all sounds. Even the voices of the dowager and Lord Whitchurch faded to nothing. Or perhaps they'd stopped talking. I didn't know. All I knew was that the door handle kept turning and turning and turning. Panic froze me to the spot. For all my bravado, I knew I couldn't talk my way out of my predicament. The dowager would make sure that I was arrested. I'd be an embarrassment to my family. My uncle would never let me leave the hotel alone again. He would forbid me from investigating. If I refused to follow his orders, I'd have to defy him and leave the hotel, perhaps never to return.

My heart seemed to stop altogether.

The set of hands clasping me from behind restarted it with a ferocious thud. I spun around to see Harry leaning in through the window, trying to encourage me to climb through. Somehow, he'd got it open from the outside.

There was no time to ask where he'd found the key, or how he knew that I was in this particular room.

I sat on the windowsill, intending to swing my legs out. Instead, Harry grasped me around the waist and hauled me through. I fell against him, my skirts tangling around me, revealing my legs. There was no time for blushes, however. He pushed me down and we lay side by side on the court-yard bricks, as close to the wall as possible.

Inside, the dowager scolded her son for being gullible and a fool. One of them closed the window, muffling her voice.

Harry put his finger to his lips to silence me, then rose to peep through the window. Without a word, he signaled for me to leave via the mews. He made sure I was on my way before he re-entered the house via the service entrance.

We met ten minutes later at the same place where we'd parted, a few streets away. I could have kissed him when I saw him striding toward me, safe and sound and looking roguish with the smudged soot on his cheek. I *wanted* to kiss him. Instead, I grinned.

It was met with a scowl. "Never again," he growled. "Next time something like that's required, I'll do it."

"But I can't haul *you* out of a window, can I?"

His jaw set firm as he indicated we should walk.

"You picked the window's lock quickly," I said.

"It wasn't locked. It was just stuck."

"How did you know I was in there?"

"I saw you through the window when I came outside to see if you'd managed to leave while I wasn't looking. I heard the dowager and Lord Whitchurch's voices and knew you'd probably heard them too. Was that the dowager's bedchamber?"

"They must have moved her things to the ground floor for the duration of her London stay on account of her frailty. It was fortunate they did."

He grunted. "It didn't seem fortunate to me. If her bedchamber had been on one of the upper floors, you would never have been in that predicament."

"I would never have found what I was looking for, either."

"You got a photograph of Rupert?"

I shook my head. "There wasn't a single photograph of him in any of the rooms, and I looked through all except for a few bedchambers. Don't you think that odd?"

"Perhaps the current Lord and Lady Whitchurch don't want any photos of him in their house. The dowager usually lives at their country manor, so perhaps they're all there."

"Or the family doesn't want anyone recognizing him.

Perhaps they removed all photographs of him when they discovered he'd become butler for the Campbells."

Harry wasn't convinced. Not that he said as much. He fell silent, sullenly and profoundly. Somehow, it made his anger seem even fiercer.

"I knew the dangers," I told him. "But if it makes you feel better, go ahead and scold me. I won't interrupt."

He kept walking, not even muttering an oath under his breath. He continued to quietly seethe, his fists closed at his sides and the muscles in his jaw throbbing. He would give himself an ache if he kept clenching his teeth like that. I didn't like seeing him so wound up, and I certainly didn't like him being cross with me, so I attempted to lighten his mood.

"I'm glad I wore my prettiest undergarments."

He stopped and grabbed me by the elbows. He'd been angry with me before, but this was different. This was unreasonable anger, far more than the situation warranted. "This is not a game, Cleo."

"I know." My voice sounded as frail as the dowager's. I cleared my throat. "I know," I said again.

He released me. "Then why are you making jokes?"

I brushed my sleeve, even though there was nothing to brush off. "Because I don't like it when you're cross with me, and I don't know how else to make you stop."

His anger cleared as rapidly as it had surfaced. He took a deep breath, then another and another. The third was more of a sigh. "I'm sorry," he murmured.

I gave him a flat smile. "It's all right. I forgive you."

"I was just worried about you."

"I know."

"If you were caught..." He looked down at his feet and shook his head.

"My uncle would ensure I was released, if I were arrested. I doubt I would have been charged. If the dowager pushed for charges to be laid, I'd simply tell her what I'd found in her desk. She would have backed down then."

"It's not an arrest that worried me. It's what Sir Ronald would do after you were released. He'd lock you away and stop us...stop you from investigating."

"I'm not a heroine from a Brothers Grimm tale, Harry. If Uncle Ronald tried to lock me away, I'd simply leave."

He tilted his head to the side. "And go where?"

"Is your old room at your parents' house still available?" The slight twitch of his lips encouraged me to go on. "I could offer to keep house for your mother in exchange for free board. She might even start to like me after a while. I'm not a bad cook."

He smiled crookedly. "'Not a bad cook?' That's hardly a solid recommendation. Do you even remember how to cook?"

"Of course. Eggs need to be boiled for an hour, don't they?"

He rolled his eyes, but his smile widened. "Let's go back to the hotel. The maintenance engineer will be wondering where his spare overalls got to."

We continued walking at a more sedate pace in comfortable silence until my nerves settled completely and I remembered I hadn't finished telling him what I'd found in the dowager's desk.

"I haven't told you the best part yet," I said. "Rupert had been sending his mother letters ever since he left the country."

"Where has he been?"

"All over the world. He sent her a letter every few months. At least, I *think* they're from him. They weren't addressed to 'Mother' or anything like that, and they were signed Oblitus."

"Oblitus? Is that Latin?"

"It sounds Latin, but I don't know what it means. I have a little French and Italian, but no Latin. I'll ask Floyd. He would have learned it at school."

"So, if it is Rupert who wrote those letters to his mother from overseas, he and Hardy can't be the same person."

"Not necessarily. The last letter was dated several weeks before Mr. Hardy started working for the Campbells. It mentioned he was in need of money. It seemed as though his earlier pleas to his mother had gone unheeded, and he was getting desperate. What if he came back to England to beg her in person, but she refused, so he took employment as a butler for the Campbells just to get by?"

"It's feasible. The timing fits."

"Then, when his brother saw him at dinner, he grew worried Rupert would be recognized in time by their friends. Not only would it jeopardize Arthur's inheritance of the title and everything that went with it, it would cause a dreadful scandal. Maybe Arthur panicked and went back a few days later to kill him."

Harry nodded slowly. "Your far-fetched theory is looking more and more likely."

We walked the rest of the way to the hotel in silence. When I realized I was spending more time thinking about how much I liked that Harry had worried about me, I pushed thoughts of him aside and concentrated on the case.

I agreed with him that my theory about Rupert and Hardy being one and the same was looking more solid after finding the letters from Oblitus and the portrait showing the tiepin I'd found in Hardy's shoe. Now all we needed to do was prove it, because I doubted we'd get a confession from Lord Whitchurch or his mother, the dowager.

* * *

MY FAMILY'S social calendar was empty for the evening, much to my relief. I needed an evening off from the whirlwind of parties and dinners. My aunt needed it too and excused herself even from a small family dinner in the restaurant. She ate in her room while the rest of us dined at our regular table. It wasn't all that peaceful, however. My uncle circulated amongst the other tables, while Floyd and I also chatted to diners who stopped by to give us their regards. Flossy wasn't as vivacious as usual. She smiled when appropriate and joined in conversations, but something was obviously wrong.

It wasn't until we finished the main course that I finally felt like we weren't at work or on display. When Uncle Ronald left us to speak to a group of Belgian guests, I asked Flossy what the matter was.

"Nothing," she muttered.

I exchanged a glance with Floyd, but he was enjoying his pudding and failed to notice. "I can tell something's wrong,

Flossy. Go on, out with it. You'll feel better when you get it off your chest."

"I won't." Flossy poked a strawberry around her bowl, drawing patterns in the cream. With a huff, she put down her spoon. "What's wrong with me, Cleo?"

"Absolutely nothing! You're sweet, kind and lively, not to mention pretty." I clasped her arm. "What's caused this melancholia?"

She sighed. "Everyone is getting married except me."

"Sometimes finding the right man takes time. Look at Miss Hessing. It took her years to find Mr. Liddicoat, but it was worth the wait. He's a wonderful man and they're well suited. The right man for you will come along one day."

"I wish he'd hurry up. Another season as barren as this one and I'll officially be on the shelf. Then I'll have to stand with the elderly spinsters at the balls." She made a face.

"Like me, you mean?" I teased.

"Not at all, Cleo! I could never compare myself to you. You'll always have dance partners, because the gentlemen are intrigued by you and they enjoy your company. You're a great conversationalist. Also, you're very pretty."

"You're never short of dance partners either, Flossy. It will be the same next year. You won't suddenly become a wallflower."

She sighed again and picked up her spoon.

Finally, with his pudding finished, Floyd joined the conversation. "Against my better judgement, I'm going to voice an opinion. The maharaja's son failed to notice you flirting with him, didn't he?"

Flossy pouted. "I don't want to talk about him."

Ah, now I understood the source of her melancholy. It wasn't Miss Hessing's pending nuptials. It was the rejection from Flossy's current object of desire.

I squeezed her hand. "Perhaps it's for the best. I have it on good authority that he will be returning to India after his studies, and I couldn't bear it if you moved away."

"I suppose," she said on a sigh. "But it would have been nice to reject him, instead of being ignored."

"Take it as a compliment," Floyd said. When we both frowned at him, he added, "His father has arranged a marriage for him back in India, so he can't marry you or any other girl, even if he wanted to. The only women he sees here are his mistresses and he has a lot of them, none of whom are the sort of girl he can be seen with in public. The fact he ignored you means he thinks you're above that and he respects you enough not to want to sully your reputation."

The effect of his words on Flossy was instant. She brightened, and with a toss of her curls, she was once again her usual unencumbered self. She tucked into her strawberries as if she were ravenous.

I mouthed "well done" to Floyd. He merely shrugged, which was as good a sign as any that he spoke the truth and hadn't made up the story about the mistresses simply to cheer up his sister.

"Speaking of mistresses," I said.

Floyd put up his hands. "I haven't got one at the moment, I swear."

"I wasn't referring to you. I'm trying to solve an old murder case that the police shelved after the main suspect went missing. The victim, the family's maid, was his mistress. My investigation uncovered some letters today that I think were written by him to his mother, although he doesn't address her as Mother and the letters are all signed 'Oblitus.' We think it's Latin."

"'We?'" Floyd echoed. "Tell me you haven't teamed up with Armitage again."

"Uncle Ronald doesn't mind," I said as I searched the restaurant for him. Spotting him well out of earshot, I felt comfortable to add, "He knows I work better with Harry. We make an excellent team."

"My father hasn't seen the two of you together. I have. I know there's mutual affection between you."

"The only mutual affection we have is for investigating. We'll never be anything more than friends and colleagues, so stop being overbearing. It makes me dislike you."

"As long as you understand he's not suitable."

It wasn't what I said or meant, but I didn't correct him. "Are you able to translate Oblitus?"

"It means forgotten or the forgotten one. If your suspect fled to escape capture years ago, the nickname fits." He stood and pushed in his chair. "Now, if you'll excuse me, I have a party to attend where some very unsuitable ladies will enjoy my attention."

Flossy made a scoffing noise as she watched him leave. "Why can men have unsuitable liaisons and women can't?"

"That is one of the greatest conundrums of our time."

* * *

WITH MY PARASOL under my arm and a wide-brimmed hat on my head, I was about to leave the hotel the following morning when Mr. Hobart intercepted me. "I received a telephone call from Harry," he said. "He wanted me to tell you that he won't be in his office until later."

That scuttled my plan to discuss my next steps in the investigation with him. Perhaps it was for the best; I was becoming too reliant on him. I needed to work alone sometimes, to remind myself that I was capable.

My uncle stepped out of the lift. He smiled at Mr. Hobart and me as he passed, then, when Mr. Hobart wasn't looking, he jerked his head at the manager, urging me to ask some questions.

I suppose it wouldn't hurt to gently probe. "I heard the position of manager is about to be filled at the Carlton."

"I heard that too," Mr. Hobart said.

"Do you know who's taking the role?"

"The Carlton doesn't confide in me, Miss Fox." He smiled, but it wasn't the most convincing one he'd ever given.

I smiled back. "It looks like a lovely day for a walk. Will you head out later?"

"I have an errand to run at lunchtime, so I'll go out then."

I waited in the hope he'd fill the silence. He did, but not with the information I wanted.

"How are you two getting along?" he asked.

"Well enough. He can be a little gruff at times, but I think I know how to manage him now. It helps to remember that he and my aunt have been good to me."

"I meant you and Harry. You seem to be spending more time together lately."

"He's assisting me with an investigation."

"So my brother told us over dinner last night. He was very impressed with your determination and intelligence. I told him that I wasn't at all surprised, that I knew you were up to the challenges of detective work. Then we all lamented that women weren't allowed to join the police force. The two Mrs. Hobarts were particularly vocal about the unfairness of it."

"At least we can have our own detective agencies."

"Then why don't you start one?"

"My uncle wouldn't allow it. For now, I need to stay on his good side. He provides a roof over my head and food in my stomach. Perhaps one day I'll have saved enough from the investigations I do manage to take on to move out of the hotel, but I think it's quite some time away."

"You could join Harry's agency for now, albeit secretly."

I laughed. "He made it abundantly clear that he won't add the name Fox alongside his and I wouldn't settle for anything less. Anyway, I think keeping our work separate is best."

Fortunately, he didn't ask why. He simply gave me a flat smile. Spotting an important guest arriving, he made his excuses. After a brief greeting, the guest went on his way and Mr. Hobart went on his.

It wasn't until I watched him join Peter that I wondered if he'd deliberately steered our conversation away from the topic of the Carlton Hotel and his lunchtime absences. He was an excellent manager of conflict, so it wouldn't surprise me if he'd manipulated me, too.

Mrs. Short emerged from the senior staff corridor and beckoned me to join her. She asked for a report on the investigation, but I refused to tell her anything.

"My work is confidential," I said. "But I'm sure your sister will update you on my progress if she wants you to know."

Her back stiffened. "Do you think we have time for socializing, Miss Fox? We're both very busy."

"She doesn't work far from here. You could meet for lunch in a teashop."

She gave me a look down her nose that could rival the pomposity of the Dowager Lady Whitchurch. "Long lunches are for those with too much spare time on their hands." She strode off without a backward glance.

In some ways, she was right. The staff rarely took long

lunches, and Mr. Hobart even less so, until lately. His recent absences in the middle of the day were in contrast to his hard-working nature. He'd denied knowing who was taking on the management role at the Carlton, which I took to mean it wasn't him. So, what *was* he doing?

It was none of my business, and unlikely to be any of my uncle's, either. Mr. Hobart was within his rights to take a full hour for lunch and not inform his employer of his move-ments. He, like the rest of the staff, was entitled to a private life.

Just as Mr. Hardy was. I decided that would be my next avenue of enquiry.

I tucked my parasol under my arm and headed for the exit. Mr. Chapman and I crossed paths in the foyer. He glared at me. I smiled back. His glare turned frostier.

The parasol wasn't needed on my walk to the Campbells' townhouse. The day was overcast and cool for July, and Harry wasn't there to tease me. I left it by the door when the maid, Betty, answered my knock and invited me into the basement service area. I hadn't seen her on my visit the previous day, and I was struck by how drawn she looked. Mr. Hardy's death must be taking its toll on all the staff.

"Mrs. Turner is in her office," Betty said, starting to lead the way along the corridor.

"There's something I'd like to ask you before I speak to her," I said.

She stopped at the open doorway to the kitchen. "It's nothing to do with me!"

Her reaction was a little strong, given I'd never suggested that any of the staff were involved in the murder. I'd not had a reason to. I wondered if I'd overlooked something. "Per-haps you could help." I turned to face the kitchen. "Perhaps you all could."

Mrs. Cook came around the central table toward me, wiping her hands on her apron. "We'll help in any way we can. Davey?"

The footman emerged from the adjoining staff parlor, a bowler hat in one hand and a brush in the other. "What do you want to know, Miss Fox?"

"Did Mr. Hardy have any friends?"

C.J. ARCHER

They all looked at each other, then shook their heads or shrugged.

"What did he do on his day off?"

Again, the cook and the maid shrugged. Davey, however, said he'd seen the butler at the local pub a few times. "I saw him twice at the Coach and Horses, the one on Hill Street, not Bruton. Friends of mine said they saw him there, having a quiet drink on his own on his afternoon off."

I thanked him and departed, armed with my parasol and a plan. It was still early, but hopefully the landlord at the Coach and Horses could tell me something about Mr. Hardy's visits. I wasn't entirely sure what I expected to learn, but it was better than the alternative—confronting the Whitchurches without evidence that Rupert was, in fact, Mr. Hardy.

I was minding the steps as I headed up to the pavement when Harry's voice once again greeted me.

"We have to stop meeting like this," he teased. "People will talk."

"Why? There's nothing to talk about."

His face fell. "Has Sir Ronald forbidden you from seeing me again?"

I'd not meant to speak harshly. I must still be smarting from Floyd's accusation that Harry and I were more than friends. "He doesn't know we're investigating together at the moment. Sorry, my mind was elsewhere." I nodded at the Campbells' neighbor's house. "Were you called out again?"

Before he could answer, the Campbells' front door opened and Davey trotted down the front steps. "You still here, Miss Fox? Just a friendly warning that I'm fetching a cab for Sir Ian. You'll want to go before he sees you."

"Thank you. Which way is Hill Street?"

"I know it," Harry said, setting off in the opposite direction to Davey. "What's in Hill Street?"

I told him about the pub and my idea to learn as much as I could about Mr. Hardy's private life. "You don't have to come with me. I can manage on my own if you have work to do."

"There's something I need to tell you. Besides, I'm enjoying your investigation more than mine."

"Murder is a little more interesting than missing cats and

122

false alarms. Speaking of which, why did the neighbor need you this time? Was it another false alarm?"

"That's what I wanted to tell you. It wasn't Mrs. Danvers who wanted to speak to me, it was her housekeeper. She'd seen me talking to you as I left there last time and asked her counterpart in the Campbell household about you."

"How nosy."

He smirked. "That's rich coming from you."

"I'm only nosy when it's relevant to an investigation. So, what do I have to do with her calling you out this time?"

"Mrs. Turner told Mrs. Danvers' housekeeper that they'd hired you to look into Hardy's death. That reminded her of something she'd overheard, and she felt you ought to know."

"Then why not invite me instead of you? Mrs. Turner could have told her that I could be contacted at the hotel."

"They like me. Besides, I think they wanted me to check the locks again."

I suspected they liked having a handsome young man around the house. It would explain all the false alarms, too. "What did the housekeeper say?"

"Two or three weeks ago—she can't recall precisely when —she was hanging washing out in the courtyard and over-heard Hardy threatening another man in the Campbells' courtyard. She recognized Hardy's voice as he did most of the talking. The other barely spoke."

"What was the threat?"

"Hardy demanded the other fellow pay him. If he didn't, it would all come out."

"All of what?"

"He didn't say." Harry indicated to turn right to skirt the northern edge of Berkeley Square with its handsome plane trees providing dappled shade from the sun.

I'd been so engrossed in our conversation that I hadn't noticed when it emerged from behind the clouds. Remem-bering how many times I'd blushed the day before, I put up my parasol and had it at the ready. "It sounds as though Hardy was in possession of information that could damage someone if it came out. We know from the letters to his mother that Rupert needed money."

"Did Floyd translate Oblitus?"

"It means the Forgotten One, which seems appropriate for a banished son."

"So Rupert needed money and Hardy was blackmailing someone for money. It fits with your theory that they're one and the same person." He indicated we should turn onto Hill Street where the Coach and Horses stood on the next corner at the intersection with a mews. "I think Hardy—Rupert—was attempting to blackmail a member of his family. Pleas for financial help to his mother failed, so he tried threats instead."

"Mrs. Danvers' housekeeper said he argued with a man, so it must be Arthur since their father died a few years ago. Considering Arthur had a lot to lose, he has just risen to the top of my suspect list. The question is, what was he blackmailing Arthur about? It can't be over Charlotte's murder. If Arthur did murder her and blamed his brother, and Rupert realized it later once he sobered up, why continue to hide in exile all these years? He could simply tell the police that Arthur did it, then come home."

"Would he be believed?" Harry said. "By all accounts, he was drunk on the night of the murder, so the police might not take his word for it. Not to mention the dowager would probably support Arthur, not Rupert, particularly now. Rupert has been gone for decades, and she might think resurrecting him is pointless when Arthur makes a fine viscount. I think Rupert would have known that the family would prefer for him to stay dead and forgotten."

I wasn't convinced Rupert would want to lie low forever for the good of the family. He'd given up an awful lot when he fled. If he'd been wrongly accused, his resentment must only have deepened over the years. It seemed like an excellent motive to threaten his own brother, and for that brother to retaliate and kill to protect his reputation and the inheritance. Families weren't always loyal, and brothers had been known to fall out spectacularly over much less.

Harry opened the pub door for me. The smile he gave me was dashing, as always, and my heart fluttered a little, knowing it was entirely for my benefit. If I wasn't careful, I would end up kissing him again.

That would not do.

I lowered my parasol, but didn't go in. "Thank you for your assistance, Harry, but I'll be quite all right from here."

"Are you dismissing me?"

"I'm simply telling you that I can manage. I'm sure you have things that require your attention. I wouldn't want to keep you from them."

He leaned back against the doorframe and crossed his arms over his chest. "Discussing cases together helps you solve them faster. Don't you want to solve this one quickly?"

"Yes, of course, but..." I didn't continue. I recognized a winning argument when I heard one.

"I know what this is about." His eyes danced and his lips tilted with his smirk.

I had a feeling I was walking into his trap, but I couldn't stop myself. "Oh? What is it about?"

"You're afraid I might solve the case before you."

Relief turned my scoff into an inelegant snort. "That's about as likely as me kissing you again." There. Hopefully, by mentioning the kiss, I'd dissolved the tension between us. Sometimes confronting one's fears is the best way to alleviate them.

I entered the pub and took a moment to adjust to the dim light. Given it was still early, there were only a few patrons, all of whom looked up when we entered. Their gazes remained on me, not Harry, as we approached the polished dark wood bar and the landlord standing behind it. Going by the patrons' clothing and the waft coming off the fellow seated at the bar, waiting for his beer, I suspected they worked in the stables or coach houses belonging to the grand townhouses. Pubs in salubrious areas like Mayfair tended to attract service staff on their days off, rather than laborers or dock workers.

The landlord passed a tankard of beer to the patron then picked up a cloth to wipe the pump clean. "Ladies' bar is through there." He pointed the cloth toward the snug where a marble fireplace would make it a cozy place for maids in winter. It was currently empty.

"My name is Miss Cleopatra Fox and this is Mr. Armitage. We're private detectives looking into the death of a butler not far from here."

The landlord stopped cleaning the pump. The patron seated at the bar swiveled on his stool to face us, while the other patrons behind us fell silent. Far from being threatening, I got the impression they were intrigued.

"We heard about that," the landlord said. "He used to come in here. The footman from the house comes in, too."

Davey must have mentioned our investigation to someone. Gossip was as rife in a place like this as it was in the drawing rooms of the houses the patrons served in.

"Did Mr. Hardy, the deceased butler, drink alone?" I asked.

"Aye. He was new, didn't know anyone."

"Except for that one time," the patron on the stool beside me said.

"The toff didn't drink with him," the landlord countered. "She asked if the butler *drank* with anyone. He didn't."

"Tell me about the other fellow anyway," I said. "How do you know he was a toff?"

"Same way I know you're one. It's obvious."

I wasn't sure if he was being insulting or not, so I ignored the comment. "When was this?"

"About two days before he died."

"Did you overhear what they talked about?"

"No, but it was clear the conversation was tense. It ended when the toff stormed out."

"What did he look like?"

"Middle-aged, gray beard, reddish moustache."

That fit the description of Arthur, Lord Whitchurch. We may not know for certain whether he was the one arguing with Mr. Hardy in the courtyard of the Campbells' house, but now we could be sure that he'd spoken to him here.

He'd claimed he didn't recognize Mr. Hardy at dinner, but we now had enough evidence to confront him and accuse him of lying.

CHAPTER 10

I wanted to speak to Lord Whitchurch without his domineering mother ordering us out of the house, so we decided to wait for him to leave. After thirty minutes, Harry gave up and went to fetch a boy to deliver a message while I wrote it on a page of my notebook. If his lordship was inside, hopefully it would flush him out.

When Harry returned with a lad in tow, I tore out the page and handed it to him. We watched him head up the steps to the front door and hand the note to the butler.

"What did it say?" Harry asked as the butler closed the door.

"'I know what you did,'" I said. "'Meet me at your club.' I left it unsigned. Arthur's imagination can fill in the name."

"Do you know which club he frequents?"

"No, but we'll soon find out."

"I'd better arrange a cab." Harry paid the lad, then set off to find a hansom.

Just as it pulled up a few minutes later, so did the Whitchurches' private carriage. Lord Whitchurch climbed in and the carriage set off at a brisk pace. I had to scramble into the cab quickly or we'd risk losing our quarry.

We followed the carriage to St. James's Street where it stopped outside White's. Lord Whitchurch alighted and looked around. Spotting us stepping out of the cab, he charged toward us, nostrils flared.

"Did you send me that message?" he demanded. At that moment, he looked like his mother. It was easy to imagine him being angry enough to kill.

Harry moved forward and a little in front of me. "Calm yourself, sir. We just wanted a brief conversation away from your family."

"Why?"

"Because what we have to say is delicate. You may not want to be overheard."

Lord Whitchurch glanced at the doorman standing on the porch of White's, pretending not to notice us. Lord Whitchurch signaled for us to move even further away.

"Go on then," he snapped. "Say your piece." He spoke to Harry.

Harry looked at me.

I cleared my throat. "Sir, you told us that you didn't recognize Mr. Hardy."

"Who?"

"The Campbells' butler. But you did recognize him, didn't you? He was altered since the last time you saw him twenty-two years ago. He was older and he'd grown a beard, but he was still very familiar to you."

Lord Whitchurch stilled.

"He was your brother, Rupert, wasn't he?"

Lord Whitchurch's eyes widened. Then he grunted a laugh. "What a ridiculous accusation."

I couldn't tell if he was lying or not, so I pushed on. "You were seen arguing with him at the Coach and Horses on Hill Street."

"By whom? A few drunks, I imagine. You can't trust drunkards, Miss Fox."

"You also argued with Mr. Hardy in the courtyard of the Campbells' residence."

"I did no such thing." He peered down his nose at me. "If you represent the quality of female detectives, it's no wonder the men get all the better cases."

Harry stepped even closer, forcing Lord Whitchurch's gaze to shift upwards. "Insult her again and I will have to force you to apologize."

Lord Whitchurch swallowed. "This entire conversation is

absurd. Good day."

Drat. If I didn't say something to make him stay, we'd lose the best, and perhaps only, opportunity to question him alone. "You lied about being in your room on the night of Charlotte's murder."

He rounded on me. "I beg your pardon?"

"You lied to the police. You weren't in your room when the murder occurred."

He stretched out his neck and pursed his lips in a show of bravado that I didn't believe. "All right, I confess. I was out of the house for a few hours before midnight, visiting…a friend. I went nowhere near the kitchen when I came home, however, and learned about the murder along with everyone else in the morning."

"Then why lie?"

"To protect my friend's reputation."

"Was it a woman?" Harry asked.

Lord Whitchurch's lips pursed again and I thought he'd refuse to answer. Then he finally gave a single nod. "I suppose it no longer matters since she became my wife. Yes, I was with her that evening until midnight. I snuck into her bedchamber after dark so no one can verify my story. Except her, of course. Ask her if you don't believe me."

"Wives don't make the best witnesses when their husbands are accused of lying," Harry said.

Lord Whitchurch's nostrils flared again, but he didn't challenge Harry. He must know he'd be a fool to do so. "She was engaged to Rupert at the time, but he'd been beastly to her earlier, so I went to comfort her. We were in love. We had been for some time and were working up the courage to tell our parents when the maid died and Rupert disappeared. The point is, I didn't tell the police because I was protecting her from scandal. I *was* in my room at the time of the murder. I didn't lie about that. Satisfied, Miss Fox?"

I answered him with another question. "If you left her at midnight and went straight home, why were you seen by one of the maids leaving your room fully clothed when the body was discovered just before dawn? It implies that you had just come in."

He slapped his hands together behind him. "I simply

didn't change. What of it? More to the point, which maid saw me?"

"I'm not at liberty to say."

He huffed. "Is it Virginia? The one who left service to get married? If so, she's lying, Miss Fox. The maids weren't allowed to wander onto the floor where the family's bedchambers are located during the night because of my brother's lecherous ways. The rule was there to protect them. If Virginia was outside our bedchambers, then she was either disobeying the rules for some nefarious reason of her own, or she lied to you about seeing me."

"Why would she lie?" I asked.

"I don't know," he said hotly. "But I do recall that she disliked the deceased maid. Virginia was a zealot, and her strict beliefs made her hateful toward anyone whose morals didn't live up to her own. She was always complaining to my mother about other members of staff that she considered unprincipled." He glanced again at the doorman on the porch of White's. "That's enough questions. Good day to you both."

He headed up the steps to his club, where the doorman greeted him and opened the door.

With a release of breath, I turned to Harry. "What do you think?"

"I think the doorman isn't a young man."

"That's unkind."

Harry took the steps two at a time and asked the doorman how long he'd worked there.

"Twenty-nine years, sir."

Harry put out his hand. "It's a pleasure to meet you. My name is Harry Armitage and this is Miss Fox. We're detectives."

The doorman looked confused but shook Harry's hand anyway, then placed his own hand in his pocket. I suspected Harry had just passed him some money. "How may I help you, sir?"

"Have there ever been any rumors about the gentleman who just entered, Lord Whitchurch?"

"Rumors, sir?"

"Amongst the staff here. Rumors about him or his brother, and a maid who was murdered in their kitchen."

The doorman's brows shot up. "There are no rumors about the *current* Lord Whitchurch. He's a good man, pleasant to the staff. His brother was…not as well liked. He was rude and abrupt, like his father." The doorman glanced at the closed door, then leaned toward Harry. His voice was so quiet, I hardly heard it. "At first, we all thought *he* done the girl in."

"The late Lord Whitchurch?"

The doorman nodded. "He kept a room here at the club for when he came to London with his wife. Lady Whitchurch stayed at the house, but he loathed her, so he slept here. He brought his mistress here sometimes. Members are allowed to, as long as they're discreet. His lordship's mistress was the murdered maid."

"Charlotte?" I blurted out.

"I didn't know she was their maid until after she died. Nasty business, it was. Caused a real stir here, amongst the staff. Some wanted to tell the police that she was his lordship's mistress, but the manager at the time forbade it. He said her death was nothing to do with Lord Whitchurch. When it came out that the eldest son ran away on the night of the murder, well, it was clear *he* was guilty, not his father, so we all stopped worrying about going to the police."

The shocking revelation sent my mind reeling. Had the late Lord Whitchurch killed Charlotte out of jealousy when he learned his son was also having a liaison with her? Had he taken his jealousy out on Rupert, too, by banishing him? This new information, coupled with Mr. Gannon's statement that his lordship's jacket had blood on it made for compelling evidence.

The revelation threw up other suspects, however. If Rupert discovered his father's liaison with his mistress, *he* could have killed her out of jealously. Lady Whitchurch may have been angered, too. Or perhaps Charlotte had tried to blackmail her ladyship and the dowager refused to pay, preferring to silence her once and for all.

How did this new information tie in with Arthur's lie about where he was that night? Or did he have nothing to do with Charlotte's murder, and was only guilty of Hardy's—Rupert's—after accidentally coming across his brother all these years later? We could be looking for two separate murderers.

Harry's steadying hand on my lower back steered me down the steps. "I think this requires a large bowl of Luigi's pasta before we return to the Whitchurches' house," he said.

I tugged my watch out of my waistcoat pocket. "I can't. I have a picnic to attend in Regent's Park. Perhaps I can think of an excuse…"

"No. Absolutely not. You told Sir Ronald you'd attend every social engagement if he allows you to continue investigating and this is no exception. You don't want to give him a reason to change his mind."

I sighed. He was right, but it didn't make it any easier to pause our investigation now. We were on the cusp of another discovery, I was sure of it. All we needed to do was apply a little pressure on the family and hopefully one of them would crack. It wouldn't be the dowager, of that I was certain. And I wasn't entirely sure if Lady Whitchurch knew the answers we sought. We'd also already just confronted the current Lord Whitchurch, so he was unlikely to give us anything else just yet.

I was beginning to see why Harry had suggested lunch at Luigi's to discuss our next steps before charging off to the Whitchurches' house. His head was generally cooler than mine, and this time was no exception.

* * *

THE PICNIC LASTED A FEW HOURS, as picnics on pleasant afternoons tend to do. We would have been back at the hotel by four, giving me plenty of time to call on Harry to discuss the case, except that Flossy and her friends decided to go to the zoo since we were close by. Not only did they want to see every animal on display, but they wanted to stop for ice creams, too. None of my attempts to gently hurry them along worked. It only made Flossy suspicious.

When I suggested for the third time that it was getting late and we had a dinner party that evening to get ready for, she hooked her arm through mine and gave me one of her sly looks. "So, who is he?"

"Who is who?"

"The gentleman you want to look pretty for tonight. The dinner is hours away, yet you want to go home and get ready now. You never usually spend more than an hour to dress, so I assume he's very special indeed."

"Flossy, there is nothing in my preparations that couldn't be done in one hour. I'm simply concerned that Harmony needs to prepare us both, and I know how long *you* take."

We stopped at an intersection of paths behind her friends while an elephant carrying six children seated on the benches across its back, and another boy on its head, ambled past alongside the keeper.

"You have a point," she murmured. "The dinner doesn't begin until eight, but Harmony does take a long time to do my hair."

"She wants it to be perfect."

"And I do want a bath first."

I didn't have to say another word. She told her friends it was time to go. When I counted heads, I noticed we'd acquired another two somewhere. Flossy offered to drive them all home.

We found our carriage in the parking area with the Mayfair's symbol of an M inside a circle painted on the door. Cobbit sat on the coachman's seat with his arms crossed over his chest and his hat pulled low. A soft snore rose from beneath the hat brim.

Flossy woke him up and gave him instructions to drive each of the girls home before returning to the hotel. There were six of us now, too many to fit comfortably inside the cabin. I decided to sit beside Cobbit. Flossy and the girls made a show of telling me we'd all fit, but I declined.

"I'd rather the fresh air," I told them.

No one pointed out that the air in London was never fresh, and they piled inside the cabin.

I accepted Cobbit's hand and climbed up to his perch. "Did you have a pleasant afternoon?" I asked him as he flicked the reins.

"Pleasant enough, Miss Fox. You?"

"Yes and no." I didn't want to go into the mixed feelings I often felt when I went to the zoo. I was fascinated by all the exotic animals and the distant lands they came from, yet seeing them cooped up so far from home saddened me. "How is the mood in the stables and coach house nowadays?"

"Well enough, although I hear another of those bloody contraptions will be stabled with the horses next week when one of the country toffs comes to stay."

"An automobile?"

"Aye. Smelly, dirty machines."

I didn't point out that horses were smelly, too. Cobbit most likely wouldn't agree, and I didn't want to spend the journey listening to him extol the virtues of the animal while denigrating the machine.

"At least not all the toffs think the same," he went on. "Many still like the traditional ways and don't want to see horses retired along with us old coachmen. Some even sought me out to tell me they support my plight."

"It's good of them to go out of their way to reassure you."

"They came to talk to the horses, not me." His fingers adjusted their grip on the reins and the two horses responded, veering right. It never ceased to amaze me that such strong creatures reacted to such light touches. Carriage driving truly was an art form.

"Do you mean they actually talk to them?" I asked.

"Some. They like to feed 'em, too, and groom 'em. For gen'lemen who grew up on country estates, horses are in their blood, and when they come to the city, they want to connect with that part of themselves again. It's like a longing deep inside, I s'pose."

We picked up the pace as we traveled along Albany Street, and I held on to the brim of my hat to stop it flapping in the breeze. "You are quite the philosopher, Cobbit."

He chuckled. "I get a lot of time to think up here." A swiftly traveling hansom cab cut in front of us. Cobbit shouted at the other driver to be more careful then resumed his philosophizing without missing a beat. "I find that a man who's good with horses is a good man, overall. He treats the staff with respect, even friendship, sometimes. Well, the outdoor staff, that is. No one respects indoor staff much. Too soft, that's their problem. Not the maids, mind. They work harder than anyone, I reckon."

I tuned out his prattling for the rest of the journey. It had just occurred to me that the list of witnesses in my bag didn't include any of the Whitchurches' outdoor staff. For some reason, the police never questioned them after Charlotte's murder. They only spoke to the indoor staff. I'd also forgotten about the grooms and coachman, a fact I wasn't proud of. I knew Rupert liked horses. Mr. Gannon had even told me as much. It was very likely Rupert had spent a great deal of time in the stables on their country estate and got to know the grooms rather well. It was also likely that the coachman and at least one of the grooms had traveled to London with Lord and Lady Whitchurch.

Sir Ian and Lady Campbell had dismissed all their outdoor staff and sold off their equipage as a cost-cutting measure, but the Whitchurches still kept them. Hopefully, they were the same ones that had worked for the family twenty-two years ago and would be willing to talk. With some of the suspects now deceased, they might not be as afraid to come forward as they perhaps were then, and hopefully they would be willing to share any secrets they might have been keeping. A little bribery might help sway them.

I checked the contents of my purse, but wasn't sure if I had enough. I wished I'd asked Harry how much he'd paid the doorman at White's.

One of Flossy's friends lived close to the Whitchurches, so instead of traveling back to the hotel, I alighted with her and told Flossy I wanted to walk the rest of the way.

As with the last time, the staff were a little reluctant to speak to me at first, but after I explained that I simply wanted to ask questions about the Whitchurches' outdoor staff, the housekeeper invited me in. She directed me to the parlor where a maid and a footman sat with their mending, cups of tea close to hand. The kitchen staff didn't join us, but I could see them working.

"How can our grooms help with your investigation into the death of the Campbells' butler?" the housekeeper asked.

"We believe it all hinges on the butler's death being linked to the murder of Charlotte twenty-two years ago, right here in that very kitchen."

The footman and maid stopped their mending to glance toward the kitchen then at each other.

"Mind yourself, Miss Fox," the housekeeper warned. "I won't have you frightening everyone."

"There's nothing to be frightened of, I assure you. You see, Rupert liked horses and was most likely on good terms with the grooms. However, the police never interviewed them at the time of the murder. I'd like to rectify that and ask them some questions."

She glanced over my shoulder at something behind me. "You think one of them helped Master Rupert escape?"

I wanted to tell her the truth, but instead, I assured her they weren't under suspicion. She might not speak openly if she was worried about incriminating them. "They may have seen something, but not know it could be a clue."

Again, she glanced past my shoulder. "I'm afraid I only know where one of them is now." She addressed the footman while pointing at the wall. "Take down that photograph, the one dated 1877."

I'd been so intent on my mission that I'd not taken note of my surroundings. There were several framed photographs on the wall of the parlor, all showing staff lined up in what appeared to be a courtyard. The maids were dressed in their black uniforms with white aprons, while the footmen and butler wore formal attire, and the grooms wore clothes more suited for working in the stables. In the bottom right corner of each picture, someone had written the address of the town-house with a date. The footman handed me the one dated 1877.

"A staff photograph was taken every five years when Lord and Lady Whitchurch came to the city," the house-keeper told me. "This one is the nearest to the date of the maid's murder, just one year prior." She pointed to the man wearing a top hat, a long coat, and knee-high boots. "The coachman died soon after I started working here." Her finger moved to the three young men all dressed in breeches, shirts, waistcoats, and flat caps. "This groom is also dead. Horse kicked him in the head. This one now works at a country manor in Kent as head groom. Young, his name is. I have his address somewhere. I don't know where the last fellow is now. I don't recognize him, so he must have left before I started. Turn it over. The names are written on the back."

I turned the photograph over and scanned the names. I recognized all the indoor staff from the list of witnesses, but one name at the very end made my heart flutter in my chest. It was the same one the housekeeper pointed to.

"Harding," she read. "It sounds like the name of the butler whose death you're investigating, Miss Fox."

It did indeed. Was it a coincidence?

I flipped the photograph back over and inspected the young man standing on the far right, looking directly at the camera without smiling, as the photographer would have instructed. Without knowing what the deceased butler looked like, I couldn't say whether they were one and the same. But others could.

"May I borrow this for a little while?"

"You may."

It was too large to fit into my bag, so I tucked it under my arm. "Thank you. This could be very helpful."

"I'll show you out."

The footman jumped up. "I'll do it."

He walked with me to the front door and even followed me outside to the steps. He closed the door behind him after glancing back inside. "I didn't want to say anything in there, but I have some information that might be relevant. The housekeeper is happy to help you with the Hardy murder, because she doesn't believe it's related to anyone here, but she draws the line when it comes to speaking ill of the Whitchurches."

"But you have no such qualms?"

"I don't know what to believe, but if I can help, then it's my moral duty to do so." He glanced at the closed door. "A week ago, the dowager and Lord Whitchurch argued."

"What about?"

"I don't know, but I did hear him tell her to 'Say something.' He spoke loudly and sounded frustrated. The thing is, I've never heard them argue before. She rules the roost when she comes to London, and he always capitulates to keep the peace. She's a mean old crow. No one likes her, not even her son and daughter-in-law. It's why Lord and Lady Whitchurch live here in London and not with her on the estate."

"Can you be more precise about the day you heard them arguing?"

"It was Saturday afternoon."

Saturday was two days before Mr. Hardy's death. It was also the same day that the landlord of the Coach and Horses had seen Lord Whitchurch talking heatedly to Mr. Hardy.

I walked quickly to the Campbells' house a few streets away. The footman's information about the argument, as well as the photograph under my arm, had given me renewed enthusiasm. I had to be careful not to let my imagination run away with me, however. Even though my instincts were screaming at me, not wanting to be ignored, I reined in my excitement.

Until I spoke to Mrs. Turner. The Campbells' housekeeper pressed a hand to her chest and took a closer look at the photograph. Then she blinked tearily at me. "Good lord. That's him. That's Mr. Hardy. He's younger, of course, and without the beard, but it's definitely him."

I drew in a deep breath, smiled and thanked her. Once again I walked, my steps brisk, my mind focused, albeit not on my destination. I wasn't at all surprised to find myself entering Broadwick Street in Soho, however. It seemed natural to tell Harry about the development in my investigation. He'd want to know that Mr. Hardy had worked as a groom for the Whitchurches at the time of Charlotte's murder, meaning he wasn't Rupert, after all.

My theory was completely shattered. I didn't mind in the least, because instead of guesses and possibilities, I now knew for certain how Hardy was linked to the Whitchurches.

CHAPTER 11

$\mathcal{H}$ arry looked pointedly at the clock upon my arrival at his office. "I thought you'd banished me for good this time and decided to continue the investigation without me." He sounded annoyed and I realized he'd been wondering when I would return. I was only supposed to be gone for lunch, but it was now almost six o'clock.

"I'm surprised you're still here this late. Were you waiting for me?"

"I had work to do." Going by the way he avoided looking at me, I suspected I was right and he was feigning indifference.

"We went to the zoo after the picnic, then I made two stops before coming here. Your presence at those stops wasn't essential. I'm sorry your self-esteem is bruised, but in all honesty, it could do with a little deflating, anyway."

To my surprise, he grinned.

I frowned. "Why are you smiling like that?"

"Because you wouldn't speak to me with such brutal honesty if you didn't feel comfortable enough to do so. I like this change in you."

Somehow, he'd managed to turn my attempts to tease him to his advantage. *He* was supposed to blush, and yet I was the one trying to hide my reddening cheeks by tugging on my hat brim.

"Where did you stop after the zoo?" he asked. He still sounded amused, drat him.

I cleared my throat. "On the journey home, I sat with Cobbit and had an epiphany."

"That sounds profound. Does it have anything to do with that?" He indicated the framed photograph under my arm.

I clasped it between both hands and turned it to show him. "Cobbit helped me realize the police missed interviewing some important witnesses twenty-two years ago."

"Cobbit did?" He frowned as he followed the thread I'd laid until he realized the mistake we'd made. "We didn't consider the coaching staff."

"I returned to the Whitchurches' house to find out if any of them still worked there. None did, but the housekeeper showed me this. It's from 1877 and shows all the staff working in the London residence during one of the visits from Lord and Lady Whitchurch."

He studied it and shrugged. "Am I supposed to recognize one of them?"

"Turn it around and read the names."

He read them aloud, stopping when he reached the end. "Harding? It's similar to Hardy, I grant you, but it's not a very good alias if he's trying to disappear."

"It *is* Hardy. I showed this to Mrs. Turner and she recognized him."

Harry sat back and studied the groom in the photograph. "So Hardy isn't Rupert."

"No. But perhaps he helped Rupert escape the night of Charlotte's murder. By all accounts, Rupert was quite drunk. He may have needed assistance. Who better to help him escape than a groom, someone he knows better than most of the other staff because they've bonded over their love of horses, someone he can trust?"

"Someone with access to a horse and vehicle," Harry added. "The question now is, who killed Hardy twenty-two years later? My money's still on Arthur. He recognized Hardy —Harding—at dinner and realized he probably helped his brother escape years ago because Harding also went missing that night. Arthur confronted him at the pub, but Hardy refused to tell him where to find Rupert, so Arthur killed him."

"Then he'd never find Rupert. And he can't have accidentally killed him in anger because if he was murdered it was with poison."

"There is still the possibility that Hardy's death is just a coincidence and he died of natural causes."

"Hmmm." I didn't like coincidences, but he was right. We had no proof that Hardy was poisoned. "There is a new suspect now. One we hadn't considered, because we thought Hardy and Rupert were one and the same."

"Rupert?"

I nodded. "Perhaps he returned to London after sending that last letter to his mother from America, learned that Hardy was also here and living under an assumed name, and decided to get rid of him because he knew what happened the night Charlotte died. Rupert may have been worried that Hardy would come forward and testify that he'd helped Rupert leave."

Harry wasn't convinced. "It doesn't seem a strong enough motive for murder. Hardy has had years to go to the police but hasn't. There's no reason to suggest he was going to speak up now."

"So you still think Arthur is the most likely suspect in Hardy's murder?"

"Or the dowager."

"The dowager? She's an old lady!"

"She's capable of poisoning someone. In fact, poison is probably the only weapon at her disposal. It doesn't require strength or agility, it simply requires cunning and ruthlessness. You've met her. Do you think she possesses those traits?"

"In spades," I conceded. Indeed, there was something I hadn't told him about the dowager yet, which might prove his theory. "The Whitchurches' footman mentioned an argument he overheard between Arthur and his mother on the same afternoon Arthur was seen arguing with Hardy in the Coach and Horses. The only words the footman caught were Arthur telling her to 'Say something.'"

Harry rubbed his jaw. "Interesting. We should confront them both and see what shakes out."

I strode to the door and removed his jacket from the stand. "Come on then."

"Now?" Harry looked at the clock again as he rose. "Don't you have a dinner party or ball to prepare for?"

"A dinner. There's plenty of time. I don't need hours to get ready."

"When does it start?"

I waved off the question. "Don't worry about my affairs, Harry." I went to open the door, but he pushed his hand against it at my head height, keeping it closed and blocking my exit.

"I will worry about your affairs when they affect me."

"How does it affect you? No one will blame you if I'm late. No one even knows I'm with you."

"It affects me because your uncle might blame your tardiness on the investigation." He lowered his hand to the door handle. The move brought him closer, so that we were mere inches apart. "He'll see the investigation as an interference, and he could forbid you from continuing. Then I won't be able to see you anymore." His voice purred deep in his chest.

I found my gaze dropping there. I wanted to place my hand on his shirt to feel his voice rumble, to slip my fingers between his buttons and touch his warm skin...

Harry drew in a sharp breath and jerked the door open. The spell broke, but it seemed to have rattled him as much as it rattled me. "My apologies. That was..." He shook his head, unable to find the right words.

"Overtly masculine?"

He gave me a cool gaze as he put on his jacket. "You know the risks as well as I do. If you want to investigate and potentially be late for the dinner and anger Sir Ronald, that's up to you."

"Thank you."

"Besides, he can try, but he can't stop me from seeing you."

I stared at him until he flashed me a smile, then I ducked my head and rushed past him to the landing. I suspected he wanted me to ask him how he would defy my uncle and still manage to see me, but I wouldn't fall for that trap. Some things are best left unsaid, particularly between Harry and me.

* * *

THE FOOTMAN who'd told me about the argument between Lord Whitchurch and his mother opened the door for us. His face fell when he saw me. "They won't want to talk to you, miss."

"Please inform his lordship that I have new evidence that the police will be interested in hearing."

He allowed us to wait in the entrance hall while he spoke to his employer. A few minutes later, he returned. "Lord and Lady Whitchurch will receive you in the drawing room. Follow me."

Lady Whitchurch sat on the sofa, her schooled features giving nothing away. The hands clasped tightly in her lap told a different story. She was anxious.

Her husband didn't bother to pretend disinterest, but his focus was on Harry, not me. At first, I thought it was because he still assumed Harry was the detective and I his assistant, but then I noticed the stance. Feet apart, shoulders back, jaw jutted forward. Challenging. He was still smarting from the scolding Harry gave him outside White's.

Then, like now, he was far from the calm man everyone claimed him to be. It seemed we'd brought out the worst in him.

"Thank you for seeing us," I said.

"I hope this won't take long," Lady Whitchurch said in her soft, ethereal voice. "I have to dress for dinner."

Lord Whitchurch rocked back on his heels. "If your evidence is the same as what you presented to me outside White's then you're wasting your time. I told you then, the witness is lying. I didn't meet that butler in a pub. I don't frequent pubs at all, Miss Fox."

Although I expected another denial, I began with that incident anyway. "You were overheard arguing with the dowager on the same day you were seen at the Coach and Horses."

He made some spluttering, blustery noises before finally

denying it again. "This is outrageous." He was about to pull on the cord to summon the butler, but Harry told him there was more.

"You might not want the servants to hear everything Miss Fox has to say."

Lord Whitchurch paused before lowering his hand, clasping both behind him. "I argued with my mother. What of it?"

"You never argue with her," I said. "You always capitulate to her."

"Not always."

Lady Whitchurch looked down at her hands.

"You told your mother to 'say something,'" I went on. "Were you referring to her speaking up about the murder?"

"The butler's death has nothing to do with any of us!"

"I was talking about Charlotte's murder."

He swallowed heavily. "Is that all the new so-called evidence you have, Miss Fox?"

"You both lied when you said you didn't recognize the Campbells' butler at dinner."

The accusation resulted in more noises of protest. "How dare you call us liars!"

I showed him the photograph that I carried under my arm. I pointed to Harding, the groom. "These servants worked here in 1877, a year before Charlotte's murder. This photograph sits on the wall in the staff parlor along with several others taken over the years, right outside in the court-yard here. I showed it to the Campbells' staff, and they recognized Mr. Hardy."

Lady Whitchurch nibbled on her bottom lip as she looked to her husband.

Lord Whitchurch drew in a deep breath. "That doesn't mean *we* recognized him. This fellow is clean-shaven, but the Campbells' butler had a beard."

"Your denials do you no favors," Harry said.

Lord Whitchurch's nostrils flared.

"He's right, Arthur," Lady Whitchurch murmured. "Tell them the truth."

Her husband studied the carpet at his feet for a moment, before meeting my gaze. "Yes, we recognized the butler. We hadn't seen him in years. I was curious as to why he changed his profession from groom to butler so I learned where he liked to drink and found him there. There's nothing more to it than that."

His wife's eyes fluttered closed and her fingers wrung together in her lap.

"It seems you don't want to tell us the entire truth," I said, "so I'll tell you what we suspect happened. The groom you knew as Harding helped your brother escape on the night Charlotte was murdered." I waited for his lordship to interject, but he didn't say a word. I suspected he was conceding that he couldn't win. "Harding also disappeared that night, something which you not only knew, but suspected *why*. When you saw him again after all this time, you worried that he'd tell the police what he knew, so you killed him."

"That's a lie! I never touched the fellow. Why would I? The police already assume Rupert murdered the girl, so it wouldn't matter if Harding went to them now with his story. What does killing him achieve?"

"It stops him from revealing where Rupert is hiding. Or perhaps his story differs from the official version."

Lady Whitchurch blinked at me. "What do you mean?"

"She means that someone *else* killed the maid, not Rupert," Lord Whitchurch said. "Which is absurd." Lady Whitchurch went very still. "I think she's trying to blame me for the murder. Am I right, Miss Fox?"

"*Are* you to blame?"

Lord Whitchurch snorted. "I knew you had nothing."

"You told us you were with your brother's fiancée—"

"Don't call her that," he spat.

Lady Whitchurch pressed her fingers to her trembling lips.

"You claimed you were with her until midnight," I went on. "But one of the maids saw you just before dawn and you were still fully clothed."

"She's lying," he growled.

"I put it to you that it wasn't Rupert who murdered Charlotte. He was too drunk. In fact, he was so drunk that he couldn't remember what happened and believed you when you accused him. That's why he fled and hasn't returned—he thinks he murdered her. But Harding, the groom, knew the truth. Perhaps he noticed the lack of blood on Rupert's clothes when he helped him flee. I don't know, and nor do I know whether it was you or your father who really killed Charlotte, but I am almost certain *you* killed Hardy to keep him quiet."

"Almost certain?" He barked a humorless laugh. "Harding could have gone to the police a long time ago or extorted money from us if he so wished. I had no reason to murder him after all this time, did I?"

"Perhaps he *has* been blackmailing you, but you couldn't find him before you saw him that night at the Campbells'. Perhaps you left him the money in secret and he has been hiding from you because he feared what would happen if you confronted him."

"There are too many guesses in your theory, Miss Fox. The police will laugh you out of Scotland Yard if you take your so-called evidence to them."

Lady Whitchurch suddenly came to life. "Arthur was with me *all* night on the night of Charlotte's murder." Husband and wife looked at one another and something passed between them. Lord Whitchurch gave a slight nod, barely perceptible, and she continued. "He didn't want to tell you because of the scandal, but he didn't leave at midnight like he says. He was with me until a little before dawn. That's why the maid saw him in his clothes."

Both looked at me, triumphant.

I shook my head. "It's noble of you, Lady Whitchurch, but I'm afraid I don't believe you. If he'd been with you all night, why say he left earlier when your version gives him an alibi?"

In fact, it gave them *both* an alibi. Now that was an intriguing notion…

"What did you think of Rupert?" I asked her.

"Me?" She glanced at her husband.

"What does it matter?" he barked. "This is nothing to do with my wife."

"I beg to differ. She just lied, attempting to give herself an alibi for the time of the murder."

Lord Whitchurch tugged on the bellpull to summon the butler. "You've said enough. Leave or I'll telephone the police."

Lady Whitchurch shook her head. "It's all right, Arthur. I want to answer her." She leveled her gaze with mine. "I hated Rupert. He was cruel to me. Oh, he was charming and a great deal of fun to others, particularly when he was drunk, but to me, he was awful. He called me all sorts of names. I was dull, you see, and he wanted to marry a spirited woman, someone to match his liveliness. His parents insisted he wed me, however, and my parents liked the idea, too. But the more time we spent together, the more miserable I became. Arthur noticed." She put out her hand and her husband took it. "He tried to cheer me up while also telling his brother to be kinder. It didn't work. All it did was bring Arthur and me closer. There you have it, Miss Fox. I loathed Rupert. I certainly wasn't jealous of Charlotte. I didn't even know they were having a liaison until after her murder. I had no reason to kill her."

"But you had every reason to blame Rupert."

"Because *he* killed her!"

I looked at Lord Whitchurch.

He glared back, thunderous. "My wife is innocent. We all are. Rupert murdered that poor girl, I know it."

"How?" I asked.

"I just do."

"What did Hardy say to you when you confronted him at the pub?"

"We never—" He cut himself off and pressed his lips together. Then he nodded quickly. "He told me Rupert did it."

I didn't believe him. There was more. There must be. "Who are you covering for, my lord? Why did you pay Hardy to keep quiet?"

The butler opened the door then and Lord Whitchurch instructed him to see us off the premises. There was no point continuing with the questions. He'd only deny it until his last breath. But that didn't mean I was giving up.

His lordship followed us onto the landing. "You have no proof of anything, Miss Fox, and certainly no proof that I paid Harding, or Hardy, money in exchange for his silence."

"Not money, no. But I do have proof you paid him. I'll fetch it and show it to you." I handed the butler the framed photograph. "Please return this to its position downstairs."

Outside, I strode away from the house, the blood coursing through my veins like a torrent. The confrontation had stoked the fire within me, and I was determined to prove I was right. I might have overreached, however.

"We don't have enough evidence," I told Harry, keeping pace alongside me with his long, easy strides. "The tiepin and watch are not definitive proof. We need more. It is a start, though, I suppose."

When Harry didn't respond immediately, I glanced up at him, questioning. I wanted his opinion.

He had an opinion, just not about the investigation. "You can't go to the Campbells now, then return to the Whitchurches. It'll take too long."

"They don't live far apart."

"You have to go home and dress for dinner."

"Not now that we've built this momentum."

"It can wait until tomorrow."

"No."

Harry caught my elbow. "I'm not joking anymore, Cleo. Go home and prepare for the dinner. It's important."

"This case is important."

"It can wait."

I jerked free. "Don't worry about Uncle Ronald. I know how to manage him."

"Do you?"

I stopped and rounded on him. "He went from forbidding me from investigating and seeing you, to allowing me to see you while I investigate, so yes, I think I do." Some of the worry in his eyes faded, but vestiges still smoldered. Seeing it dampened my ire. I couldn't stay angry when his demands were the result of genuine concern. I clasped his arm. "There's no need to worry, Harry. I can manage him. Now come on. We're getting very close to a confession."

He gave in with a sigh.

* * *

THE BASEMENT SERVICE rooms of the Campbells' household were busy, but Mrs. Turner was willing to spare a few minutes since she wasn't required to assist with dinner or setting the dining room table.

"It smells delicious," Harry said as we passed the kitchen.

The young assistant giggled, and the cook thanked him before gently scolding the girl and ordering her to continue stirring the pot on the stove.

We waited in the empty parlor while Mrs. Turner went to fetch the tiepin and watch. From there, we could hear the cook giving her assistant instructions. During a lull, the assistant poked her head through the doorway. She smiled shyly at Harry.

"Hello," he said, smiling back. "What's your name?"

"Birdy."

"That's a pretty name."

She emerged from behind the doorframe, her hands buried in her apron pocket. "I know a secret."

"Birdy!" Mrs. Cook marched over, waving a wooden spoon. "Stop bothering these nice folk and get back to work before the sauce goes lumpy." She clicked her tongue as she watched the girl return to the stove. "Don't mind her. She's simple."

Davey rushed in and stopped short upon seeing us. "You again, Miss Fox? Can't stay away, eh?"

"I'm just collecting something," I said. "You look flushed."

"I'm looking for Betty. She hasn't set the table. Have you seen her?"

Mrs. Turner bustled up, having heard him. "She's not upstairs?"

Davey shook his head.

The housekeeper muttered something under her breath. "I'll go look for her." She handed me the tiepin and watch. "Keep them safe, Miss Fox. I still hope the next of kin will come out of the woodwork. Now." She sighed. "I'll check Betty's room. That girl will be the death of me."

As we headed into the corridor and made our way to the front door while Davey and Mrs. Turner went in the opposite direction, Betty came down the service stairs. She looked exhausted, her youthful vigor erased by dark smudges under red-rimmed eyes.

Mrs. Turner planted her hands on her hips. "And where

have you been? The table needs setting. Go and do it, then come and see me in my office. It's time for a chat about your attitude."

Betty burst into tears.

Harry and I left before we heard Mrs. Turner's reaction.

"I'm glad I never had to enter service," I said as we walked back to the Whitchurches' house. It was high summer, so the sun hadn't yet set, but the shadows were long. It was growing late, and I worried Harry would once again urge me to abandon the mission and return to the hotel.

Fortunately, he seemed to have stopped beating that drum. "You would have been a terrible maid."

"Why do you say that?"

"You don't like being told what to do." It would seem he hadn't stopped beating it, after all.

"I don't mind if there's a valid reason and the person ordering me about isn't worrying over nothing."

"Nothing!" He huffed a humorless laugh and shook his head. Thankfully, he didn't say another word until we reached the Whitchurches' house.

While we didn't quite have to muscle our way inside, the footman was very reluctant to let us in. He called the butler and the butler threatened to telephone the police.

I told him to go right ahead. "They'll be very interested in what we have to say."

The butler's lips thinned before he agreed to show us through to the drawing room.

"We'd rather wait in the dining room," I said.

He baulked. "Why?"

I strode past him and headed up the stairs. "Please inform Lord and Lady Whitchurch that we're waiting for them."

Harry and I were both studying the portrait of the late Lord Whitchurch and the dowager hanging above the fireplace when the current Lord and Lady Whitchurch entered. It was clear that his anger hadn't dissipated in our absence. He opened his mouth and looked like he would blast us for wasting his time, so I cut him off before he could begin.

"Please don't bother asking us what the meaning of this is or telling us we're barking up the wrong tree then ordering us out." I removed the tiepin and watch from my bag. I opened my palm to display them.

Lady Whitchurch looked at the pieces. "I don't understand."

It was Lord Whitchurch's reaction that interested me more. His gaze lifted to the portrait. His wife's followed it. She gasped and clutched her throat.

"Where did you get that?" Lord Whitchurch demanded.

"These were in Mr. Hardy's possession." I turned to look at the portrait of the previous Lord Whitchurch wearing the same tiepin. "It's a distinctive piece. There can be no doubt it belonged to your father."

"*This* is your proof that Hardy was blackmailing me, Miss Fox?"

I arched my brows. "How else did these get into his possession?"

"He stole them." He went to take the tiepin off me, but I closed my hand into a fist and tucked both items back into my bag.

"Unlikely."

He scoffed. "It's time you left. This is over. You have nothing, Miss Fox."

"I have enough to interest Scotland Yard, my lord."

He looked uncertain whether to believe me or not. Or perhaps he was weighing up if he had enough influence to stop the Yard paying renewed attention to the case.

I pressed home my advantage. "Who are you protecting, my lord? Yourself? Your wife?"

"My wife is innocent! She was as much a victim of Rupert as Charlotte was."

Lady Whitchurch pressed a handkerchief to her chin, but it continued to tremble. "Stop it," she whispered.

Her husband didn't hear her and barreled on. "You need to leave, Miss Fox. NOW!"

His wife jumped with fright.

Lord Whitchurch finally took notice of her. "Sit down, my dear." He drew out a dining chair and gently steered her to it. "You've upset my wife, Miss Fox. You need to leave before you make it worse."

"No, Arthur," Lady Whitchurch said. "It's time for this to end. Stop protecting her. She doesn't deserve your loyalty."

"My dear, you don't know what you're saying."

"I do. I know this is her fault. Isn't that what the Campbells' butler told you? I know she's not innocent. She's a mean, horrid woman, and I *hate* her for how she treats us. How she treats *you*."

"That's just her way."

"She still prefers Rupert over you, even after all this time and what he did. You'll never be good enough in her eyes."

He opened his mouth to protest, but a thin voice from the doorway stopped him.

"It is true." The dowager looked feeble standing there, leaning heavily on her walking stick, her stooped back making her look even smaller. But there was nothing feeble in the way she addressed me. It was blunt and bold. "You want to know what happened, Miss Fox? Then I will tell you."

CHAPTER 12

*L*ord Whitchurch left his wife's side to assist his mother into the dining room. The dowager's pace was slow, her steps unsteady as she relied on her walking stick, yet she waved her son away.

"Stop fussing, Arthur. It's tiresome."

Lord Whitchurch self-consciously fidgeted with his cufflinks as he watched her settle on a chair. "I think it's best to say nothing to Miss Fox, Mother."

"Don't tell me what to say in my own house!"

Lady Whitchurch appealed to her husband, but when he remained silent, she dared to speak, albeit softly. "It's Arthur's house."

The dowager turned her icy glare on her daughter-in-law. "You do have a voice, I see. If only you'd found it twenty-two years ago, this would all have turned out differently."

Lady Whitchurch gasped, then lowered her head.

Lord Whitchurch stepped forward. "None of this is her fault."

"Isn't it?" his mother bit off. "If she'd been more interesting, Rupert's head would never have been turned by that foolish girl."

"Charlotte?" I said, more to cut off Lord and Lady's Whitchurch's gasps and protests than any uncertainty on my part.

The dowager's hand rubbed the top of her walking stick.

She wore no gloves. They wouldn't have fit over her swollen knuckles and gnarled fingers. "Rupert had an abundance of energy. As a boy, he wanted to be outside riding, rowing, running...every athletic activity he tried, he excelled at. He was intelligent, too. He graduated from Oxford with first-class honors. He was handsome, and could be charming when he wanted to be. Naturally, girls adored him. He could have his pick." She sighed. "When a gentleman has so many virtues, he has a wider choice and it can be difficult for a young man to be discerning. So we chose a bride for him." Her gaze turned cool again as it shifted to her daughter-in-law.

Lady Whitchurch's head lowered further. She sniffed.

"Their marriage was set to take place in the autumn of '78, but it all began to unravel in the summer. Rupert wasn't interested in his fiancée. You can see how plain she is, Miss Fox."

"Mother," Lord Whitchurch chided as he gently patted his wife's shoulder.

The dowager ignored him. She continued to address Harry and me. "She was always better suited to Arthur. A plain, dull girl for a plain, dull man."

"Mother!" He did not go on. He didn't defend his wife or himself, or their love for one another. He didn't chastise his mother for her cruel words or throw accusations back at her. His half-hearted protest was that of a man who'd been made to feel inferior to his older brother for decades, even after his disappearance. In a way, it may have been better for Arthur if Rupert had stayed and inherited the title. In time, his excesses and arrogance would probably have led to his own ruination. Perhaps then their mother would have appreciated her steady younger son more.

She stamped her walking stick on the floor again, making Lady Whitchurch jump. "You see me as the dragon in this story, but everything I did, I did for the good of this family."

Lord and Lady Whitchurch both looked away, unable to meet the dowager's piercing, accusatory gaze. I suspected they knew what she was about to say next.

I also suspected I knew where they'd learned of her involvement. "Mr. Hardy told you the dowager was responsible for Charlotte's murder, didn't he, my lord?"

"I was *not* responsible," the dowager snapped. "You silly girl. You have it quite wrong."

I continued to press her son. "That's what you and Hardy talked about in the Coach and Horses, and again in the courtyard of the Campbells' house. He accused your mother, and you became cross and angry with him."

"First of all," Lord Whitchurch began, "I did not have an argument with Hardy in the courtyard. But you are correct about most of the rest, except that Mother didn't murder Charlotte."

The dowager gave me a challenging look, daring me to prove her guilty. I didn't rise to the challenge. I didn't have to. Lord Whitchurch seemed keen to talk. All I had to do was prompt him.

"You'd better start at the beginning. When you recognized Hardy at dinner."

"There's not a lot to tell. My wife and I recognized Harding, our former groom, and he recognized us. It was a shock. I knew he'd disappeared the night of Charlotte's murder, of course, and I suspected he had something to do with Rupert's disappearance, but then I forgot all about him until I saw him at dinner. At the end of the evening, I asked Sir Ian about him. He said they'd gotten him from an agency. He was inexpensive on account of his limp, and the Campbells are struggling financially. Hardy's references were all aboveboard. He used to work as a butler at some country manor or other and as a footman before that. Sir Ian didn't know he'd once worked for us. He didn't even know he'd been a groom. His references hadn't gone back that far."

"You told Sir Ian that you suspected Hardy had helped your brother escape," I said.

He nodded. "I wanted to speak to the butler, but privately, not at the house. Servants have ears. Sir Ian suggested I follow Hardy on his afternoon off, so I did. I followed him to the Coach and Horses, where I asked him what happened that night twenty-two years ago. He didn't want to say at first, but after I bribed him, he opened up."

He looked at his mother, a frail yet stoic figure, staring straight ahead as if she were sitting for her portrait. She gave nothing away, but she didn't interrupt his confession either.

Lord Whitchurch seemed to take heart from his mother's silence. He puffed out his chest and spoke in a louder voice. "Harding told me that Rupert did kill Charlotte. It was an accident, but he did it. He had blood all over his clothes and hands. Rupert told Harding later that she'd tried to blackmail him, and he'd grown angry with her. She was carrying his child, you see."

The childless Lady Whitchurch wiped away the tears sliding down her cheeks with her handkerchief.

Lord Whitchurch patted her shoulder. "Rupert offered to support the child, but Charlotte wanted more. She wanted marriage."

"Stupid girl," the dowager spat. "She could have lived well on what we'd pay her. If she hadn't overreached…"

I bit my tongue. I wanted Arthur to keep talking, so urged him with a nod.

"Rupert became angry with her demands," he went on. "Knowing him, he wouldn't have liked being pushed into a corner. They argued. According to Harding, Rupert claimed Charlotte pushed him first. Rupert retaliated by grabbing the first thing at hand, the knife, and stabbed her with it." His gaze slid to his mother. "He always did have an uncontrollable temper. It only came out occasionally, and only when he was drunk. Few saw it, but when he unleashed it, he was like a wild animal."

"He was frightening," Lady Whitchurch whispered.

The dowager huffed. "His temper was only ever unleashed on those who pushed him too far."

I'd had enough of her blaming Charlotte, but Harry spoke before I could. "No matter how much she angered him, Charlotte didn't deserve to be murdered."

"He was drunk. He didn't know what he was doing."

"That's not an excuse, particularly if he knew how violent drink made him. Something you both knew, as well as your husband."

The dowager rubbed her hand over the walking stick and continued to stare ahead.

Lord Whitchurch glanced at the portrait of his parents above the fireplace. "My father was nearby and overheard."

"Why was he in the vicinity of the kitchen?" I asked.

"What does it matter why?" the dowager snapped.

"Perhaps he got hungry during the night," Lord Whitchurch said.

"He was fully clothed," I said. It was speculation, but probably true given Mr. Gannon had seen blood on his jacket. "As if he was meeting someone there. He kept a room at White's, so must have made a special visit back to the house to meet someone. Was it Charlotte?"

Lady Whitchurch blinked at her husband. Her husband stared at his mother. Clearly, neither knew his father was also having an affair with the maid. The dowager knew, however. It was obvious from her lack of a denial.

A curious smile appeared on Lady Whitchurch's face. Her mother-in-law had cruelly told her she wasn't interesting or pretty enough for Rupert and blamed her for his affair. But now she knew the dowager had the same problem with her husband, and with the same mistress, too. I suspected Lady Whitchurch was storing the information away to use another time.

"My lord?" Harry prompted. "Harding told you that your father heard the argument."

"Uh, yes." His lordship cleared his throat. "He tried to save Charlotte, but it was too late. She bled out."

That explained the blood on the inside of his jacket. It had likely happened as Harry and I guessed; his lordship had thrown the jacket over her in an attempt to keep her warm as she bled to death.

"My father decided what was to be done next," Lord Whitchurch said. "He ordered Rupert to leave and never return. He knew how it would look, how the police would discover Charlotte was with child. There'd be a trial. It would be a scandal. But if Rupert couldn't be found, there'd be no trial and it would be easier to sweep Charlotte's death under the carpet, so to speak. My father had contacts in the House of Lords who had contacts in the highest ranks of the Metropolitan Police. Scotland Yard ended their investigation swiftly and made no real attempt to find Rupert."

That explained the incompetence of the lead detective. The outdoor staff weren't questioned, and any mention of the pregnancy, which would have been revealed in the autopsy, was suppressed.

"My father woke up Harding in the stables. He knew Rupert and Harding got along, and that Harding had no family. If he went missing, too, nobody would look for him. My father told Harding what happened and instructed him to take Rupert to Dover and put him on a boat at the earliest opportunity. Harding did, then he disappeared, too. He changed his name to Hardy and found work as a groom, but after getting kicked by a horse, he decided he no longer wanted to work in stables. He was a good mimic and had seen how the footmen spoke and behaved, how they worked. So he became a footman, then eventually a butler, but his limp held him back from working in the best houses. He moved to London a month ago and that's when the Campbells took him on. I didn't know any of this until I spoke to him at the Coach and Horses."

"Where were you on the night of Charlotte's murder?" I asked. "You weren't with your future wife, were you?"

He closed his eyes and shook his head. "I'd rather not say."

Lady Whitchurch covered his hand with her own. "It's all right, dearest. You have no reason to be ashamed." To us, she said, "He realized when he came to me that night that he… required a more thorough understanding of…relationships. He'd heard of a woman with a certain reputation. A widow who took young gentlemen under her wing and…educated them."

"You visited a whore?" the dowager cried. "Honestly, your brother would never have needed to stoop so low."

"She wasn't a whore," Lord Whitchurch growled. "She was a lady."

"Did you pay her?"

His cheeks flamed and he turned away.

His mother gave them both a look of satisfaction, having proved her point.

It lit a fire under her daughter-in-law, albeit a small one. "That's not all Harding told Arthur," she said defiantly. "When Arthur asked him if he knew where Rupert was now, Harding said to ask her." She nodded at the dowager.

"That's the argument your staff overheard," I said. "When you urged your mother to 'say something,' you wanted her to go to the police and confess that you knew the whereabouts of Rupert."

The dowager adjusted her grip on the head of the walking stick. "Just because that man said I knew where Rupert was doesn't mean I did."

"You knew."

She looked at me sharply, then narrowed her gaze. "You say that with conviction, Miss Fox. Why?"

Harry must have been worried I'd admit to finding the letters during the supposed gas leak because he spoke before I could. "You had a good relationship with Rupert. He knew you'd worry, so Miss Fox is merely guessing that he wrote to you."

She stared at Harry then me for several moments before conceding. "He did write. He never returned to English soil, however. He died two months ago in America."

Rupert's last letter had a New York postmark, but it hadn't mentioned he was ill. He'd asked for money. Begged, in fact.

"How do you know he died?" I asked. "Did an acquaintance of his write to you?"

"Nothing like that. His last letter worried me. He needed money. He sounded desperate. I was afraid he was going to return to England and claim what was rightfully his."

"My title," Lord Whitchurch clarified.

"He'd face a murder charge," Harry pointed out.

Lord Whitchurch grunted. "Knowing Rupert, he'd think he could get away with it after all this time. He'd had years to make up a convincing story."

"A story that would lay the blame at my late husband's feet," the dowager said. "It's easy to blame a dead man."

Indeed.

"After I received his letter, I employed the Pinkerton Agency to find him so that I could write and attempt to convince him to remain in hiding. They did find Rupert, but he'd died a few days earlier. A drunken accident, apparently. He fell off a railway platform and was struck by a train."

"Do you have the agency's report?" I asked.

"I threw it away. It was…unpleasant. Final. I've kept Rupert's letters, however, if you'd like to read them." The dowager's gaze drilled into me. "Or is that unnecessary?"

I returned her gaze with a level one of my own. "So Rupert didn't return to London and kill Hardy?"

"No!" Lord Whitchurch snapped. "None of us killed him. What was the point? He'd stayed silent all this time and he promised me he would continue to stay silent."

"Why? Because you paid him with your father's tiepin and watch?"

He huffed out a breath. "First of all, the watch is neither mine nor my father's, nor Rupert's. Ours are engraved with our initials. Secondly, I hadn't seen that tiepin in years before you showed it to me. I can only assume my father was wearing it on the night of Charlotte's murder and he removed it on a whim to pay Harding to help Rupert get away." He looked to his mother.

She nodded. "I didn't notice the tiepin was missing for some time, but when I did, he confessed that he'd given it to Harding. He had to pay the groom something. He assumed Harding would exchange it for a ticket to the continent, but it seems he held on to it. He must have used his own savings instead, or perhaps Rupert had money in his pockets."

Lord Whitchurch squared up to Harry and me. "There you have it. The truth. None of us killed Charlotte or Harding. The police could charge my mother with being complicit in Rupert's disappearance and covering up the truth, but it's doubtful they'd arrest an elderly lady years after the event."

The butler appeared in the doorway and cleared his throat.

"Yes?" Lord Whitchurch snapped.

"Your guests are arriving soon, my lord."

Lord Whitchurch checked the time on his watch. "Darling, we have to dress." He turned to Harry and me. "Can I rely on you not to let anything we just told you leave this room? Or do I need to give you a family heirloom, too?"

Harry scowled at him. "We'll see ourselves out."

"The butler will see you out." He signaled to the butler then turned his attention to his mother, rising from her chair. "I'll take you back to your room."

His wife sighed heavily as she watched her husband assist the dowager to stand, while the dowager scolded him for fussing like a ladies' maid.

Outside, dusk bathed the elegant townhouses in an ethereal glow. A flock of birds flew overheard in the direction of Hyde Park, and a carriage rumbled past. The street was otherwise quiet, serene almost. It was that peaceful time after the men arrived home from working in their city offices and before the evening's social events began. Ladies and gentlemen were inside, dressing for dinner or a party, while the servants worked tirelessly downstairs. From the outside, the world of the upper classes seemed genteel and unencumbered, where polite manners and pleasant compliments were uttered by polite, pleasant people.

Over the course of my six months in London, I'd learned the elegant townhouses hid the same problems suffered by people everywhere, in all walks of life. Behind the facades, people could be as miserable and cruel as the lowest dock worker from Whitechapel. Perhaps more so, because they couldn't show it. They must always pretend.

It was that pretense that played on my mind as I thought through what we'd learned from the Whitchurches. "'It's easy to blame a dead man.'"

"Pardon?" Harry asked.

"That's what the dowager said. 'It's easy to blame a dead man.' Of course, she was referring to Rupert returning to London and blaming his father for Charlotte's murder. But it could very well describe what the dowager and Lord Whitchurch just did. Blame Rupert. If he is dead, then perhaps they just did the same thing to him that he may have done to his father."

"I don't know. Everything they said in there makes sense." Harry set off at a swift pace. "But Rupert was her son. Do you think she'd really lay the blame at his feet if he wasn't guilty?"

I picked up my skirts and rushed to catch up to him. "I think she'd do anything to protect the family's reputation." I started to trot. "Harry, slow down."

"It's late, Cleo."

I checked the time on my watch. "Oh lord!" I started to run. "See you tomorrow," I called over my shoulder.

I turned into a much busier thoroughfare and slammed into a slim youth lounging against the wall around the corner. I would have fallen if he hadn't caught me.

He grasped my arms, steadying me. "Miss? You all right?"

"I'm fine, thank you."

He picked up my bag and handed it to me. I set off again, this time with a little more decorum and less frenzy.

It was so late in the day that Frank and Goliath had finished their shifts, as had Mr. Hobart. Peter was still there, looking very comfortable as he strolled around the foyer, greeting guests with nods and smiles. Harry's shoes were big ones to fill, but Peter was doing a fine job. Soon, the regular guests would stop lamenting how they missed Harry and start treating Peter with the same fondness they'd given his predecessor.

He approached when he saw me, a grim set to his jaw. "They've been looking everywhere for you."

"Who?"

"Sir Ronald, both your cousins, Harmony... She's very cross."

"Is my family cross, too?"

"They will be when they see you're alive and well. Earlier they were simply worried. Miss Bainbridge told her father that you'd decided to walk back to the hotel, but when you failed to arrive...I'm sure you can imagine her panic. Harmony wanted to tell them you were most likely investigating, but Goliath and I thought it best not to until we were sure you wanted them to know."

"I'm sorry to put you through that, Peter. It's been a long, exhausting and frustrating day." The lift door opened, and two guests emerged. I signaled to John to wait for me then offered Peter an apologetic smile. "I'll fill you in tomorrow."

Upstairs, my suite was busier than the foyer. Uncle Ronald, Flossy and Floyd occupied the sitting room, while Harmony was in the bedroom. She emerged upon hearing me arrive, one of my evening gowns in her arms. She glared at me but stayed silent.

My family did not.

"Where have you been?" Floyd demanded.

"Investigating," I said, keeping an eye on my uncle to see his reaction.

His gaze narrowed. "Alone?"

"With Harry."

His gaze narrowed further.

"I was so worried!" Flossy whined.

"Why? I go out alone all the time."

"You were out alone after *dark*—"

"It's not dark."

She looked pointedly at the window. The curtains were still open and the sky had slipped from twilight to night since I'd come inside. Harmony closed the curtains.

Flossy picked up the gown that Harmony had put down on the sofa and gave it to me. "Next time, just tell me if you're going to be late, so I don't worry."

"I don't always—" I bit my tongue and forced a smile. "Of course, Flossy. I'm sorry you were worried." I kissed her cheek and thanked her for helping Harmony choose a dress for me.

The last vestiges of her frostiness thawed. "Thank goodness you've got a little bit of time before we leave. Fortunately, I'm ready and you don't take long. I've just got to put on some jewelry."

She left. Floyd glanced at his father, then followed her, leaving me alone with Uncle Ronald.

He was a man who wore his heart on his sleeve, so I was quite sure he wasn't angry. His face would have been red by now and he would have scolded me, no matter who was present.

Instead, he touched one of the lacy frills trimming the capped sleeve of my ball gown. "Your aunt worries about you when you go out without a chaperone at all hours." I suspected he wasn't referring to just my aunt. "Cleopatra, in future, if you don't plan on going directly home, don't tell your cousin that you are going directly home."

I wasn't aware that I had told Flossy that, but I couldn't recall my exact words to her. My mind had been elsewhere at the time.

"As for you being out until all hours with Armitage—"

"It's not *all* hours, Uncle. And Harry is a gentleman, you know that."

"Not in the strictest sense of the word, and that's the problem. If people see you always in his company, they will talk."

"Let them."

"And he'll get the wrong idea. Is that what you want?"

I sighed. I loathed it when his demands had logic behind them. "Harry knows how I feel about not marrying. As do all of you." It was time to end the discussion before it became tiresome, so I kissed his cheek. "I will be home before dusk from now on."

Harmony was the only person who would have seen my crossed fingers behind my back, and she was a loyal friend. She took the dress from me and headed into the bedroom, a subtle move that would signal it was time I dressed and my uncle should leave.

He grunted. I wasn't sure if that meant he believed me or not. "Did you learn anything?"

"Pardon?"

"You said you were investigating Hobart's absences, with Armitage's assistance. Did you learn where he goes during lunch and why he leaves early?"

The reason he was not angry about my tardiness became clear: he thought I was investigating on his behalf. I did not correct his false assumption. I didn't want to test whether he'd be angry if I admitted I was in the middle of a different investigation. "Mr. Hobart leaves work on time, Uncle. I did learn something about him though, as it happens. I learned that his business is private and has nothing to do with the hotel." What did one more lie matter after I'd told him so many?

"Hmmm," was all he said. "You should dress. There'll be a *suitable* gentleman there tonight and I have it on good authority from your aunt that you'll be seated next to him."

I smiled at him.

Once he was gone, I collapsed onto the sofa with a sigh. "Is it too late to feign illness?"

Harmony emerged from the bedroom, grabbed my hand and hauled me to my feet. "Yes, and it's also too late to do your hair properly. I only have time to add a few pins to tuck in the loose strands. It's a shame the *suitable* gentleman won't see you at your best, but so be it."

I groaned. "That was my uncle's thinly veiled attempt at saying Harry isn't suitable, wasn't it?"

"Not so thinly veiled. A herd of elephants has more subtlety."

I laughed, despite everything. As she helped me dress, I told her what we'd learned that day about the two murders. By the end, my mood had flattened again. Harmony was no help when it came to deciding whether the Whitchurches spoke the truth. If true, their story sewed up all the holes, leaving a watertight case that pointed to their innocence.

So, if the Whitchurches didn't poison Mr. Hardy, who did?

CHAPTER 13

The following morning, Harmony eyed me dubiously as she carried our breakfast tray into my room. "Either you had a very good night after imbibing a little too much wine, or you had a terrible night. It's not always possible to tell which with you."

I followed her into the sitting room and flopped onto a chair. "I slept poorly. I couldn't stop thinking about the case. Both cases, actually—the murders of Charlotte and Mr. Hardy."

"We still don't know if Hardy was murdered." She lifted the lid on the platter and passed me the plate of toast. "You'll feel better after you've eaten something."

"I'll feel better after coffee." I reached for the silver pot and poured the steaming contents into the matching cups.

"You'll *look* better after you've dressed and done your hair." She gave me another dubious glance. "And perhaps a little powder under your eyes to cover the dark circles. Do you want to discuss the thoughts that kept you awake?"

"Inspiration didn't strike, so unfortunately I don't have any new theories. Let's discuss something else instead. I need a distraction."

"A distraction in the form of Harry Armitage?"

"Absolutely not. I mean, he's not distracting. Not in the least. He's simply…a friend."

"Friends don't kiss."

I eyed her over the coffee cup. "I regret telling you about that now."

She chewed her toast thoughtfully. "If he's merely a friend, why did you involve him so much in this investigation? Could it be that you want to see more of him and the investigation is a good excuse?"

"He's helpful. Can we discuss something else?"

"How was the 'suitable gentleman' at dinner last night?"

"A perfect gentleman and eminently suitable. The son of a wealthy heiress and an earl, no less. He stands to inherit a title *and* a fortune."

"What more could a woman want?"

"He was also quite good-looking, didn't get drunk, and didn't speak about himself overmuch, although on three occasions, he did manage to inform me how one day he'd be wealthy and titled."

"You can't blame a fellow for ensuring a lady knows his best traits. So, what was wrong with him?"

"What makes you think something was wrong?"

"There always is with you."

"That's not true!" I plucked a piece of toast from the platter. "But in this instance, you're right. He asked me what plans I have for the future."

Harmony groaned. "You told him you want to be a private detective."

"Lord, no. My uncle would loathe it if I told yet another gentleman about that. No, I simply told him I don't plan on marrying. He spent the rest of dinner speaking to the lady on his other side."

Harmony laughed.

"What about your evening?" I asked. "Did you and Victor discuss *your* plans for the future?"

"He was working the dinner shift, and I was in bed by the time he finished, so I didn't see him. Even if we did make plans, it would only be to discuss the Hessing-Liddicoat wedding. Unfortunately, I don't think I'll be given the opportunity to organize it, unless Mr. Bainbridge is handed the task, but it seems Mr. Chapman has a tight grip on managing the preparations, despite how poorly he handled the engagement dinner."

"The reception will be here and not at the Savoy, after all? What a relief!" Miss Hessing must have spoken to her mother after all. "Mr. Chapman won't give up control easily, it's true, but I'm afraid it will be a disaster unless he starts listening to the bride's mother. The wedding reception needs to please her, not Miss Hessing. She's the one paying for it. She's the one who will be returning to the hotel, year after year. It is noble of him to think that Miss Hessing's wishes matter, but even she says he ought to do as her mother wants."

"She should tell him that."

"I told her to speak to him, but I don't think she will. I think she wants to avoid conflict at all costs." A lifetime of having her opinions disparaged by her mother had made her terrified of speaking up.

Harmony sighed. "Perhaps she'll find some courage."

"Or you could approach my uncle and suggest *you* assist Mr. Chapman. Remind him that you did most of the work for the restaurant's opening, not Floyd, and tell him everything we just discussed about Mr. Chapman's reluctance to follow Mrs. Hessing's directives. I'd go to him on your behalf, but you told me not to." I watched her carefully for signs she secretly wanted me to. There were none.

Her answer didn't encourage me, however. "Sir Ronald barely even knows I exist and won't see me, anyway." She cracked the shell of her boiled egg with the back of a spoon. "Let's change the subject. What are you going to do today now that the investigation has stalled?"

"I'll return Mr. Hardy's belongings to Mrs. Turner for her to pass on to his next of kin, if any are found. They're probably worth quite a bit, particularly the tiepin. The watch is rather plain, although still a handsome piece."

"May I see the tiepin? You made it sound beautiful."

I fetched my bag from the desk and dug through it for the pieces. They weren't there. I tipped the contents out onto the desk. No tiepin or watch. I cursed under my breath.

Harmony came up behind me. "Did you leave them with the Whitchurches?"

"No. I remember returning them to my bag, because Lord Whitchurch wanted to keep the tiepin and I wouldn't give it up. His father gave it to Mr. Hardy as thanks, so it no longer belonged to the family." I closed my eyes and squeezed the bridge of my nose, trying to recall where I could have left the pieces.

But I'd not taken them out since leaving the Whitchurches, nor had I set the bag down anywhere until placing it on the desk upon my return. It wasn't an evening bag to carry to dinner. I'd used a small, beaded purse last night. There were only two explanations. Someone had entered my room while I was at dinner and removed them from my bag, or the youth I'd bumped into on my way home was an excellent pickpocket and had fished them out when he picked my bag up off the pavement. He may have even had an accomplice. I'd not really taken much notice at the time. I'd been distracted by the lateness of the hour. The spare hotel room keys were kept secure when the maids weren't cleaning, and we rarely had a problem with thieving staff, so I was inclined to think the youth was the culprit.

Either way, the pieces were gone.

* * *

Davey answered my knock on the basement service door, but didn't immediately let me in. He glanced over his shoulder, along the corridor. "I'd leave if I were you, Miss Fox. Mrs. Turner's in a right mood today. She was yesterday, too, after you were here. Don't know what happened, but she was suddenly real angry with me."

"Does it have something to do with you leaving them in the lurch?"

"Don't you start. I've had enough of that from the others."

"Sorry, your employment is none of my business. When is your last day?"

"Friday." He stepped aside. "Enter at your own risk."

Mrs. Turner emerged from her office before I reached it. Davey was right to warn me. She crossed her arms under her bosom and looked at me as though she already knew I'd lost Mr. Hardy's valuables. She couldn't possibly know, however. Nor could she be in a bad mood because of me.

"Good morning, Mrs. Turner. May I speak to you in private, please?"

She hesitated before inviting me into her office. She closed the door, but didn't offer me a chair. "I see you didn't receive my message yet. I asked my sister to pass it on."

"I haven't seen Mrs. Short this morning. Is everything all right?"

"We—the other staff and me—don't want you to continue with the investigation."

"Why not?"

"You said yourself there's no evidence Mr. Hardy was murdered. There doesn't seem any point in continuing."

"But you were so sure, Mrs. Turner."

"I no longer am."

She must have heard about my confrontation with the Whitchurches, and learned Mr. Hardy was indeed known to them, as she suspected, but they didn't have enough motive to kill him. "Were the Whitchurches here last night? Did Davey overhear them informing the Campbells of their innocence?"

"They weren't here and I haven't heard anything. I'm sorry for taking up your time for nothing, Miss Fox." She rounded the desk and used one of the keys on the bunch at her hip to unlock a metal box. "I can pay you a little for what you've done so far."

"No, please don't. I can't take any fee when there's been no outcome. Mrs. Turner, I don't understand why this sudden change of heart if you didn't know what I learned from the Whitchurches."

"If they're innocent, then it's clear I made a mistake, isn't it?" She moved past me and opened the door. "Thank you, Miss Fox, but I have work to do."

I was so stunned by her change of heart without giving a reason that I was halfway down the corridor before I remembered the tiepin and watch. "Mrs. Turner, I almost forgot." I strode back to her.

She scowled. "What is it?"

"You haven't asked me for Mr. Hardy's tiepin and watch."

"Oh. Of course." She put out her hand, brows arched expectantly.

"I, er, I'm afraid they've been stolen. I'm so very sorry, Mrs. Turner. I believe it was a pickpocket—"

"There are thieves everywhere in this city. Never mind, it can't be helped. There appears to be no next of kin anyway, so no one will miss them. Good day." She returned to her office and closed the door.

"Good day," I muttered.

I headed back along the corridor. As I passed the kitchen, I hesitated. Birdy had her back to me, and Mrs. Cook merely glanced up at me, nodded a greeting, then returned to her recipe book. Betty sat on a stool in the corner, cradling a cup of tea in both hands. She watched me over the rim with bloodshot eyes. She'd been crying again.

Outside, I began to walk away, but paused at the neighbor's house. This time, Harry didn't trot down the steps as though he was a favorite guest of Mrs. Danvers. Unlike me, he didn't come and go through the basement service entrance. The lady of the house welcomed him with smiles and refreshments, while I was treated abysmally by the Campbells when I'd met them.

Disappointment at not seeing Harry settled like a stone in my stomach.

That would not do.

I turned around and marched up the main steps of the Campbell residence and knocked on the front door. Davey opened it.

"Miss Fox! What are you doing up here?"

"Are Sir Ian and Lady Campbell at home?"

"They are, but are you sure you want me to announce you?"

"Yes. Actually, no. I'll announce myself."

He moved aside to let me pass. "She's in the sitting room at her writing bureau," he whispered. "I'll fetch Sir Ian."

Lady Campbell did not look up from the letter she was writing upon my entry. "Who is it, Davey?"

"Miss Cleopatra Fox, private detective," I said.

She spun around in the chair, her eyes wide. "You have a nerve coming here after the last time."

She wore a plain dress with a small bustle that was at least ten years out of date, and no jewelry to speak of. She wasn't expecting visitors or she would have dressed in her finest clothes. For a morning at home alone, she'd reverted to older outfits. It seemed Lady Campbell couldn't afford to have them altered to newer styles, and it was likely Mrs. Turner and Betty didn't have the skills required for such a complicated task. The Campbells couldn't afford highly skilled maids.

I heard Sir Ian's heavy footsteps coming down the stairs moments before he burst into the sitting room. Davey followed him in and remained by the door, standing quite still so as not to attract attention.

"What is the meaning of this?" Sir Ian demanded. "Davey, send for a constable."

"If you do that you won't know what I have to say," I said. "I think you'll want to answer *my* questions rather than Scotland Yard's."

"The Yard! What the devil?"

Lady Campbell stood and put out a hand to silence her husband. Her icy composure was on full display as she jutted her chin forward. "Is this about the butler's references again? You can't have them. That's his private information and his death doesn't change his need for privacy. When his next of kin are found, you can bring it up with them."

"I don't want to see them," I said. "I know you destroyed them."

Sir Ian's jowls wobbled with indignation, but his wife's reaction interested me more. Lady Campbell's gaze slid to her writing bureau where the other employee files were kept.

"You don't know a thing," Sir Ian spat.

"Protecting your friends is a commendable trait, sir. You shouldn't feel ashamed."

"I don't," he bit off.

Again, his wife put out her hand to silence him. "I'm sure the references are here somewhere, but I have neither the time nor the inclination to look. What does any of this have to do with your investigation into Hardy's death?"

"From natural causes," her husband felt compelled to remind me.

I ignored his comment and answered her question. "Lord Whitchurch told you, Sir Ian, that he recognized Hardy. He used to be known as Harding, a groom at their country estate who'd gone missing while in London, on the night their maid, Charlotte, was murdered."

None of that seemed to be news to either of them, so I assumed Sir Ian had informed his wife about it after Lord Whitchurch approached him.

"Charlotte was murdered by Rupert, who fled London that night. His escape was aided by Harding, but at the time he spoke to you, Lord Whitchurch didn't know that for certain. He hadn't seen Harding or Rupert in twenty-two years, and he wanted answers. Then Mr. Hardy died, and I came here asking to see his references after learning of a connection between Hardy and the Whitchurches. Is that when you decided to destroy his file?"

Sir Ian grunted. "We don't have to answer your questions."

I pushed on. "You believed you were protecting the Whitchurches, yet Mr. Hardy's references never mentioned that he worked there as their groom years ago under a different name. So why bother?"

Sir Ian wagged a finger at me. "Now see here, you are upsetting my wife."

Lady Campbell's jaw hardened. She'd given me an icy glare, but the one that now bored into her husband was positively venomous.

I suddenly realized I'd get more from her than him if I played my cards right. It meant placing pressure on what mattered to her. In this case, her friendship with the Whitchurches—and their money and influence—mattered more than her husband's pride.

"Did you destroy the references with or without the Whitchurches' knowledge?" I asked.

Sir Ian clicked his fingers at Davey. "Escort Miss Fox out."

Davey hesitated.

"Lady Campbell?" I pressed. "You can see how this looks for them."

Sir Ian clicked his fingers again. "Get out, Miss Fox!"

"Stop it," his wife hissed. "You're making it worse."

He fell silent and signaled for Davey to leave. The footman exited and closed the door behind him.

Lady Campbell drew in a deep breath and let it out slowly.

"Destroying the references was a mistake." She said it more to her husband than to me. "It makes them look guilty, when they're not. After Arthur—Lord Whitchurch—told Sir Ian about our butler's connection to the murder of the maid, I had luncheon with Lady Whitchurch. She told me everything. How Rupert killed the maid and his father had it covered up, how the girl was carrying Rupert's child and had tried to blackmail him into marrying her. He wasn't yet married at the time so it was possible, although it was never an option as far as the Whitchurches were concerned." She stretched out her neck and pursed her lips. It was obviously distasteful to her to even discuss it. "The upshot is, Rupert stabbed her in a moment of drunken rampage, not only taking her life and his baby's, but ruining his own life, too. It's horribly tragic. And all because of a pretty face who lifted her skirts for any man with deep pockets. Stupid, *stupid* man," she spat.

"Men," I said. "Charlotte was with the late Lord Whitchurch, too."

Sir Ian reached out to the nearest chair and sat down heavily. Lady Campbell clutched her throat. Perhaps I shouldn't have confided that information to them, but I was in no mood to be discreet anymore. Discretion didn't lead to clues. It seemed this discussion wasn't giving me new clues either. It had been worth trying, but it was time to bow out as gracefully as possible.

Lady Campbell pressed a hand to her narrow waist and drew in another breath. "Once she told me the story, I realized she and her husband were quite innocent in the entire affair, and that destroying Hardy's references after you came here asking for them was unnecessary, as they revealed nothing. When we spoke to you, Miss Fox, we didn't know the story. We thought we were protecting our friends."

Sir Ian got to his feet. "My wife's telling the truth. The Whitchurches have been kind to us. We thought we were repaying that kindness, but as it turns out, we needn't have bothered." He opened the door, taking Davey by surprise.

"One more question." I addressed Lady Campbell. "Do you, or did you, own a silver watch?"

She looked at her husband.

He removed his watch from his waistcoat pocket. Both it

and the chain were gold, the case engraved with a crest. "This is mine. Why?"

"I came across one with Mr. Hardy's belongings. The case was plain, not engraved. It's not yours?"

"You can see that it's not."

I thanked them and left.

"Well?" Davey asked when we reached the front door. "Did you learn anything, Miss Fox?"

I sighed. "Not a thing." I was about to walk out, but stopped. "Davey, do you think Mrs. Turner is right to end my involvement? Or do you still think Mr. Hardy was poisoned?"

He scratched the side of his clean-shaven jaw. "Well, I've never seen a person die before that night, but I would have thought poisoning would show some signs."

"Not hyoscine."

"Then how can you know he was poisoned?"

"Without an autopsy, you can't. But the coroner won't perform an autopsy and look for hyoscine poisoning unless there is a suggestion of foul play. Which there no longer is. The Whitchurches had no reason to murder Mr. Hardy."

He gave me a flat smile. "At least Mrs. Turner can get on and not dwell or mope. I reckon she was half in love with him." A bell rang in the depths of the house, and he sighed. "Goodbye, Miss Fox."

"Goodbye, Davey. Good luck in your new position."

Speaking to the Campbells' servants reminded me that there were other servants who'd helped me understand the link between Mr. Hardy and the Whitchurches. They deserved to know the full story behind Charlotte's murder. I also had nothing else to do that morning, and if I didn't distract myself, I was in danger of wandering to Broadwick Street in Soho.

* * *

I PRETENDED to be interested in the tie display while Mr. Gannon finished serving a customer. Once he was free, he approached and pointed to a lovely blue silk tie.

"This color will look very fetching on him," he said.

"Who?" I asked idly.

175

"Mr. Armitage, of course. He could wear any color, really, and I'd wager he'd look just as dashing in a navvy's neckerchief." He smirked. "Perhaps more so. Shall I wrap the blue one up for you?"

"No, thank you. I wanted to let you know that your information about the former Lord Whitchurch's blood-stained jacket was helpful. We confronted the dowager and she admitted that her late husband tried to save Charlotte by keeping her warm, but it was too late. He then helped Rupert escape with the assistance of one of the grooms."

"One of the grooms? Must have been one of the lads from the country estate. I didn't get to know them. How intriguing. Thank you for coming here and telling me, Miss Fox. I've often thought back to my time there and poor Charlotte's murder. I know I should have spoken up about the bloody jacket, but I also know it wouldn't have gone well for me afterward. What would it have solved, anyway? Lord Whitchurch would see that the evidence was destroyed, then he would have ruined me. Besides, speaking up wouldn't have brought Charlotte back."

As much as it galled me that Mr. Gannon hadn't come forward at the time, he had a valid point. If he'd done the right thing, he'd have been dismissed without a reference, and all for nothing, as it was unlikely old Lord Whitchurch would have faced justice over his part in helping Rupert escape.

"What a family they turned out to be," he said with a shake of his head. "They had the seemingly perfect son in Rupert, but his actions could have destroyed their reputation if not for his father's intervention."

And his mother's continuing intervention over the years, I could have said. I did not tell Mr. Gannon about the dowager's letters from her son. With Rupert dead, it no longer mattered.

"Are you sure I can't tempt you to purchase the tie?" he asked when I made to leave. "They say the way to a man's heart is through his wardrobe."

I laughed. "I'm quite sure that's not the way."

"It is for me," he muttered.

"I have no interest in Mr. Armitage's heart anyway, so no

thank you, although it is a nice tie. I'll return for my uncle's birthday and perhaps you can sell it to me then."

I left the shop and stopped to buy a box of chocolates from a confectioner's before catching an omnibus to Bloomsbury. I found Mrs. Hatch looking the same as she had on my last visit, propped up by pillows in bed in her room at The Female Servants Benevolent Society shelter. She was pleased to see me, particularly when I gave her the chocolates.

"How thoughtful of you, Miss Fox, although you needn't have. Your company is enough for me." She removed the box's lid and wiggled her fingers at the array of choices. She made a selection and popped it in her mouth. Her eyes fluttered closed as she hummed in pleasure. When she opened them again, she offered me one.

I declined and sat on the chair beside the bed. "I came to thank you for your assistance the other day. It was most helpful to learn that Arthur hadn't been in his room on the night of the murder. I was able to use that information to pressure the family into giving me answers, although it turns out that he wasn't involved in Charlotte's murder. His father, however, helped Rupert escape."

"And the dowager? She must have had something to do with it, surely."

"Why do you say that?"

"She's the type, that's all. It wouldn't surprise me if she instructed her husband. She was wily, that one. S'pose we'll never known the truth, especially with his lordship gone. She has no reason to admit it."

"I just thought I'd drop by and let you know that you helped me complete the picture of what occurred that night," I went on. "I appreciate your assistance."

"I would say it was my pleasure, but there's nothing pleasurable about murder, is there?" She shook her head and sighed. "I sometimes wonder where Charlotte would be now if she'd lived, but I always come to the same sad conclusion."

I suspected I'd regret asking, but I did anyway. "And what conclusion is that?"

"She would have given birth to several children by now, all by different fathers, and all adopted out because she couldn't, or wouldn't, take proper care of them." She set aside

177

the box and picked up a framed photograph of a young woman dressed in a maid's outfit standing on some familiar-looking stairs. "Children are a gift, Miss Fox. Mr. Hatch and I only had the one daughter, but Betty is everything I could have wished for in a child."

Betty?

"May I have a closer look?" I asked.

She passed me the photograph, smiling proudly. "You can't tell from that, but she has lovely hair."

I stared at the girl's face, hardly believing the coincidence. Or *was* it a coincidence? I tried to think back to the previous conversation with Mrs. Hatch and couldn't recall mentioning the name of the Campbells to her. "Is this photograph taken at your daughter's first placement?"

"Yes, the Campbells of Mayfair. She has nothing to do with Sir Ian or Lady Campbell, but she likes the other staff and says the housekeeper is kind. She's very content there."

That wasn't the Betty I'd seen. The girl always looked like she'd been crying. "This picture wasn't here when I last called on you."

"I knocked it off the table and the frame broke. I placed the photograph in the drawer until Betty bought another. Isn't she pretty?"

"Yes," I murmured. She was even prettier in person, I could have added but did not. I didn't want Mrs. Hatch to know that her daughter worked in the house where I'd been investigating the death of the butler. I wasn't yet sure why I withheld that information. It might not be important.

I needed to think it through to decide if the connection mattered. Actually, I needed to *talk* it through with someone. And I knew just the person.

CHAPTER 14

I may have been determined not to see Harry today, but circumstances had changed. I couldn't jeopardize the investigation based on my decision to put some distance between us. It would be wrong of me.

That's what I told the voice in my head that sounded remarkably like Harmony.

I stopped at the Roma Café before going up to Harry's office. Luigi signaled for me to wait while he finished serving a trio of women seated at one of the tables. Dressed in housemaids' uniforms, they spoke in rapid Italian until Luigi joined them, at which point they fell silent. The younger one smiled sweetly at him as he set down a cup of coffee in front of her.

When he walked away, the other two women gave the third girl teasing looks that made her blush.

Quite oblivious to the byplay, Luigi returned to his usual position behind the counter where the two elderly men sat on their stools, openly watching me as if I were an exhibit in the zoo. I ignored them. I was used to them staring by now.

"Will it be two coffees, Miss Fox, or would you like a cup of dirty water?" Luigi asked.

"Not tea, just coffees, please. I need something strong to get me through the day."

One of the elderly men withdrew a battered old flask from his inside jacket pocket and offered it to me.

"*Grazie*, but I'll just take the coffees as they come," I said.

179

Luigi reached for the pot warming on the stove behind him and poured coffee into two cups. "How's the detective business coming along?"

"All right, I suppose."

"That's what Harry says." He nodded at the ceiling, to indicate Harry's office, above. "You'd be busier if you joined together. Two heads are better than one, and you could cast your net wider."

"I used to think the same thing, but I'd rather work alone now."

"Why?"

"It's complicated."

He looked past me to the women seated at the table. "It often is."

With my bag hooked over my arm and my parasol tucked under it, I headed upstairs to Harry's office, balancing one cup on the other to free a hand to open the door. The door was jerked open from the other side, however, causing me to lurch forward. Coffee would have spilled over the floor if Harry hadn't smoothly whisked the top cup off.

"That was close," he said, returning his hat to the stand.

"I see you prioritized rescuing the coffee over rescuing me." I nudged the door closed with my foot. "Nice to know what's most important to you."

"Don't be so tart. Coffee *is* important. Besides, you were my second priority, above both the parasol and the bag."

"A true gentleman."

He sat behind the desk and smiled into his cup. After a decent sip, he set it down. "I tried telephoning you this morning, but Uncle Alfred said he'd seen you leave. I thought you might come here, but that was over an hour ago."

"I wanted to return the tiepin and watch to Mrs. Hardy. You weren't required for that. As it turned out, I couldn't give them back. They were stolen."

"When?"

"After you and I parted yesterday. I bumped into a youth around the corner. He must have taken them from my bag."

Harry swore under his breath, then picked up his cup and finished his coffee. "I'll go there now," he said, rising. "If it's his usual haunt, he could be there again today."

"Sit down, Harry. You and I both know he won't return to the same corner."

He sat, but looked decidedly annoyed about staying put.

"Mrs. Turner no longer wants me to investigate," I went on. "She says there's no point."

"I suppose there isn't. The Whitchurches are probably innocent of Hardy's murder."

"She'd made up her mind *before* I told her that."

He arched his brows. "What reason did she give?"

"She said there's no proof it was murder."

"That didn't stop her from hiring you to begin with."

"I spoke to the Campbells, too," I said. "They admitted destroying Hardy's references. They thought they were protecting the Whitchurches."

"Congratulations on getting that much out of them. Very impressive. So…is that all? Are you leaving the investigation there, as Mrs. Turner suggested?"

I tapped my finger on the cup's handle and nibbled on my lower lip.

A crooked smirk cast him in a rather wicked light. "I didn't think so."

"There's no client anymore," I reminded him.

"That hasn't stopped you before."

"There's also no real evidence that a murder has occurred."

"Except your instinct is telling you otherwise. Isn't it?"

I didn't answer that. I wasn't sure whether my instincts were entirely trustworthy. "And there's almost no reason to think he was murdered now that we proved the Whitchurches had no motive."

"First of all, are we sure that's put to bed?"

"What do you mean?"

"That's why I telephoned you this morning. I was thinking after you left last night that we shouldn't believe the dowager's claims that Rupert died in New York. She could have been lying."

I shook my head. "She seemed genuine to me. A lot of what they told us was rather humiliating to admit, so why admit it if it wasn't true?"

"Even so, you should check."

"How? Send a telegram to each of the New York cemeteries and ask if a man named Rupert Whitchurch was buried there in the last two months? And what if he went by an assumed name? It's an impossible task, Harry."

"It'll be difficult, but involving Scotland Yard will speed up the process considerably. I thought you could approach Forrester."

Detective Sergeant Forrester was one of Harry's father's former colleagues at the Yard and had been helpful before. But this was an old case that had been brushed aside by his predecessors after the late Lord Whitchurch pressured them. I wasn't sure he'd get approval.

"He could telegram his counterparts in New York," Harry went on. "The former lead detective is deceased, as is Lord Whitchurch, and the dowager doesn't have the same influence as her husband. I doubt it will be buried this time. And don't you want to know for sure?"

"All right, I'll call at the Yard and speak to him, but I do genuinely believe the dowager when she says her son is dead. So, what's your second point?"

"You tell me, Cleo. You said '*almost* no reason to think he was murdered', which implies you believe there is still a reason to keep investigating."

"It may be nothing…"

"If it was nothing, you wouldn't have come here to discuss it with me." He leaned back in the chair with that wicked, crooked smile again. It was both annoying and devastatingly attractive at the same time. "Unless you made something up so you had an excuse to come here."

"Would you like me to confide in you or not?"

My heated response wiped the smile off his face. He put up his hands. "I'm all ears."

"After speaking to the Campbells, I called on Mr. Gannon and Mrs. Hatch to thank them for their assistance and tell them how their information had helped. Given they both knew Charlotte, I thought they'd want to know. Anyway, Mrs. Hatch had a photograph on her side table that wasn't there during our last visit. It was of her daughter, Betty, the Campbells' maid."

He drummed his fingers on the chair arm, frowning.

"That's quite a coincidence, but it's possible the Campbells employed her because the Whitchurches recommended her as a favor to their former maid, Virginia Hatch, or Fryer, as she was known then."

"Mrs. Hatch hasn't been employed by them in years. Not only that, it's very unlikely they'd recommend someone who has never worked for them, even if she is related to a former member of staff."

"Perhaps Betty was inexpensive. You said yourself the Campbells don't have a lot of money."

It was a valid point, yet it still didn't explain the coincidence. "Why would the Whitchurches recommend her? And why are they making up a basket for Mrs. Hatch once a month?"

"Perhaps Lady Whitchurch is just nice."

"And why is Betty always in tears, or close to tears?" Now that I thought about it, that was odd. The first time, she could have still been in shock over Mr. Hardy's death. But the shock should have worn off. Tears like that implied more. It implied she was deeply saddened. Why would a housemaid be deeply saddened by the death of a butler much older than her, who she had only known for a month? "And don't forget Mrs. Turner's change of heart about me investigating."

Harry nodded slowly, beginning to agree. On their own, each piece of information wasn't suspicious. But lined up one beside the other, they pointed to guilt.

Harry gathered up our cups and rose. "We'll question Betty and Mrs. Turner together. You're not leaving me out this time."

"I wasn't planning to. It's why I came. Besides, a little masculine charm might be required. After all, except for Davey and Sir Ian, it's a household full of women, who think you're rather handsome."

He scowled at me, but didn't offer a quip in response. I'd found commenting on the reactions of women to his good looks and charm was often a way to silence him.

With a coffee cup in each hand, he held the door open for me. "Can you fish my key out of my top pocket?" He indicated his full hands.

Removing the key would bring me closer to him than I

C.J. ARCHER

dared get. There may be layers of clothing between my fingers and his chest, but I knew without a doubt that it would be unwise to comply. I suspected he hoped the nearness would spark something in me, too, going by the way his eyes gleamed with mischief.

I took one of the cups. "Fish it out yourself."

I waited for him downstairs on the pavement and we returned the cups to Luigi. As we set off along Broadwick Street, Harry asked me if I'd made it home in good time the day before. "I assume you didn't get into trouble for being late, or you wouldn't be here now. Or did you sneak out of the hotel without Sir Ronald's knowledge?"

"I arrived home at a decent hour. Nobody minded," I lied. "Do you know, I haven't needed to sneak out in some time. It's rather dull being good."

"Let me know if you want me to liven things up for you."

I only had myself to blame for walking into that trap.

* * *

I WASN'T TERRIBLY surprised when Mrs. Turner refused to let us in to see Betty. I'd suspected she was thwarting my attempts to find answers after she'd canceled the investigation and now, when she told us that Betty was too busy, I was sure. The maid hadn't looked busy the last few times I'd called.

As Mrs. Turner began to close the door on us, I put my hand out to stop it. I hadn't wanted to ask my next question to the housekeeper at the front door, but she left me no choice. "Betty has a lover, doesn't she? At least, she used to."

"Whether she does or doesn't is none of your affair." Mrs. Turner tried to close the door again.

I pushed back on it. "It is our affair if her lover was Mr. Hardy."

Her jaw dropped before snapping shut again. "Don't be absurd!"

I let the matter rest. I'd warned Harry as we walked that she was going to try to block any further investigation into Mr. Hardy's death, so we'd formulated a plan. He now put it into action.

184

"Mrs. Turner, may we speak privately?" he asked. "This is nothing to do with the investigation. It's about the hotel where your sister works. I used to work there, too."

Her features softened at the mention of her sister. She opened the door wider for him to enter, then closed it in my face.

I waited several seconds before I cracked the door open and peered along the service corridor. It was empty. This next phase of the plan was the trickiest. I crept along the corridor until I reached the staff parlor. I peered around the doorway, but the parlor was empty. I continued on, knowing the kitchen would not be empty. Once again, I peered around the doorway. Mrs. Cook had her back to me as she worked at the stove.

Birdy, however, saw me. She smiled and waved.

Bloody hell. One word from her and the cook would turn around and alert Mrs. Turner. I put my finger to my lips and mouthed 'Our secret'.

Birdy's grin widened. She put her finger to her lips, too, and nodded.

I continued on, up the steep, narrow service stairs, all the way to the top level. It was easy to identify the bedchamber belonging to Betty and Birdy. Where the rooms used by Mrs. Turner and Mrs. Cook were somewhat practical in their plainness, the girls had tied ribbons to the bedposts, and had collected feathers, shiny buttons and other pretty objects that took their fancy. My hunch was confirmed when I saw one of the photographs on the dressing table was of Mrs. Hatch and a man who must be her late husband.

My hopes of finding a diary or letters were dashed after a search of the dresser drawers, cupboard, and old suitcases above the cupboard. There were no mementos or photographs of Mr. Hardy, and nothing to indicate Betty had been given the maid's position because of her mother's connection to the Whitchurches.

Harry would be winding up his conversation with Mrs. Turner soon, so I searched the next logical hiding place—under the mattress of the bed the girls shared. Instead of paper, my fingers touched cool glass. I removed the small bottle and opened the stopper.

A vaguely familiar minty scent wafted out. I'd smelled the same odor mere weeks ago when I was investigating the murder of the polo player. I'd not known what it was then, but Harmony had.

I returned the stopper to the bottle and closed my fingers around the glass. It was small enough to fit in my palm.

I hoped to see Betty on the stairs as I headed down, but I met no one. Harry's deep voice could be heard quite clearly from Mrs. Turner's office as he spoke loudly for my sake. He was expounding on the virtues of employment at the hotel, telling her that any of her staff would be welcomed there if they found the Campbells no longer had any need of them. She interrupted him, telling him she already knew that from her sister, but he continued on as if she hadn't spoken, to draw out the conversation. He was doing his best to give me more time, but not even Harry could keep going much longer.

I ought to leave before Mrs. Turner realized what we were up to, but the glass bottle in my hand couldn't be ignored. Or, rather, its contents couldn't.

Betty wasn't in the kitchen, either, but this time, Mrs. Cook saw me. "Everything all right, Miss Fox? Are you looking for Mrs. Turner?" Not only did she not attempt to throw me out, but she was being agreeable. Mrs. Turner must not have told her that I was essentially banned from the investigation, and therefore the house.

I took full advantage of the miscommunication and entered the kitchen. It wasn't the cook I wanted to talk to, it was her assistant.

I smiled at Birdy. She smiled back, completely without guile. I felt a little guilty for asking her not to say anything earlier, and I was wondering how to make it up to her when she started to lightly clap her hands.

"That was a good secret," she said, grinning. "I like secrets."

Yes, she did. She'd told me on one of my visits that she knew a secret, but I'd dismissed her. I'd not taken her seriously, rather like a busy adult brushing off a child who wants to play. It had been rude of me. Even if I'd thought she could tell me nothing, I should have indulged her for the sake of making her smile. If she knew something important, I deserved the delay my carelessness had caused.

"Do you have a secret you'd like to share with me?" I asked her.

Mrs. Cook placed a hand on her hip and glared at her assistant. "Don't you go telling stories now, Birdy."

Birdy shook her head vigorously. "It's not a lie. I do know a secret. I know that Betty had a row with Mr. Hardy before he died." She placed her hands at her throat and made a choking noise. She finished the little act by sticking her tongue out of the corner of her mouth and closing her eyes.

Mrs. Cook nudged her in the arm. "All right, that's enough of that. Have some respect for the dead. Tell Miss Fox about the argument. Where did it happen?"

Birdy pointed to the butler's office next to Mrs. Turner's near the end of the corridor. I'd half expected her to say it was in the courtyard outside. Mrs. Danvers' housekeeper had told Harry she'd overheard Mr. Hardy arguing with a man out there, but perhaps she was mistaken, and it was a woman.

"What did they argue about?" I asked.

Birdy shrugged, then glanced past me to the doorway.

I spun around, preparing an excuse for Mrs. Turner, but it wasn't the housekeeper who stood there, staring at us through swollen eyes rimmed red. It was Betty.

I took her hand lest she run off. "Just the person I wanted to see. Come with me into the parlor."

She allowed me to lead her to the staffroom. I closed the door that led to the kitchen and the second one that led to the corridor. "Will this take long? I have work to do."

"I just have a few questions." I opened my hand to reveal the bottle in my palm.

Tears filled her eyes.

"I found this oil of pennyroyal under your mattress. It's used to abort a pregnancy."

She sat on a chair and burst into tears.

I almost crouched before her, but if she were the killer, it was a vulnerable position to be in. Instead, I remained standing and kept my distance, ignoring my instinct to offer comfort. I passed her a handkerchief instead, then stepped back again.

"You're with child, aren't you?" I asked.

She buried her face in the handkerchief to smother her sobs.

"Given how upset you are, I assume the father is Mr. Hardy, and that you were in love with him."

She stopped sobbing and lowered the handkerchief. "No! Not him."

I wasn't entirely sure if she was lying or not. Her denial was vehement, but that could mean she was violently opposed to the idea of having intimate relations with Mr. Hardy, or it could simply be her eagerness to make me believe her lie.

"You were overheard arguing with him before his death. What did you argue about?"

"He guessed I was with child and blamed me. He said this is what happens to girls with loose morals. He demanded to know who the father was, but I refused to say. He got cross with me and called me all sorts of horrible names. But I didn't kill him, Miss Fox. I didn't!"

I set that line of questioning aside for now. I had others I wanted to ask and I was running out of time. "How did you come to be employed here?"

The abrupt change of subject ended her tears altogether and she blinked at me with damp lashes. "My mother heard about the position and suggested I apply."

"How did your mother hear about it?"

"I don't know."

"Have you met Lady Whitchurch?"

Yet another sudden subject change ended her tears completely. "No." She wiped my handkerchief across her eyes. "She sends a basket of food once a month to my mother in the shelter, but she doesn't deliver it herself."

"Do you know why she sends your mother a basket once a month?"

"She's kind."

"Your mother hasn't worked for the Whitchurches in years. Why would she send her food now?"

"I s'pose because my mother's spirits are low after her accident, and we're very poor. My wages aren't enough and if this baby stays in my belly..." Her face crumpled, but she

188

didn't cry. "If you see my mother, Miss Fox, please don't tell her. She doesn't know. She'd be so angry with me for succumbing to temptation. She thinks fallen girls are sinners, you see. She won't understand."

"That you loved him?"

She looked down at the handkerchief scrunched in her fist.

"If the father isn't Mr. Hardy, who is it? Why doesn't he marry you?"

She lowered her head even further. "I haven't told him yet."

The door to the kitchen suddenly flew open and Mrs. Turner stormed in, wagging a finger at me. "I told you Betty was too busy to talk to you. Off with you, Miss Fox! Or I'll have Davey throw you out."

While I would have liked the opportunity to speak to Davey, I relented. Causing a scene that alerted the Campbells to my presence wouldn't help my cause. Besides, Harry looked at me apologetically over the top of Mrs. Turner's head, and I didn't want him to feel as though he'd failed. It was my fault for taking so long.

Mrs. Turner wagged her finger at him next. "I knew it was strange you informing me about the hotel's staffing policies when my sister could do it."

He attempted a smile, but it was too late. She was furious.

"Get out, the both of you! Go on! And you, Betty, get back to work."

As I passed her, I pressed the bottle into Mrs. Turner's palm. She would treat Betty kindly and advise her rather than blame her. Mrs. Turner frowned, but I didn't stay to see her reaction when she sniffed the contents. I hurried along the corridor, Harry at my heels.

"Well?" he asked me as we walked away from the house. "Was it worth it?"

"It was. I learned that Betty is pregnant and doesn't want to or can't keep the child."

"And Hardy's the father, which is why she's upset and can't keep it? There's no one to support her?"

I frowned as I shook my head. "She says he's not the father, and I think I believe her."

"Then who is it?"

189

"She didn't say, but I think it's Davey. I presume she's hopelessly in love with him, but he's leaving the Campbells' employ to work elsewhere."

"Meaning he isn't in love with her." He sighed. "Poor Betty."

Poor Betty indeed. "She had an argument with Mr. Hardy before his murder. She claims he was scolding her about her condition and demanding to know who the father is. She denied killing him out of anger, but..."

"You don't believe her?"

"It's a very strong motive. She grew up in a religious household with a mother who is vehemently opposed to men and women having relations outside of marriage. Mrs. Hatch condemned Charlotte for it, and might be equally cruel toward her own daughter if she knew. She might desert her at a time when Betty needs her most."

Harry turned to me, his face alight as an idea occurred to him. "What if Hardy threatened to tell Mrs. Hatch? He might think it was the right thing to do, but Betty knew it would destroy her relationship with her mother. Or worse, destroy Mrs. Hatch's love for her. That gives Betty an even stronger motive to silence him."

It did indeed. It would be another strong reason for her to consider getting rid of the baby.

CHAPTER 15

*H*arry returned to his office, leaving me to visit Detective Sergeant Forrester on my own. He claimed he didn't want to step on my toes, since it was my case. I hadn't been sure the detective would meet with me without his former colleague's son present, but Forrester listened intently to the entire story, and even came up with a better suggestion. He agreed the new information about Rupert's escape was relevant, even though the case was an old one, but he would ask for assistance beyond the New York police. Given that the Pinkerton Agency were the ones who reported to the dowager that her son was indeed deceased, he said he'd go to the same source in the hope it would save time. He was a thorough and clever detective. It was no wonder he and D.I. Hobart had become friends, despite the generational age gap.

I returned home, feeling a little restless. Perhaps I'd suggest a picnic, since we had no luncheon engagement. The day was growing warm, however, and I didn't expect Flossy to agree. She loathed the heat.

I smiled at Frank as he opened the door for me. He frowned, which was not unusual for Frank. His warning, however, was. "I'd look out if I were you, Miss Fox."

"Look out for what?" I tried to think of all the things Uncle Ronald could be cross with me about, but gave up. There were quite a few.

Before Frank could respond, Mr. Chapman swooped on me. "A word, Miss Fox."

Frank muttered an apology as he slipped back outside and closed the door.

"Have you been waiting for me?" As I asked it, I glanced behind Mr. Chapman to Peter, hovering not far away. He nodded grimly. "I can see you have something you'd like to get off your chest, so I think it's best if we do this in private."

Mr. Chapman led the way to the staff corridor, but didn't get as far as his office before rounding on me. "What is the meaning of this?" he hissed.

"I'm afraid I don't know what you're talking about."

"You had Sir Ronald give the Hessing-Liddicoat wedding reception to Mr. Bainbridge."

"I did no such thing! If he has asked Floyd to do it—"

"He has."

"Then it was my uncle's decision. No one makes up his mind for him, especially me."

"You have influence over him, more than everyone else except Lady Bainbridge."

"Rubbish."

He pointed a finger at me. "You may not have told him directly to give it to Mr. Bainbridge, but you must have had a hand in it. He never changes his mind once it's made up. There's always a reason."

"Perhaps the reason is that he knew Floyd would do a better job of it. With Harmony's assistance, I assume."

"Ha! I knew this was for her benefit. You wanted Miss Cotton to coordinate the event because she's your friend, so you whispered in your uncle's ear." As if he realized how mad he looked and sounded, he cleared his throat and lowered his voice. "You shouldn't have interfered, Miss Fox."

"I didn't," I ground out. "In fact, I told Miss Hessing to come and speak to you about her wishes for the wedding feast. Her wishes being that you listen to her mother in all things. I tried to *help* you, Mr. Chapman. Why do you continually think I want to thwart you?"

He tugged on his cuffs, his throat moving with his hard swallow. It would seem I'd got through to him.

He might *look* a little sheepish for accusing me, but he

wasn't prepared to apologize. "Well," he said huffily, "it's too late now." Mr. Chapman pushed past me and headed back along the senior staff corridor.

"Too late for what?" I called after him.

He turned left into the restaurant, where the luncheon service would begin in another hour. With the staff setting tables, it was too public to continue our argument in there.

I drew in a deep breath and returned to the foyer. Mr. Hobart and Peter were in conversation with a large group of guests, although Peter's concerned gaze followed me.

Goliath, pushing a luggage trolley, stopped suddenly before we collided. "What did the floor do to you, Miss Fox?" He chuckled.

I frowned. "Pardon?"

He pointed at my parasol. I'd not noticed that I was using it as a walking stick, stabbing the end into the floor tiles with each step. I tucked it under my arm.

"Have you seen my uncle?"

"He has been upstairs all morning."

I thanked him and continued on. I took the staircase to the fourth floor, even though John was on the ground floor, waiting for passengers. I wasn't in the right mood for idle chatter with him as we rode up slowly in the lift.

I was a little out of breath when I arrived, and purposely slowed my steps before I expired. It was quite warm on the fourth floor. Modern luxury hotels kept cool in summer using advanced ventilation systems that sucked in the outside air, which was then cooled by passing it over blocks of ice before sending it into each room, but the Mayfair was an old building that was once a family-owned mansion. It would require an enormous renovation to install such a sophisticated mechanism.

I opened the door to my suite only to pause upon seeing a folded piece of paper on the floor that had obviously been slipped under my door. It was from Uncle Ronald, summoning me to his office immediately upon my return.

It was clear from the stern way he greeted me that he was cross. Just how cross wasn't as easy to determine. He didn't bellow, which was a good sign. If he was boiling with rage, it would be obvious. He wasn't very good at hiding his emotions.

"You wanted to see me, Uncle?"

He indicated I should sit, then, with more force than each move required, slotted his pen into the stand and flipped the inkpot lid closed. "Cleopatra. Your aunt and I are aware that you're not our daughter or ward, and that you came to us after a liberal upbringing that has shaped you into a young woman with...different ideas to ours. As such, my wife has pointed out that I must be patient with you." As if to illustrate how frustrating this was, he stretched his fingers wide before clasping his hands on the desk in front of him. "I have allowed you to indulge your whim to investigate; I haven't forbidden you to see Armitage when investigating, against my better judgement."

I bit my tongue so hard I drew blood.

"I let you roam around the city on your own, even after dark, something which I should remind you is very unwise. London is not Cambridge."

"It was dusk when I returned, not nighttime," I felt compelled to point out.

"But I draw the line at you breaking and entering into the offices of the senior staff, even if it is for an investigation."

So this was what Mr. Chapman meant by being too late. He'd already informed my uncle that I'd searched his office. I didn't think mentioning the office door wasn't locked would change anything, so I kept my mouth closed.

"I thought you were investigating Hobart's disappearances," he went on.

"Mr. Hobart doesn't disappear during work hours."

"He wasn't there the night of Miss Hessing's engagement dinner. He should have been there."

"Uncle, if you are unhappy with his work, tell him."

He suddenly thumped the desk with his fist, making my nerves jump. "I asked you to look into it!"

I pressed a hand to my rapidly beating heart. "And I told you I wouldn't."

He stroked his thumb and forefinger over his moustache three times before he regained some composure. "My apologies for shouting. However, I think I made it clear that your first priority should always be to the hotel."

"Perhaps I didn't explain myself very well, Uncle, so let me do so now. I adore my family, and my home here at the Mayfair. I appreciate everything you and Aunt Lilian have done for me. But my first priority is to myself and that includes my conscience. Mr. Hobart is a friend, and I won't spy on him. Not even for you or the betterment of the hotel."

To my surprise, he said nothing. He studied the papers on his desk as if he were contemplating picking one up and pretending to work.

"May I go now?" I asked.

"No." His gaze lifted to mine. The anger had almost entirely faded, thankfully. The only good thing about his temper was that it was quickly over. "There is still the matter of Chapman's office. He mentioned you were looking for information about someone called Mrs. Campbell."

"Lady Campbell, and her husband, Sir Ian." I breathed a sigh of relief to be heading down a path I could manage better. "I've been investigating the death of their butler. When I saw Lady Campbell take afternoon tea here, I watched her closely. Before she left, Mr. Chapman tried to speak to her and I wanted to know why."

"Then why not ask him?"

"He wouldn't have told me."

"Then ask me."

"Would you have told me?"

"Of course! You're family, Cleopatra, and family have privileges that staff don't. You have access to information about guests. As long as you keep it to yourself and don't tell anyone, including investigation assistants, then I have no issue with telling you something you need to know." He plucked out his pen from the stand. "Next time you have a question about one of our guests or a regular diner, come to me. There's no need to sneak into the staff's offices. Now, should I be worried that a murderess has been taking tea in our sitting room?"

I smiled, more from relief than amusement. "Lady Campbell is most likely innocent. She hasn't got a motive to kill the butler."

"Not unless he was going to tell the world they're in financial difficulty. That's why Chapman wanted to speak to her. She has a line of credit with us so she can take afternoon tea from time to time with her friends. She and Sir Ian pay a sum off each month, but they're three months in arrears. Chapman wanted to speak to her about it that day you saw her here."

"I had surmised they were in some difficulty, but I don't think their butler was about to let anyone know it, if he even knew it himself. Of course, there could be a motive that I've missed," I added with a frown. The thought was troubling. "I know so little about Mr. Hardy's private life. I don't even know if he had a lover, for example."

Uncle Ronald looked at me fondly. "You're clever, Cleopatra. I doubt you've overlooked anything. But it's true that employers don't know everything that goes on in our staff's private lives." He sighed, no doubt thinking about Mr. Hobart and his frequent disappearances.

I needed to steer the conversation away from that topic before he became cross again. "Speaking of Mr. Chapman, he thinks I told you to take the planning of the Hessing-Liddicoat wedding off him and give it to Floyd."

"Ah, well, it was Miss Hessing herself who asked that of me. I can't deny a guest's wishes, especially not one with a mother like hers. Besides, she had an excellent point. The restaurant opening was a triumph and the engagement dinner was a little disappointing. I have no doubt Floyd will make the wedding reception an event to remember."

I leaned forward, expectant, but he didn't mention Harmony's involvement.

"Do you want me to set Chapman straight?" he asked.

"No, it's all right. I think he believed me when I told him I didn't suggest it to you, and I don't want him thinking I ran to you to complain about him. I want him to think I fight my own battles."

"I'm sure he knows, Cleopatra," he said gently. "It's an admirable trait of yours."

He smiled fondly, then suddenly concentrated on his paperwork. He attempted to write something but found the pen nib dry. He flipped open the inkpot lid as I rose to leave.

"Wait. Take this down to Mrs. Short, will you?" He signed his name on the bottom of a note then passed it to me. "It's a directive to free Miss Cotton from her maid's duties until the wedding is over."

I smiled to myself as I flapped it to hasten the ink to dry.

"Then would you mind informing Florence that Miss Cotton may not have time to do her hair for the next few weeks? She's going to be busy helping Floyd, and you know how upset Florence will be to lose her favorite maid. You're better at calming her than me."

I was feeling quite thrilled for Harmony's sake, so I dared make a quip. "You mean I'm better at fighting your battles as well as my own?"

He laughed lightly. "When it comes to my children, yes, you are. Now, off with you. I have work to do and you have an investigation that requires your attention."

If only it did. The problem was, moving forward required putting pressure on Betty to urge her to confess, but I didn't have the heart for it. She had enough burdens already. I didn't want to add another.

* * *

As I EXPECTED, Flossy didn't want to go out for a picnic. She lay sprawled on the sofa in her sitting room with a damp cloth across her forehead and her eyes closed. An electric fan whirred in the corner, but it merely pushed warm air around.

"It's much too hot, Cleo," she whined. "I can't face walking anywhere at the moment."

"It's nicer outside than up here." I crossed to the window and looked down at the groups picnicking beneath shady trees in Green Park. "If we go to Hyde Park, we could dangle our toes in the Serpentine."

"But it's *such* a long walk to Hyde Park and the hotel coaches won't be able to take us at short notice. They're always busy on days like this."

"We could take a cab."

She wrinkled her nose. "No, thank you."

"The walk wouldn't feel so arduous if we removed our corsets—"

"Cleo!" She sat bolt upright, causing the damp cloth to fall onto her lap. "That's too daring, even for you." She reached out a hand to me. "Let's have the kitchen send up ice cream."

I was about to speak into the brass tube that connected her room to the kitchen when there was a knock at the door.

"Floss, let me in," came Floyd's voice.

I opened the door, and he stumbled inside. "You look dreadful, Floyd."

"Good morning to you too, cousin." He attempted to do up a cufflink, but gave up and thrust out his wrist to me.

I did up both cufflinks but drew the line at fixing his shirt. I pointed my finger at the buttons. "You missed one. And you're missing your tie."

"I know that."

"And you need a shave, and your hair is...interesting."

He licked his palm and smoothed it over the hair behind one ear, but it was the side that was already plastered to his head. It was the other that stuck out.

Flossy called to us to join her in the sitting room. "If you're going to have a conversation, then have it here where I can hear you."

"I was just telling Floyd how awful he looks," I said when we joined her.

She wrinkled her nose at her brother. "Why have you come to my suite smelling like a drunken chimney in need of a bath?"

"Interesting imagery, Sis." He flopped onto an armchair and sank into the cushion. "I'm hiding."

"From Father?"

"From Harmony. She's due to return to my suite in a few moments, after I sent her away almost..." He removed his watch from his waistcoat pocket and checked the time. "...thirty minutes ago."

"Why did you send her away?" I asked.

"I'd just woken up and wasn't ready for our meeting."

Flossy glanced between her brother and me, realizing I knew what he meant. She must feel left out. "What meeting? What's going on?"

"Father has asked me to organize the Hessing-Liddicoat wedding, with Harmony's assistance, of course. She wanted to get the ball rolling this morning and make a list of things to do, but I'm not ready. I haven't even had breakfast." He looked around the suite, perhaps hoping to find some left-overs the maid hadn't cleared away.

"I don't know why she bothers involving you at all," Flossy said. "She did the restaurant opening all on her own."

"She did not!" He sniffed. "I had an important role. Perhaps *the* most important role."

"You made a guest list, Floyd," I said with a roll of my eyes.

"If the most important and fashionable people hadn't come, it would have been a disaster, and you know it, Cleo. Don't worry. I gave Harmony the credit she was due, and I will do so again when this wedding turns out to be a bloody marvel." Spotting a jug and cups on a side table, he waved a lazy hand in their direction. "Be a good girl and pour me a glass, will you?"

I wasn't sure whether he was asking Flossy or me, but since we were both seated as far from the jug as he was, neither of us was going to indulge him. Flossy ignored him and I told him to fetch it himself.

He merely sighed.

Flossy lay down, then suddenly sat up again. "Does this mean Harmony won't be able to do my hair anymore?"

A knock on the door postponed that drama. Since neither of my cousins rose, I answered it. Harmony stood there in a skirt, blouse and waistcoat ensemble that suited her better than the maid's dress.

"You look smart," I said.

She flattened her hand over her stomach. "Thank you. Is Mr. Bainbridge here? He isn't in his room, and we're supposed to have a meeting."

"He's here," I said, loudly so that Floyd could also hear. "He's avoiding you."

"I am not!" he called back. When Harmony and I joined them, he said it again. "I couldn't do up my cufflinks and I didn't want to meet you looking like a wastrel who'd just got out of bed."

Harmony took in his missing tie and messy hair. Although she didn't say a word, Floyd looked like a boy who'd been scolded by his teacher. He cleared his throat and attempted to flatten his hair again. It didn't make a difference.

"Harmony," Flossy began, "last time you helped Floyd, you managed to find time to do my hair of an evening. Will you be able to do that again?"

"I'm sure I can, Miss Bainbridge."

"And Cleo's."

"Of course."

"Harmony is going to be very busy," I told her. "We can't expect her to be at our beck and call."

"It's only our hair, Cleo. We'll have the other maids fix our outfits for us if needed. Thank you, Harmony. You're wonderful. And you're going to do an excellent job with the wedding, I just know it. I can't wait to see what the ballroom will look like."

"Thank you, Miss Bainbridge."

"Yes," Floyd added, "thank you, Floss. I think *we're* going to do a marvelous job of it."

Flossy snorted. "Stop pretending you'll have anything to do with it, Floyd. Everyone knows Harmony will be the driving force of the entire thing. All you'll need to do is be present in the meetings with Mrs. Hessing. She's such a snob that she'll insist on having a Bainbridge in charge so she can boast about it to her friends. I'm sure that's the only reason Father is including you at all."

Floyd was so taken aback by her insult that he was rendered quite speechless.

Harmony quickly spoke before he could recover and begin a duel with Flossy where insults were the weapon of choice. "I've set up a lunchtime meeting with Mrs. Hessing in the small sitting room at two, which will give you and I enough time to discuss our thoughts beforehand. Shall we return to your suite to work, sir?"

Floyd removed his watch again and flipped the cover open. "Excellent plan. I'll have tea sent up. I'm parched." He rose to leave, but the gold of his watch flashed in the sunlight coming through the window, catching my eye.

"May I see your watch?" I asked, taking the device before he could pocket it.

The gold chain was short, so I had to step closer to take a

proper look. The watch's case was engraved with an elaborate swirl that included his initials. Inside the cover, the watch-maker had engraved Floyd's date of birth.

"If you're going to steal it, you should wait until I'm not wearing it," Floyd said, sounding amused.

"Is it a clue?" Harmony asked.

"A clue for what?" Flossy said.

I briefly told her about Mr. Hardy, including the tiepin and watch I'd found hidden in his shoe. I mentioned that the tiepin was a gift, but I wasn't sure about the watch, and I'd wondered if he'd stolen it. "If he had, shouldn't it have an engraving like yours, Floyd? The initials of the man it once belonged to, or of the person who gave it to him. But it was quite plain."

"Did it have a silversmith's mark?" Floyd asked. "Or a watchmaker's?"

"I didn't look that closely, and I can't check now. It and the tiepin were stolen from me."

"That's a suspicious coincidence," Harmony said.

I frowned but didn't have the opportunity to explore that line of thought further as Floyd made another valid point.

"Good quality silver watches aren't common. You could go to the best watchmakers and describe it to them, and they might remember who they sold it to. It would be time consuming, but if you're at a loss and you think it's impor-tant, it might be worth it."

I had a better idea. "There was a box of receipts in Mr. Hardy's office. If he did purchase it, the watchmaker's receipt might be among them. If not, then I'll assume he stole it and send some friends out to as many watchmakers as possible in the city to make inquiries."

"What friends?" he asked.

I tucked the watch back into his waistcoat pocket, then stood on my toes to kiss his cheek. "Well done, Floyd."

He gave his sister a smug smile. "See, I am good for something."

"Yes, dearest brother. You're good for ordering ice cream for me from the kitchen before you leave."

* * *

Mrs. Turner's change of heart bothered me. Her sudden opposition to me continuing with the investigation was quite aggressive. Perhaps her reasons were financial, and she realized she couldn't afford to pay me, and when I'd continued to investigate, she'd become annoyed with me. It was understandable. I had been persistent.

But I suspected her reasons weren't financial, that something else lay at the root. I wasn't yet sure what.

For now, the reason didn't matter. The fact remained that none of the Campbells' staff would allow me to enter the house, let alone Mr. Hardy's office. Harry was known to them all now, too, and would be in the same boat. His charms wouldn't be of any use. Even so, I went to his office to ask his advice.

He wasn't there.

I headed to the Campbells' residence on my own. By the time I arrived, I'd decided the only way I could get in unobserved was through the back door, accessed via the rear courtyard. There were no outdoor staff, and of the few staff they did have, only two had a good reason to be in the courtyard. Davey, to carry deliveries in, and Betty, to hang up washing. The back door was also closer to Mr. Hardy's office. Indeed, I wouldn't need to pass any other rooms to get to it.

I entered the courtyard off the mews and crept to the rear door of the house. Finding it unlocked, I slipped inside and tiptoed down the stairs to the basement. The house was quiet except for Birdy humming tunelessly in the kitchen.

I tried the handle of Mr. Hardy's office door, but as I expected, it was locked. I removed my lock-picking tools and got to work as quickly as I could. Fortunately, it was a simple mechanism. Moments later, I entered the office and closed the door softly behind me.

The box of receipts was in the same place, in one of the desk drawers. I rifled through the bills of sale from vintners, tailors, and haberdashers, all of whom Mr. Hardy would have engaged on behalf of the Campbells. If the watch was purchased for Mr. Hardy, not Sir Ian, there was a possibility the receipt would be in his own room. I'd not seen it there when I'd gone through his belongings on the day Mrs. Turner engaged my services, but as the pile in the box grew smaller, my hope of finding it in his office faded.

Just as I was about to give up, I found it near the bottom. According to the handwritten receipt, Mason and Sons had sold a watch matching the description of the one I'd found in Mr. Hardy's shoe three weeks before he died for the sum of twenty pounds. It wasn't an enormous amount, but it would have been out of reach on a butler's wages, especially one who was supposedly inexpensive to employ due to his limp. Mr. Hardy's name appeared on the receipt, written in the same hand as the watch's description. The watchmaker had definitely sold it to him, then. Mr. Hardy hadn't stolen it, nor had he received it as a gift.

So where had he gotten the money to buy it? Was he blackmailing the Whitchurches, after all? Or someone else? Or had he inherited money?

Even more curious, why store it in his shoe and not the lockbox?

The more I considered those questions, the more I realized I didn't know enough about Mr. Hardy. Did he have anyone in his life who may have left him an inheritance? A former employer, perhaps, or a friend? There were no personal letters or photographs in his bedchamber or office, and the other staff hadn't known of anyone.

I returned the box to the drawer and rounded the desk. As I reached for the door handle, it began to turn. Someone was entering from the other side.

I was trapped.

CHAPTER 16

*S*eeing Betty enter the butler's office was an enormous relief. The panic that had tightened my chest began to ease. Poor Betty, however, emitted a small cry upon finding me in a room she thought was empty.

"I'm sorry I frightened you," I said as I slipped behind her and closed the door. "I was looking for a clue."

She glanced over her shoulder at the closed door. "Does Mrs. Turner know you're in here?"

"No. She doesn't want me to investigate anymore, but I want to take this through to the end now. Mr. Hardy deserves it. Don't you agree?"

She didn't respond, which was perhaps understandable, given that he'd spoken cruelly to her. "I have to count Sir Ian's port before I take Mrs. Turner her tea." She held up a key and indicated the sideboard where Mr. Hardy locked the most expensive bottles for safekeeping.

I stepped aside to allow her to pass. She knelt on the floor and unlocked the sideboard. "It's Davey, isn't it? He's the father of your unborn child."

She sat back on her haunches, but kept her back to me.

"Betty," I said gently. "I'm not here to make your life more difficult. I merely want answers."

"I don't understand what my predicament has to do with Mr. Hardy's death," she said, her voice trembling.

"I don't know if it does have anything to do with it. But

knowing how he treated you gives me a better understanding of the man. Do you know if he had any family?"

She shrugged.

"Friends? Anyone from his past that he spoke to you about?"

"He didn't speak to me about anything like that. I was beneath him. The only time he talked to me was to give me orders and to tell me I had loose morals."

"When he learned about the baby?"

Her shoulders slumped forward, and she burst into tears again, but she did manage a nod.

I laid a hand on her shoulder, but the gesture felt woefully inadequate. She needed more than my sympathy. She needed money and support. But if she was guilty of murder, nothing could help her.

"Betty, did *you* kill Mr. Hardy?"

She spun around. "No!"

I grasped her shoulders and leveled my gaze with hers. "Is Davey the father of your baby?"

The door suddenly opened and Davey stood in the doorway. He must have heard us. Had he been listening at the door or had he merely wandered past when Betty blurted out her denial?

He took in the both of us and the open sideboard. He put out his hand to Betty and gave her a gentle smile. She stared back at him, her eyes huge. Something passed between them. Something I'd not noticed before.

"It's mine," he said as he assisted her to stand. "And I'm going to take care of everything. You all right, Betty?"

"Yes," she murmured.

He handed her his handkerchief. "Dry your eyes."

She took it gratefully and wiped the tears away.

Davey turned to me. Where he'd always been boyishly jovial, he was now quite serious, and mature. "Hardy knew about us and the baby. He confronted me."

"In the courtyard," I said.

He nodded. "But I didn't kill him. After we had words and both calmed down, we had a good conversation. That's when I decided to make an honest woman of Betty." He clasped his hands over both of hers as she clutched the handkerchief. "This was some days before he died. I never killed him, Miss Fox. I never went near this office that day."

Outside, a clock chimed. Betty gasped. "I have to fetch Mrs. Turner's tea."

"I'll lock up," Davey said. "You go."

She pressed the sideboard key into his palm and raced out of the office.

"We're sorry we didn't tell you earlier, Miss Fox," he said as he locked the sideboard. "It's a sensitive topic, you understand, and to be honest, we're both in a bit of shock about it."

"I imagine you are." I followed him out of the office into the corridor. "Thank you for telling me."

A bell rang and he sighed. "I have to go." He headed up the stairs and out of sight.

I decided to leave via the front door, not the back away, so walked along the corridor. I'd be seen, but I no longer cared. I'd found what I was looking for, so if Mrs. Turner had me thrown out, it wouldn't matter. I even waved to Birdy as I passed the kitchen.

I reached the top of the external basement stairs and saw the now-familiar sight of Harry outside the neighbor's house. He wasn't leaving this time, however. He'd just arrived. We were so comfortable in each other's presence that we no longer bothered with greetings and pleasantries.

He launched into his questions. "Aren't you banned?"

"I snuck in the back way."

"Why did you need to look inside?"

I told him Floyd's theory about the watch and my success at finding the receipt. "Hardy didn't steal it," I finished. "He purchased it."

"On his wages?"

"Precisely. And what's more, I learned that Davey is the father of Betty's baby."

He didn't look surprised. "I've been called out to Mrs. Danvers' place again. It's probably another false alarm, but I assured her I'd give the entire house a thorough search for signs of an intruder."

"May I join you?"

"I don't see why not." He led the way up the steps and knocked on the door.

The housekeeper greeted Harry with a smile, which widened when he introduced me. "So you're Miss Fox! You're just how I pictured you."

I arched my brows at Harry. "He mentioned me?"

"Oh, yes. Often."

"Not that often," he countered. "And only in relation to your own investigation next door."

The housekeeper, who Harry had introduced as Mrs. Lund, winked at me, then ushered us inside. "Go through to the sitting room and I'll join you in a moment. I've just made a fresh batch of those biscuits you like."

"I can see why you come here a lot," I said as we parted ways with the housekeeper.

Mrs. Danvers did not rise when Harry and I entered the sitting room, but her features lifted upon seeing him. She sat by the fireplace, her delicate frame swaddled in mourning-black crape. A large white tulle cap covered much of her gray hair, and she clutched a black silk fan in one hand. The unrelenting black of her dress made her sunken features look even paler. She reminded me of the Dowager Lady Whitchurch, except Mrs. Danvers had the wrinkles of a woman who'd smiled through much of her life, where the dowager's wrinkles had settled into a pattern formed by decades of frowns and scowls.

Harry kissed her cheek and introduced us, speaking loudly into her ear. An ear trumpet was within her reach on the table beside her chair, but she left it there. The sitting room was neat and tidy, with a faint smell of polish. The furniture, however, was quite out of date. The simple, solid lines were popular sixty years ago, whereas nowadays ornate decorative elements were added to everything. The room probably hadn't been updated since Mrs. Danvers moved in as a newlywed.

To my amusement and Harry's embarrassment, she repeated what Mrs. Lund said. "So you're the famous Miss Fox! You're as pretty as I imagined. Sit, sit. Mrs. Lund will bring biscuits and tea." Once we were settled, she wanted to know all about me.

I spoke loudly, but even so, she had to lean forward to hear.

When Mrs. Lund bustled in carrying a tray, she scolded her employer. "Use the trumpet. That's what it's for."

Mrs. Danvers cupped her ear. "What did you say?"

Mrs. Lund set down the tray and picked up the ear trumpet, giving Mrs. Danvers a good-natured scold for being too proud to use it. I was surprised to hear her call her employer by her first name.

Mrs. Danvers placed the trumpet in her ear only to put it down again when her housekeeper passed her tea and a biscuit. "These are Mr. Armitage's favorite," she said to me. "Nel always makes them for him, don't you, Nel?"

The women exchanged sweet smiles. The age difference between them must be at least fifteen years. They were dissimilar in other ways, too. Mrs. Danvers was frail, whereas Mrs. Lund was stout. She assisted Mrs. Danvers to sit up straighter, then fluffed the cushion at her back. She then settled a tray across Mrs. Danvers' lap to give the elderly woman something to balance her cup and saucer on.

"There, now," she said before taking a seat herself, cup of tea in hand. "We'll all enjoy a nice chat before we show you the Cure-All tonic, Mr. Armitage."

Harry and I glanced at one another, but we didn't rush the conversation. The women asked me questions about living at the hotel and my family, before Mrs. Lund suggested she show us why they asked Harry to come.

Leaving Mrs. Danvers in her chair, Mrs. Lund led us upstairs to the master bedchamber. Like the sitting room, the furniture was simple in design, without the modern opulence of the hotel suites. A portrait of a young gentleman hung on the wall opposite the bed. On the bedside table, a photograph of Mrs. Lund and Mrs. Danvers taken in a studio took pride of place.

Mrs. Lund opened the cupboard door and pointed to a brown bottle on the top shelf, out of her reach. "Be a dear and bring that down," she said to Harry. "You'll save me getting the stool."

Harry plucked it off the shelf and went to hand it to her, but she shook her head. He removed the stopper and sniffed the contents then passed it to me. The bottle label read DR. GOODBODY'S CURE-ALL. The next line claimed it could cure headaches, stomach complaints, and nervous disorders in less than twenty minutes.

"It smells all right to me," I said.

"The contents are fine, as far as I can tell," Mrs. Lund said. "That's not the problem. The doctor prescribed the tonic to Mrs. Danvers for her headaches, but he warned me that too much could be fatal for a frail thing like her. So I keep it up there and give her a dose when she needs it. I don't want her accidentally taking it too soon after her previous dose. She can be forgetful, and it wouldn't surprise me if she made a dreadful mistake like that."

"Very wise," Harry said. "Some tonics contain hyoscine. It can be poisonous in large doses."

"Well, that bottle wasn't on that top shelf yesterday when I went looking for it," she went on. "It was on the shelf below, pushed toward the back. I know I didn't put it there. Not only that, it's nearly empty."

"Are you sure Mrs. Danvers didn't take it without your knowledge?"

"The bottle was full when I last saw it. To have taken almost the entire thing would have made her sick, or worse."

"When did you last see the bottle?" Harry asked.

"Nearly two weeks ago, I'd say."

Harry and I exchanged glances. The timing fit.

Mrs. Lund frowned in thought. "First the jewelry was moved, and now this. Yet you've found no evidence of a prowler and the house has been secured at night."

I asked Mrs. Lund if I could keep the bottle for a while and she handed it to me. "Was the tonic the only thing that was stolen? None of the jewelry was taken?"

"That's correct. The jewelry was moved, but none of it is missing."

It wasn't a thief then.

Harry had remembered, however. "The jewelry was paste."

Mrs. Lund nodded. "Mrs. Danvers sold it all off years ago and had some of the nicer pieces replaced with fakes." She placed a hand to her throat. "Do you think the intruder knew they were paste, that's why he didn't take them?"

"I do. When he or she realized each piece of jewelry was

worthless, they returned them, but placed them somewhere odd, so you'd assume Mrs. Danvers put them there during one of her forgetful episodes."

"So we do have a prowler." She pressed her lips together to stop them trembling.

"Have you given your key to anyone?"

"No."

I placed an arm around her shoulders. "We're going to find who did it, Mrs. Lund. In fact, I think I already know."

She took my hand. "Be careful, Miss Fox. Whatever you do, don't confront them alone. Take Mr. Armitage with you. He's very capable."

I smiled at Harry. He did not smile back. He looked troubled.

After we said goodbye to Mrs. Danvers, without telling her about the intruder, he apologized to Mrs. Lund as she saw us out. "I'm sorry. I should have been more thorough."

She took his hands as she'd taken mine and shook them as if she were trying to shake sense into him. "You *were* thorough. You cannot stop someone who isn't here when you come. Now, don't fret anymore about it. Go and catch the thief and put him behind bars."

It wasn't just a thief we were about to catch. It was a murderer, too.

Harry and I discussed our theories as we stood on Mrs. Danvers' front porch. It didn't take long. We had the same theory. Forming a plan took a little longer. Harry wanted to go to the Campbells' residence alone, but I wouldn't allow it. For one thing, it was my investigation. For another, the plan required both of us to be present. One to catch the killer, the other to explain to the rest of the household in the meantime. I didn't argue with him when it came to dividing the roles between us.

I took the stairs to the Campbells' front door while Harry descended to the basement. Mrs. Turner answered my knock herself. Before she could refuse me entry, I pushed past her.

"Miss Fox, I must protest!"

"There's a thief and a murderer in your household."

She covered her mouth and shook her head vigorously. "No. Don't do this."

I grasped her shoulders. "It's not who you think. Fetch Sir Ian and Lady Campbell and I'll explain."

I waited in the drawing room while Mrs. Turner returned with her outraged employers. I couldn't blame them for their irritation at seeing me yet again. I'd not only been something of a pest, but I'd also exposed the secrets of their dear friends, unnecessarily as it turned out.

"Please, just listen to what I have to say. The police will be here shortly." The small lie was enough to quieten them so I could ask the remaining questions I still needed answers to. "Have any of you noticed valuables going missing lately?"

Sir Ian and Lady Campbell glanced at one another and shook their heads.

"What about things that have moved? Particularly something a thief might think is valuable, but on closer inspection isn't?"

Lady Campbell sat down on the sofa. Her husband came up behind her and placed a hand on her shoulder.

"No," he said.

"What about the jewelry?" Mrs. Turner asked her mistress. "The diamond necklace and matching earrings were supposed to be toward the back of the top drawer of your dressing table, but we found them near the front. There was that brooch, too, and hair combs. Miss Fox, are you suggesting someone stole them only to return them?"

"I am."

"But why?"

"Because they're not real, Mrs. Turner."

Her mouth formed an O and her gaze slid to Lady Campbell, sitting quietly on the sofa.

"The thief realized they were fake, so left them," I went on.

Sir Ian clicked his heels together and stretched out his neck. "It was the butler. Must have been."

"No!" Mrs. Turner blurted out. "He was a good man."

"It must have been him. How else do you explain the watch in his possession? He must have stolen it from his previous employer."

"But they wouldn't have given him references if he had, would they?"

Sir Ian patted his wife's shoulder but made no further comment.

"They didn't check the references," I told the housekeeper. "Mr. Hardy was...inexpensive, so they simply hired without digging further."

"It's none of your business," Sir Ian growled at Mrs. Turner.

She surprised me by jutting her chin at him in defiance. Something had changed in the household, and I wasn't yet sure what had caused it.

"The tiepin was given to him by Lord Whitchurch on the night he helped Rupert escape," I said. "The watch he bought himself. The receipt is in his office."

"How could he afford such a piece on his wages?" Sir Ian snapped.

I checked the clock on the mantel. Harry should have had ample time to apprehend the thief. "Let's go downstairs. I'll explain everything there."

"Why?"

"Just come with me." I walked out of the drawing room and headed for the service stairs hidden behind one of the wall panels on the landing.

Lady Campbell and Mrs. Turner followed without question, but Sir Ian refused.

"Is it one of the other staff?" he demanded.

I didn't answer as I headed down the flight of narrow stairs.

"Do you mean to tell me we've been living with a thief and murderer under our very roof?" he thundered.

I found Harry in the kitchen explaining the situation to Mrs. Cook, Birdy and Betty. There was no sign of Davey.

At my arched brows, Harry shook his head. "He's gone."

CHAPTER 17

$\mathcal{T}$he collective gasps of the staff and their employers filled the kitchen. Only Mrs. Turner looked relieved, however. She blew out a shuddery breath as she clasped Betty's hand. Betty didn't seem to understand why, but I did.

"Explain yourselves," Sir Ian demanded. "What makes you believe the footman had anything to do with the thefts?"

"And Mr. Hardy's murder," Mrs. Turner added. Now that she knew Betty wasn't in any danger of being arrested, she no longer cared about thwarting me. Davey's guilt was obviously a more palatable option than Betty's.

Harry handed me a notepad that I hadn't noticed him carrying. It was open to the last page where an indentation of the words written on the page that used to be above it had been exposed by using a pencil to lightly shade over the top.

"'Pay up or else,'" I read. "Mr. Hardy wrote that and gave it to Davey. He was threatening to expose Davey's thieving. That's why Davey killed him. He'd already paid Mr. Hardy a considerable sum for his silence, but clearly Mr. Hardy was asking for more and Davey either couldn't pay or didn't want to anymore."

Mrs. Turner asked to see the notepad. "That's Mr. Hardy's handwriting." She shook her head. "I cannot believe it. I thought he was a good man."

"That's how he could afford the silver watch," Lady Campbell murmured.

"It also explains why he hid it in his shoe," I said. "He was afraid Davey would break into his room and steal it. Even though he had a lockbox, he knew not to keep valuables in it. A lock wouldn't keep Davey out."

"Nor did it," Mrs. Turner said. "Mr. Hardy knew someone had been in his room. I suppose Davey didn't find what he was looking for and gave up."

"I'm not entirely sure about that," I said. "It's possible Mr. Hardy had evidence that proved Davey was the thief."

Mrs. Turner's eyes widened. "The button! Davey was missing a button! Mr. Hardy told him he found it. Then they went into his office and had words."

I'd forgotten about the argument Mrs. Cook reported hearing. Davey had even admitted it was over a missing button, but he'd simply explained that Mr. Hardy scolded him for losing it and that the butler expected better standards.

Sometimes, the best lies are the ones containing a measure of truth.

I took up the explanation. "Mr. Hardy must have found the button somewhere it shouldn't have been, like Lady Campbell's bedchamber after she'd discovered her things had been moved. I suspect Davey's very good at picking locks and that's how he got into Mr. Hardy's room." It also explained how he got into Mrs. Danvers' house, but I didn't mention that. "After Mr. Hardy confronted him, Davey searched the butler's room and took back the button, which he found in the lockbox. He didn't continue his search for other valuables, because he didn't know about the watch and tiepin and he'd got what he needed. He didn't know there was a tiepin and watch at all until he saw you give them to me, Mrs. Turner."

She gasped. "He was standing right there when I handed them to you!"

"He stole them," Harry added with certainty. "He had a friend follow Cleo, and when she was alone, the friend bumped into her and stole them from her bag."

"That cur. I cannot believe we all trusted him. We liked him!"

I glanced at Betty, but her face revealed only shock,

confirming my suspicion. Before I had a chance to ask her, however, Sir Ian had a question.

"Are you saying he poisoned Mr. Hardy? But there were no signs."

"Hyoscine poisoning can be mistaken for death by natural causes," I said. "It's harmless in small doses, given to otherwise healthy people, and is included in some medicinal tonics and powders to relieve headaches and other conditions."

"Such as seltzer salts?" Mrs. Turner asked. "But you had Mr. Hardy's bottle tested and the contents were harmless."

"It was probably in the tonic Davey acquired elsewhere. I'll hand over the bottle to the police for testing. I'm quite sure they'll find it contains hyoscine, and an autopsy will find traces in the body."

Poor Betty turned quite pale.

"Are you saying Davey administered a large dose and Hardy didn't notice?" Sir Ian asked.

"He probably placed some in Mr. Hardy's tea." I turned to Mrs. Turner. "Did he take tea to the butler sometimes?"

"He did."

"I'd wager Davey also placed the tonic in Mr. Hardy's food, and perhaps his wine or spirits, too."

"Mr. Hardy wasn't a drunkard."

"I suspect he liked to imbibe, Mrs. Turner. When I looked in the sideboard in his office earlier, there were fewer bottles than I would expect to see in a house like this. Betty, do you recall Davey coming in this morning as you were about to count the bottles in the sideboard?"

"I do. I never did count them. Do you think Davey stopped me on purpose?"

"Yes, although he had another reason for interrupting us."

Before I could explain, Lady Campbell cut in. She seemed to have recovered from the shock of discovering her footman was a murderer and once again wanted to exert her authority. She looked down her nose at me. "Are you suggesting that a healthy man in the prime of his life was poisoned by a medicinal tonic?"

"Perhaps he wasn't as healthy as everyone assumed. An autopsy will reveal if he had another condition, such as a

215

weak heart, which wouldn't have helped. Even so, an over-dose of the tonic is what killed him."

"But I take tonics from time to time."

"If you're careful to only consume the dose prescribed by your doctor, they're quite safe."

I wanted to return to the conversation between Betty, Davey and me in the office, so I continued before Lady Camp-bell could divert the conversation in another direction. "I noticed you and Davey exchange glances in the butler's office, Betty. At the time, I thought it was love, after he claimed…" I trailed off, not wanting to reveal her secret to the others.

Betty was quite open, however. "After he claimed he fathered my child," she finished.

Only the cook gasped. Birdy had lost interest in the conversation some time ago and wandered off. Lady Camp-bell and Sir Ian clearly knew. I suspected Mrs. Turner had made Betty inform them.

"But he's not the father, is he?" I asked.

"I don't understand," Mrs. Cook said. "Why admit it if he isn't?"

"Because it gave him a reason for a second argument he had with Mr. Hardy, this one outside in the courtyard. He *claimed* Mr. Hardy discovered he'd got Betty with child, and he promised he'd do the right thing by her, hence eliminating any motive we assumed he'd have to kill Mr. Hardy. But their conversation wasn't about that at all, so he had to get Betty to comply with his lie when he told it to me. The look he gave her encouraged her to agree with everything he said."

Betty's face crumpled. "I know lying's a sin, but I didn't know what to do. He just said it, right there in the office, and I couldn't think fast enough. I thought he was helping me, you see. I thought he was my friend."

Mrs. Turner put her arm around the girl's waist. "There, there."

"He was using you to buy himself some time," I said. "He just needed to mislead me, so that I'd leave. That would give him time to pack his things and disappear." I looked to Harry, who nodded.

"All his personal belongings are gone," he confirmed.

"He knew you'd admit you lied eventually, Betty," I went on. "He knew you couldn't live with the lie for long and would realize why he'd said it, so that's why he left immediately."

Mrs. Cook placed her hands on her hips and glanced between Betty and Mrs. Turner. "So, if he's not the father, who is?"

Betty's instinctive glance at Sir Ian betrayed her.

Mrs. Cook lowered her hands to her side and bit her lip. Mrs. Turner showed no surprise, nor did Lady Campbell. The latter merely pinched her lips and headed back up the stairs, her head high.

Sir Ian pretended he wasn't the focus of everyone's attention. He cleared his throat. "Did you say the police are on their way, Miss Fox?"

"They will be, once I tell them everything I know."

He grunted. "Tell them this must be handled with the utmost discretion. None of this is our fault, and yet we are the ones who will suffer when the investigation is reopened."

"Not just you," I pointed out.

He pointed a finger at me. "You should have left well enough alone. Look at the damage you've caused!"

Harry pushed Sir Ian's finger away and squared up to him. "You've caused a lot of damage yourself. I hope you'll do the honorable thing and take care of your responsibilities."

Sir Ian merely sniffed and followed his wife up the stairs.

"He tried to *take care* of it," Mrs. Turner spat. "He bought her the oil of pennyroyal."

"I didn't use it," Betty whispered through her tears. "I couldn't do it."

Mrs. Turner patted Betty's shoulder. "Go and dry your eyes, girl, then get back to work. We'll have a chat later and decide what to do next."

Mrs. Turner, Harry and I watched her go, while Mrs. Cook returned to the kitchen.

"I'm sorry I didn't realize earlier that Davey was guilty," I said.

Mrs. Turner sighed. "You weren't to know."

"He mentioned he hadn't been in Mr. Hardy's office on the day he died, but of course he had. He'd delivered the poisoned cup of tea. He actually had no reason to lie and pretend he wasn't there, as it was perfectly natural to take in tea to the butler, but in the heat of the moment and feeling the pressure, he'd accidentally lied when it was quite unnecessary."

"Never mind. You worked it out in the end."

"You thought it was Betty, didn't you? You thought she killed Mr. Hardy, then became upset afterward. That's why you wanted me to stop investigating. You didn't want me to catch her."

She nodded. "I thought that was the reason for all her tears, and I didn't want her to hang for it. She's a kind, sweet thing." She huffed in frustration. "I should have trusted my instincts and known she couldn't poison anyone, even if she had good reason. When I finally confronted her not long ago, she told me who the father was. Well, you could have knocked me down with a feather, you could! It never occurred to me it would be Sir Ian. Like you, I thought it was Davey." Her gaze wandered to the staircase Sir Ian had just taken. "I told Lady Campbell immediately. She thinks Betty's lying and told me to mind my own business. That was the last straw for me. I'm going to give my notice just as soon as I find a new position. I can't stay on here working for people like that."

"And Betty?"

She sighed again. "I don't know. I'll go with her later to tell her mother. Betty's terrified of what she'll say, but what mother wouldn't want to help her daughter at such a time?"

"Mrs. Hatch does love her daughter," I said. "But this will test their relationship. Betty will need your support. If she does have the child and finds she needs work, tell her to ask Mrs. Short at the hotel for a position."

She shook her head. "My sister doesn't like loose girls."

"If anyone can convince her that Betty isn't loose, merely the victim of an employer who took advantage, you can."

She walked with Harry and me to the front door. "You think you know the people you work with, but this just goes to show that some folk keep things close to their chest."

"Don't blame yourself for not seeing Davey for the thief he is," Harry said. "He was an excellent liar."

"I was talking about Mr. Hardy. I liked him. I felt sorry for him that he had no one in his life, no family or friends. But he was a blackmailer, which probably explains why they'd all cut him out of their lives." She gave yet another sigh, this one weighty, as if she was weary to her bones. "I'll pay you your fee, as agreed, Miss Fox. I don't have it on me, but I'll give it to my sister to give to you." She huffed a humorless laugh. "Glad I didn't keep it here, now, what with Davey being a thief and all." She opened the door and peered up at the stairs. "Do you think we have to worry about him coming back?"

Harry shook his head. "He'll be long gone by now. Scotland Yard will give a description of him to the newspapers, so hopefully no one else will employ him, but I doubt they'll catch him. The criminal world takes care of its own."

Harry and I walked together only as far as his office. He was quiet much of the way, but that could have been because I did all the talking. I went over every detail of the case, all of which he already knew. It was a waste of breath, but it was a good deterrent. The last time we'd ended an investigation together, he'd kissed me.

I couldn't allow that to happen again. Endings of investigations were proving to be a somewhat heady and irrational time for us.

Instead of going to his office, I made sure to say farewell while we were still on a public thoroughfare. Broadwick Street was too quiet, too intimate, whereas the throng of pedestrians and vehicles near Piccadilly Circus ensured he would not kiss me again.

"Well, that's that then," I said, inching away from him. "Bye, Harry, and thank you." I waved and hurried off.

I resisted the urge to turn around and see if he was still standing there, watching me. It wasn't easy, but it helped that I saw the omnibus that would take me to Scotland Yard about to pull over. I ran to catch it. Once safely on board, I expelled a measured breath. I felt like I'd been holding it ever since leaving the Campbells' house.

* * *

C.J. ARCHER

I SPENT some time with D.S. Forrester. He insisted I repeat everything for his superior, who then insisted I help their sketch artist draw a likeness of Davey. They would make copies and send it out to as many stations around the city as possible. They didn't sound hopeful of catching him. At least they listened to me and took me seriously. I suspected I had D.S. Forrester to thank for that. He assured his superiors that I'd helped solve murders before, and that I was a friend of D.I. Hobart's. Harry's father still had a great deal of respect from his former peers.

I arrived back at the hotel before afternoon tea. After a brief exchange with Frank, then Goliath, I took the stairs to the fourth floor. I poked my head into Flossy's suite and told her I'd join her for afternoon tea in the sitting room as soon as I changed, then I headed to my own suite.

My mind was not altogether in the present moment, as I was still thinking over the events of the day. That was my excuse for not noticing someone had been following me. I'd barely had a chance to remove my key from the door when a hand clamped over my mouth and I was ushered inside.

"Don't make a sound, Miss Fox." Davey forced me into the sitting room, but did not remove his hand.

I tried to wriggle free, but he was too strong. I tried stomping on his toes but missed. My shouts were muffled. No one could hear me. No one had seen him capture me. I was alone and at a distinct disadvantage.

His grip tightened. "Quiet! I have a knife, but I don't want to harm you. I just want to explain."

I opened my bag and eased my hand inside. I kept a small knife with me at all times for just such an emergency.

Davey ripped the bag out of my grip and threw it on the sofa. The contents scattered on the floor. "Just let me explain!"

I put up my hands in surrender.

"I'll let you go, but don't shout. All right? I don't want to cut you, but I will if I have to."

I nodded.

He let me go and eased away. "It wasn't me, Miss Fox. I didn't do anything."

With my hands still in the air, I slowly turned to face him.

He held a knife in his white-knuckled grip. "Of course you did, Davey. Don't take me for a fool."

He wiped his sweating brow with the back of his hand. "All right, I did it, but I didn't mean to kill him. I just wanted to make him sick and scare him a bit into keeping mum. But he died. I swear, I didn't give him much of the stuff, just a bit more than the dose it says on the label."

"You gave him nearly an entire bottle. I saw it in Mrs. Danvers' house."

"Those old crones don't remember how much they started with."

"Mrs. Danvers' housekeeper is as sharp as a knife. She remembers everything."

He swore and started to pace the floor.

"Davey, why did you come here? Am I your hostage? That won't go well for you in court."

He wiped his forehead with the back of the hand that gripped the knife. "I like you, Miss Fox."

"And I liked you, Davey. That's why I'm urging you to give yourself up. If you explain that you didn't want to kill Mr. Hardy, the judge might give you a lighter sentence."

"Ha! Ain't no chance of that happening." He lunged toward me, only to stop when I yelped in fright and backed away. "Listen, this is what we'll do. I'll walk out of here and go into hiding. You return to Scotland Yard and tell them you made a mistake."

"You saw me go there?"

"Aye, but I couldn't stop you. I missed the bus you caught and had to take a cab to follow you. Once you got out at the Yard, I had to keep my distance. It was too public and there were too many pigs around for me to speak to you. So I bided my time until you came out again, then I followed you here. That snobby old doorman wasn't going to let me in, but I got past him." He adjusted his grip on the knife handle as he thrust it in my direction, more with the intention of frightening me than harming me. "You tell them I'm innocent, Miss Fox. They'll listen to you. You're an heiress—"

"I'm not."

"You must be connected to someone important to be able to afford to stay here."

I didn't correct him. It was safer if he thought I was merely a guest. "I'll do my best, Davey, I promise."

"Good. Right. I'll take myself off now. Give me time to leave then—"

At that moment the door to my suite opened and Harmony entered. "Cleo, what—" She gasped, as Davey instinctively turned toward her, knife at the ready.

I took advantage of his momentary lapse in concentration and lunged at his outstretched arm, forcing it back with the entire weight of my body. He cried out in pain and dropped the knife. I kicked it in Harmony's direction. She stepped over it as it skittered toward her and grabbed his other arm while I still gripped his right. Between us, we forced him back into the wall and pinned him there.

"Bloody hell." Floyd had been a little behind Harmony and missed the capture. "What the devil, Cleo?"

"This man is a murderer," I told him. "Telephone the police."

His mouth fell open and he stared at me until I snapped at him. "But you don't have a telephone in here." At my glare, he nodded quickly. "Right. My father's office is closest. He has one."

"Floyd!" I shouted. "Are you mad? Don't let him know about this. He'll ban me from investigating."

Davey tried to push against Harmony and me, but between us, we managed to hold him against the wall. He gave up with a frustrated groan.

"May I make a suggestion, Mr. Bainbridge," Harmony said. "Use the speaking tube to ask the kitchen to send up Victor and any other cooks they can spare. Once this man is secured, we can sneak him out without Sir Ronald seeing, then take him to Scotland Yard ourselves."

Floyd wagged his finger at her. "There's a reason you're good at organizing things. You manage to keep a cool head when the rest of us don't."

"My head is quite cool," I shot back. In truth, he was right. I certainly wasn't as calm as Harmony. If Floyd left to use the telephone, as I suggested, we would have been more vulnerable.

He managed to get the urgency across without telling

whoever was on the other end of the tube what was happening. The more we contained the gossip about this incident, the better. A few minutes later, Victor and two other burly cooks entered.

Harmony and I handed Davey over to them. She directed the cooks to take the service stairs to the kitchen, then out of the hotel the back way. "I'll go first and keep an eye out."

"I'll send for a carriage to collect him in the lane," I told her.

Harmony wagged a finger at Davey. "If you utter a sound, Victor will punch you in the mouth to keep you quiet. Is that understood?"

A forlorn, defeated Davey appealed to me. "Miss Fox, remember your promise to speak to the Yard. You tell 'em I didn't mean to kill him. You tell 'em!"

"I'll do my best."

Part of me felt sorry for him, but I only indulged that thought for a brief moment. He was a murderer, despite his somewhat charming manner. I wouldn't be offering any defense on his behalf. That was something he could bring up himself at his trial.

I clasped my cousin's arm as I passed him. "I have to go to the Yard, too. Please tell Flossy that I can't meet her for afternoon tea." I stood on my toes and kissed his cheek. "And do not, under any circumstances, tell your father about this incident."

He dusted his hands as if he'd taken care of the entire situation himself. "You keep my secrets safe, and I'll keep yours."

It seemed a good deal to me, considering I was amassing quite a number of secrets lately.

CHAPTER 18

wo days later, I finally got to enjoy afternoon tea with Flossy. Floyd hadn't told her why I'd postponed, and she was none the wiser that a murderer had briefly held me captive in the suite next to hers. She was once again her cheerful self, having gotten over her heartache after the maharaja's son's rejection. We didn't have an opportunity to discuss it alone as we sat with several of her friends, their mothers and Aunt Lilian at the table beside us.

As I popped the last macaron into my mouth, I felt as though I was being watched. I peered through the fronds of the potted palm next to me and saw Lady Whitchurch at another table with three other women. When she realized she'd been caught staring, she looked away.

I did not expect her to acknowledge me, so was surprised when she approached as we were both leaving. She made a small sign that she'd like to speak to me alone.

I drew away from the others. "Good afternoon, madam. I hope you enjoyed your afternoon tea."

She offered me a small, if somewhat anxious, smile. "I didn't know you came here."

"I live here. My uncle owns the hotel."

She pressed her fingers to her lips. "Oh! You never mentioned it."

"If you're concerned about what I learned during the

course of my investigation, then let me assure you that your secrets are safe with me. My family and their friends are none the wiser and will remain so."

She lowered her hand to her stomach. "Thank you. Your discretion is appreciated." She caught my arm as I began to move off. "There's something else I want to thank you for. My mother-in-law is moving back to the country estate."

"I thought the dowager needed to be in London, close to her doctor."

"He told her that, but she's stubborn and does as she pleases." She gave me a wry look. "She's dying, and she'd rather do that there, in the place she considers her home, surrounded by the things she loves."

"But her family is here."

"As I said, surrounded by the things she loves."

Poor Lord Whitchurch. "Do you think I had something to do with her moving back there?"

"Quite possibly. You may not have realized it, but she was involved in a battle of wills with you. It was a case of who would give up first. Would you stop digging into the past, or would she be forced to offer up the family secrets? She lost." Lady Whitchurch smiled. "She hates to lose."

I considered asking her if she believed the dowager's claim that Rupert was dead, but decided not to. She seemed so happy that her mother-in-law was leaving her and her husband in peace; I didn't want to throw cold water on her contentment by suggesting the man she'd loathed, whom she'd almost been forced to marry against her will, might be alive. Of all the people I'd met throughout the investigation, Lord and Lady Whitchurch had not only been amongst the most innocent, they'd also been two of the most sincere.

She walked with me past Mr. Chapman, who politely thanked her and said he hoped to see her again soon while simultaneously managing to give me a glare. There wasn't a great deal of iciness in it, however. I'd seen him leave his office this morning with Harmony. She was clearly involving him in the wedding arrangements, and I knew she'd make sure he was doing the parts that he loved to do, while she continued with the rest.

Lady Whitchurch eyed her friends, waiting for her in the foyer. "Have you seen the Campbells lately, Miss Fox?"

"No." Two days ago wasn't lately, surely. "Why?"

"Lady Campbell was supposed to join me here today, but she sent a message to say she wasn't feeling up to it. She's been quite out of sorts this last day or two. I can't think why. It can't be the death of her butler, or she'd mention it. Never mind. I'll call on her tomorrow. She'll be so surprised when I tell her you're related to the Bainbridges of the Mayfair Hotel." She thanked me again and left to join her friends.

I walked back to Flossy. The moment I was within earshot, she and her friends wanted to know who I'd been speaking to.

"Lady Whitchurch," I said.

Cora Druitt-Poore's eyes widened. "The one whose brother-in-law went missing years ago?"

"Wasn't he her former fiancé?" Felicity Digby asked with a smirk and waggle of her eyebrows.

Aunt Lilian's friend, Mrs. Mannering, told the girls to hush. "How do you know Lady Whitchurch, Miss Fox?"

I was saved from answering by Peter trying to get my attention. I made my excuses and joined him at the post desk. "You want to see me?"

"Not me, Mrs. Short. She's in her office."

I knocked on her door then entered upon her summons. "Peter said you wished to see me."

"I have something for you from my sister." She opened her desk drawer and removed an envelope. "Your fee."

I'd already made up my mind I wouldn't accept it. It wasn't right. Mrs. Turner and the other staff needed the money more. They could ill afford to pay me. "Please, give it back to her. I can't accept it."

She hesitated, staring at me as if trying to get my measure, then lowered the envelope to her desk. "She won't take it back. Nor should she. She employed you to do a task and you performed it. This belongs to you." Mrs. Short offered me the envelope again.

"Do you know The Female Servants Benevolent Society on Southampton Row?"

"I do."

"Would you mind donating it to them, please? I'd prefer not to do it myself. There's someone staying in one of their rooms who I'd rather not see."

She picked up her pen and concentrated on her roster chart. "That'll be much appreciated, I'm sure, although I can't say it's good of you to think of them." This last part, she added in a mutter.

I wasn't sure if she'd wanted me to hear it or not. "I suspect I won't like the answer, but do tell me why you think that, Mrs. Short."

She put down the pen and leveled her gaze with mine. "Giving money to the poor is only a kind deed when a person can ill afford it. Otherwise, it's one's duty."

Clearly, she thought I was an heiress, too. "Good day to you, Mrs. Short." I turned to go, but stopped at the door. "Do you know, when I first met Mrs. Turner, I only saw the physical resemblance between the two of you and I thought how alike you were! But now that I've got to know her a little, I see that you're very different."

She picked up her pen again. "Thank you for noticing."

Perhaps it was just as well that she didn't understand the insult in my comment.

My uncle hailed me as he emerged from Mr. Hobart's office. "Good to see you taking an interest in the hotel affairs, Cleopatra." He nodded at Mrs. Short's office, then glanced over his shoulder at Mr. Hobart's. He caught my elbow and drew me away, out of earshot. "Come and see me later. I've got your fee for you on my desk."

"Fee?"

"For helping me with Hobart."

It took a great effort, but I managed to refrain from rolling my eyes. "You know I didn't investigate, Uncle, and as much as I'd like to take your money for doing nothing, I can't."

"Your morals do you credit. You may not have investigated Hobart, but you did help. You encouraged me to speak to him. We just had a good chat, as it happens."

"Wonderful! I'm so pleased. So... is everything all right?"

"Quite well, for now, and a little while longer. He was considering retiring, but changed his mind."

What a relief! I'd been so worried imagining all the

terrible things that could be causing Mr. Hobart's absences, illness being chief among them. "That is good news."

"Indeed. He was spending his lunches and some evenings talking to his bank manager and lawyers about selling his house and moving to the seaside."

"That sounds very pleasant. Why did he change his mind?"

"His wife decided against the idea. She said she didn't want him under her feet just yet, and that he'd be bored away from the hotel. Apparently, her sister-in-law had something to do with it. Her husband has recently retired and he's trying his wife's patience."

I couldn't help laughing. I could picture Harry's mother getting annoyed with D.I. Hobart for getting in her way. He was a man who needed to be active, and being at home all the time was going to be a trial for them both.

"I told Hobart that he can't retire until Peter is ready." Uncle Ronald gazed out to the foyer where Peter stood chatting with a guest. "He's some way off from that, I'm afraid. If only Armitage hadn't left. He could step into Hobart's shoes at a moment's notice." He sighed, then shrugged. "I told Hobart to take a holiday instead."

It seemed he'd conveniently overlooked the fact that he'd dismissed Harry. It was pointless to correct him. "That's an excellent idea. I'm sure a week or two will do him wonders."

"Just as long as he waits until after we return from our family holiday in Brighton. The hotel will need him in my absence." He patted my arm and headed off to speak to some guests he recognized in the foyer.

I was considering whether to follow him or speak to Mr. Hobart when my mind was made up for me. My name was whispered from behind.

"Cleo, a word."

I spun around to see Harry standing there with Detective Sergeant Forrester. They must have arrived in the senior staff corridor via the service lift at the end. "Did you come in through the kitchen entrance?"

"I thought it best to avoid the front door."

"Very wise." I eyed D.S. Forrester, who was looking guilty for sneaking in. "You haven't been banned, only Harry."

"I feel conspicuous," he said, indicating his plain suit.

"You grow accustomed to it," Harry told him. "Don't worry, we're just going to my uncle's office. Is he in there, Cleo?"

"I believe so. Wait here." I knocked on the door then, when Mr. Hobart invited me in, I signaled to Harry and D.S. Forrester to follow me.

We slipped inside before anyone saw and closed the door.

Mr. Hobart blinked in surprise. "Harry! What are you doing here?"

Harry introduced D.S. Forrester. "We need to speak to Cleo. Can we use your office?"

Mr. Hobart stood and indicated his chair. "Please do. I'll walk the floor for a little while."

Harry took the chair his uncle vacated, while the detective and I occupied the guest chairs. Harry looked comfortable in the manager's seat. It ought to have been his one day. It would have been, if I hadn't changed the course of his life. Sometimes, when I allowed myself to dwell on my mistakes, the magnitude of that one haunted me.

"Are you all right, Cleo?" Harry asked. "You look a little peaky."

"I'm fine."

Even so, D.S. Forrester poured a glass of water for me from the jug on the sideboard. He handed it to me with a smile.

Harry narrowed his gaze as he watched on.

"Thank you, Detective," I said, returning the smile.

"Please, call me Monty."

"Then you must call me Cleo."

Harry cleared his throat. "Forrester telephoned me to give me some news. I thought you should hear it, since it's about your investigation." He indicated that Monty should take over.

The detective removed a notepad from his inside jacket pocket and flipped it to a page with a series of notes written in an untidy hand. "I haven't yet heard back from the New York police, but I did receive a telegram from a Pinkerton agent, after I sent the agency a message. This particular agent was hired by the Dowager Lady Whitchurch to find her son,

Rupert. The agent confirmed that his investigation led him to discover that a man named Rupert Whitby died after being struck by a train on April twenty-ninth this year. Witnesses claimed he was drunk and fell off the station platform. At the dowager's request, the Pinkerton agent made further inquiries and discovered that Rupert Whitby had indeed sent letters to England on a regular basis from his local post office. He also had a photograph in his possession of a younger version of himself standing beside a horse in front of an English country manor. Someone had written 'Rupert and Midnight at Deensbury House' on the reverse of the photograph." Monty closed the notebook. "Deensbury is the name of the Whitchurch's country estate."

"So Rupert *is* dead," I murmured.

"The dowager spoke the truth," Harry said. "I wasn't sure I believed her until now."

"It certainly draws a line under that mystery. Thank you, Monty. What will happen now?"

"I've sent a report to my superior. He'll most likely officially close the case without making further inquiries. I also have news about the death of Hardy, the Campbells' butler. Based on your evidence and the capture of Davey, the investigation has been re-opened. Yesterday, the body was exhumed, and tests were run on it, as well as the bottle of Cure-All tonic you gave me. The tonic contained hyoscine hydrobromide. Traces of the substance were also found in the body, more than should be there if he'd simply taken a normal dose. His heart also showed early signs of disease. The excessive dose of hyoscine most likely caused it to fail altogether."

"Then Davey may have told the truth when he said he didn't want to kill Mr. Hardy, merely frighten him by making him unwell."

"It might be enough to save Davey from the noose," Harry said. "Although he'll spend a number of years in prison. That's two cases solved, Cleo. Well done." He rose and extended his hand to the detective. "Thank you, Forrester."

"I should be the one thanking Miss Fox. I mean Cleo." He smiled sheepishly at me. "You make me look good to my superiors."

Harry had been about to open the office door, but paused. "Cleo should be credited with solving those cases."

"She is! I do credit her! Sir." Poor Monty hastily said his goodbyes and hurried out of the office under Harry's watchful gaze.

"Harry," I chided. "Did you have to come across quite so gruff? You frightened him."

"He's a policeman. He shouldn't be so easily frightened." I went to exit the office, but he put his hand out to stop me. "I haven't finished with you yet."

I crossed my arms over my chest and arched my brows pointedly at the doorway. He stepped aside so that I could pass if I wanted to. I ought to leave without listening to him. What if he kissed me again? But I got the feeling he wanted to speak to me, not kiss me. "Go on then."

"Why didn't you tell me Davey was here?"

"Oh. You heard about that. There was no point. He was apprehended quickly and taken to Scotland Yard by Victor and that was the end of it."

"You should have told me."

"Why? What would it have achieved?"

"Nothing, but I'd still like to know. I was involved in the investigation, for one thing. But mostly because we're friends and, as your friend, I want to hear about things that happen to you. We are friends, aren't we, Cleo?"

Was it a trap? Would I somehow stumble into admitting that I had feelings for him if I answered him truthfully? I spent so long considering my answer that he gave up with a shake of his head. He stormed out of the office only to return a moment later before I'd had a chance to move.

His temper had gone off the boil, but it still simmered as he regarded me with a searing intensity that had my insides melting. "When I heard, I was worried. That's why I wanted to know."

"And that's precisely why I didn't tell you. I knew you'd worry and it would have been needless because it was over quickly and I was in no danger."

"Even so, I *want* to know, and I want to hear it from you, not third hand from Forrester. From *you*, Cleo, face to face, where I can see that you're fine. It will ease the worry."

"That makes sense, I suppose. I'm sorry. Next time, I'll tell you in person or telephone you."

"Good." He frowned. "But don't let there be a next time." He made no move to go. I could tell he was warring with himself about something else. Perhaps now the kiss would come.

My stomach fluttered, part in panic, part with desire. Each emotion grappled with the other until panic came out on top. "You should leave via the front door."

"I plan to." He still didn't move, however. He did not attempt to touch me, but the look he gave me was as thrilling and terrifying as any touch or kiss. "I am a patient man, Cleo."

He walked off before I could say another word, leaving me staring at his straight back and broad shoulders, my nerves shredded.

I drew in a deep breath as I smoothed my hand over my still-fluttering stomach. Then, with a toss of my head and a determined stride, I followed a few feet behind him. I watched as he crossed the foyer to say goodbye to Mr. Hobart. He greeted Goliath, had a few words with Peter, then shook the hand of a guest he must have known from his time working at the hotel. He even nodded at Uncle Ronald.

My uncle nodded back. He did not throw him out nor storm up to him. There was no fury in his gaze. For once, I couldn't read his thoughts.

After Harry exited the hotel, Uncle Ronald approached me. "Was he here to see you, Cleopatra?"

"We had a case to discuss. It's finished now."

"So you won't have any need to see him again."

"No."

"Until the next time you work together, that is."

I didn't say so, but I wasn't sure there should be a next time. Harry was too much of a temptation. If I was going to move beyond desire and forget about him, I'd have to do a better job of avoiding him.

Available 3rd December 2024 :
MURDER ON THE BRIGHTON EXPRESS
The 9th Cleopatra Fox Mystery

Returning from a seaside holiday, Cleo sees a woman board the train but not get off. Where did she go? And why did she send Cleo a blackmail note?

A MESSAGE FROM THE AUTHOR

I hope you enjoyed reading MURDER AT THE DINNER PARTY as much as I enjoyed writing it. As an independent author, getting the word out about my book is vital to its success, so if you liked this book please consider telling your friends and writing a review at the store where you purchased it. If you would like to be contacted when I release a new book, subscribe to my newsletter at http://cjarcher.com/contact-cj/newsletter/. You will only be contacted when I have a new book out.

ALSO BY C.J. ARCHER

SERIES WITH 2 OR MORE BOOKS

The Glass Library

Cleopatra Fox Mysteries

After The Rift

Glass and Steele

The Ministry of Curiosities Series

The Emily Chambers Spirit Medium Trilogy

The 1st Freak House Trilogy

The 2nd Freak House Trilogy

The 3rd Freak House Trilogy

The Assassins Guild Series

Lord Hawkesbury's Players Series

Witch Born

SINGLE TITLES NOT IN A SERIES

Courting His Countess

Surrender

Redemption

The Mercenary's Price

ABOUT THE AUTHOR

C.J. Archer has loved history and books for as long as she can remember and feels fortunate that she found a way to combine the two. She spent her early childhood in the dramatic beauty of outback Queensland, Australia, but now lives in suburban Melbourne with her husband, two children and a mischievous black & white cat named Coco.

Subscribe to C.J.'s newsletter through her website to be notified when she releases a new book, as well as get access to exclusive content and subscriber-only giveaways. Her website also contains up to date details on all her books: http://cjarcher.com She loves to hear from readers. You can contact her through email cj@cjarcher.com or follow her on social media to get the latest updates on her books:

facebook.com/CJArcherAuthorPage

x.com/cj_archer

instagram.com/authorcjarcher